Little Girl

I0601015

A Novel

Courtney Vigo

Acknowledgments

Thank you to my wonderful husband, Jeremy, who stood by me for all the edits and rewrites of this novel.

Thank you to my attacker. You broke me, confused me, made me think in twisted ways, but through it all, I've come out stronger and happier than ever before.

Little Girl

Chapter 1

The director of the foster care facility sat in the corner of the office. She eyed me over the top of her unflatteringly small glasses. She had to be present during my therapy sessions. Apparently the government was in charge of me and they needed someone to act as my guardian since I'm a minor.

In reality, they're saying I can't be left alone with a man. First of all, they're totally overreacting. Second of all, this guy has so many wrinkles even an iron would be completely useless.

"Miss Harper," the psychiatrist started, his nasally voice already grating on my nerves, "you're not going to *improve* if you don't open up."

I looked at the director. Her name was Stacy. It didn't fit her. She looked like a Helen to me. She sighed and looked at her nails, a poor excuse of a manicure. This was what felt like my hundredth (although I think it was only my second, maybe third) session and I hadn't talked about my issues. I looked back at the psychiatrist. He showed no signs of frustration with me. His eyelids drooped over kind eyes. His eyebrows were relaxed, not gnarled with impatience.

I decided these people were not going to budge at any time. They could see through my lies, the armor I'd put up. I wasn't going to get out of here unless I *did* open up. And really, it did seem like I could trust this man. I wasn't so sure about the director, but I don't think she was even listening.

"Kay, fine. What do you want to know?"

"Whatever you feel comfortable sharing. You could start from the beginning."

"The beginning of what? Of the day? Of my life? Of all time?"

I knew what he meant, of course, but I wanted to push him. To see if he'd break.

He didn't falter. "The beginning of what you think caused this behavior."

"'This behavior'?" I raised my voice, irritable.

"The behavior that got you here. Seducing older men."

"You can be blatant like that with me. Don't treat me like I'm some fragile creature," I mumbled, losing steam.

"That was never my intent, Miss Harper."

A beat of silence. Another. I looked back at the director. She doodled on her notepad. Spirals. Triangles. Back to the doctor. He blinked, slowly.

"Well," I sighed, "I guess the beginning would be when my uncle was living with us."

He stared expectantly, but without rushing me. The director didn't look up from her triangles. I'd never talked about what had happened with my uncle before, except with my closest friend, Ashley, so I guess this would be as good a time as ever.

Chapter 2

My uncle, Glen, came to live with us when I was seven or eight, I can't remember exactly. My dad left when I was six. He just went to work and didn't come home again. My friends at school told me he left because he hated me, and I believed it. Every night I prayed to every god I knew and wished on every star I saw that he would come back so I could say I was sorry for being such a disappointment.

My mother made sure to remind me what kind of disgrace I was too.

When Uncle Glen came, though, he told me my dad was in heaven. He said that my dad didn't leave me, that he was a hero. My uncle showed me newspapers from the day it happened. My dad fought fires and saved lives. That day, he saved everyone else's lives but couldn't save his own.

That was the moment I started resenting my mother. For lying to me about my dad leaving. For instilling in me a self-hatred. Mostly, though, I resented her for not mourning him.

She didn't care about what I wanted or needed. Closure would be nice, but I wasn't allowed to talk about him or even look at pictures of him. If she would have been saddened by the memories, I could have understood. She wouldn't cry though; she'd just get mad at me, like I'd done something wrong.

Being curious about what had happened to the man I looked up to was punishable.

But Uncle Glen. That man gained all my trust and respect from the moment he told me the truth. He spoke softly, yet his voice carried a powerful boom and hum with each word. It comforted me, hearing him talk, having him there to hold me, to tell me I was beautiful and smart and that I would make a difference in the world one day. That I'd already made a difference in the world.

"How?" I asked.

"Well, little girl, every interaction you have with someone changes their world. You can either change it for the better or for the worse. In your case, since you're such a sweet little girl, it's been for the better every time." He flicked the end of my nose with his rough finger.

"But how?"

He chuckled, deep in his throat. "Just like that! You might not understand it now, but think on it and you'll get it. You bring joy to people's lives. People need joy. There's so much sorrow in the world already."

"Did I bring joy to Daddy's life?"

He squeezed me tighter. "Of course you did, little girl. You made his life worth living."

The more I saw my uncle, the less I saw my mother. It was like they were trading places. He hung around more, started making sure I ate my meals, got me dressed, took me to school. She would leave and not come back for a few days at a time. She'd watch TV, do her hair, maybe eat a microwave meal. I always remember her smoking a cigarette on the porch, slowly, taking deep breaths, staring at the ash, completely lost in her own mind. Then she'd leave again, like she was just visiting her extended family for the weekend.

My mother was so beautiful to me while I was little. My favorite was watching her get ready for her day, taking notes for myself. I loved when she'd pin her hair up into a messy bun. I loved the way she flicked and tucked the pieces effortlessly into place, as if each strand already knew where to go on its own. She'd fill in her eyebrows with a special pencil, making them bold and striking. I admired the way she swept jet black liquid liner over her lids, making perfect wings every time. It took her half a second, yet when I'd sneak into her makeup bag, I'd end up with black swirls covering my irises and pupils. She used to laugh and hug me to her chest before rinsing my eyes out with water, but after my uncle moved in, she hardly noticed that I was getting better. I made it onto my eyelids rather than in my eyeballs, uneven and shaky at first, but then, they were almost as perfect as hers were.

I loved the way her nose was flawlessly straight until it had just the slightest little upturn at the end. She had about five perfectly-spaced freckles on that perfect nose. I had none on my own button nose; a nose I must have gotten from my father's side of the family. My uncle had it too, but his was wider and more manly. She'd had me when she was nineteen, and no wrinkle had touched the corners of her eyes, the sides of her mouth, the space between her colored-in eyebrows. She was in her prime and she was my queen.

I remember she always smelled like lilacs, even after chain smoking in the back yard. Lilacs followed us everywhere. Even when she was gone, I still caught little pockets of lilacs throughout the house, like she was just out of reach, haunting the corners and the spaces.

Eventually, I grew up. My mother wasn't beautiful to me anymore. She didn't bring springtime wherever she went. Instead, she brought a chill that I couldn't shake. I saw her for who she was, or at least, for who she had become after my father's death. She was shallow, flippant.

It was weird, and I know how it sounds, but it was almost like she became jealous of me, especially when I was around my uncle. When he'd laugh with me or pat my leg, I'd catch her giving us sideways glances. I'm not sure she wanted Glen so much as wanting all the attention the world could offer her. That's why she was gone so often. She couldn't get the attention she needed within the house.

While my uncle left her wanting, searching elsewhere for men's sweet observation, he provided me with more than enough charm.

When I was little, he was fatherly. He made my lunches for school and carried me to my bed when I fell asleep in front of the TV. As I developed, it changed. I'd catch him looking at me from the corner of his eye. He didn't realize I could see the glances, but I saw each and every one of them. Once it started, I didn't want to be around him anymore.

I had no choice, though. I was hardly even twelve, which meant I had to do what authority told me. Authority told me I was pretty, developing nicely. Authority told me to be a good girl, to sit on his lap.

As I noticed my uncle's lingering stares, I started noticing glances from other men. Boys my age didn't notice anything related to the female species yet. They were too involved in video games and burning ants with matches.

Those older men, though, they certainly noticed. I saw the way their eyes lit up when I flipped my hair, or smiled at them sweetly. I started noticing the way their wives' chests turned red, or the way their mouths tightened, with jealousy.

And I started to like it.

I liked the control I had over men and the women on their arms. I was shedding my shyness, like a snake sheds its skin. I could have whatever I wanted.

By thirteen, I'd had my first period, and it was as if men could sense it. Their glances turned into outright stares. My hips were filling out; my breasts did the same. I had curves. Deep, beautiful curves that got sexier by the day. I couldn't wait to have an hourglass figure like my mother.

I learned that men liked coy girls. Girls who seemed shy, but weren't really. Girls who gave the signal to have men make the first move. Girls who flaunted it, but didn't give it up.

Acting like this allowed me to have anything I wanted. From free candy to free concert tickets to free booze. They didn't even care that I was underage. In retrospect, very clearly underage. Thirteen-year-olds don't look like they're twenty-one, no matter how much we thought we had filled out, or how much makeup we caked on.

But I didn't want any of these things, not really. What I truly craved was simply the attention, just like my mother. I suddenly understood the high she got from it. I liked being the object of desire, of making men's knees turn to Jell-O and their brains turn into that creepy cymbal-clapping toy monkey.

That's exactly what happened to my uncle. When he saw me, his brain took a lunch break and his penis took over. Since I'd flowered, glances had become a thing of the past. He put me on birth control and then, he got handsy.

The first time it happened, I was in the kitchen washing the dinner dishes. I felt him staring at me, and instead of feeling confident and coy, I retreated within myself. He had raised me and he was family. My dad's brother. I didn't want the attention from him. I wanted him to tuck me in at night and protect me from men like him.

In my less-than-perfect world, it wasn't like that. He wanted me to look at him or at least acknowledge him in some way that night. I refused to turn around, despite his eyes burning holes into my back.

Finally, he broke the silence."Well well, little girl, I must say," he said quietly, stepping forward into our cramped kitchen, "you have grown up so much since I've been living here."

The walls and ceiling felt so much closer than they had before. I opened the window over the sink, leaving soap suds on the sill. I didn't answer him, but I wanted to say, "Yeah, dipshit, that's what happens to living things; they grow," but something stopped me. Stopped up my throat and clamped my mouth closed.

"I know you know what I'm talking about." He stood right up behind me, breathing in the smell of my shampoo.

I was torn. I didn't want him, yet I wanted to impress him. I needed him to be a father figure rather than this pervert, yet I'd been trained my whole life to obey authority.

He grabbed my ass and squeezed. "This. This right here." He gave it a tap and walked away, laughing.

I finished washing the dishes in silence. I stood there, running water over chipped ceramic, in a fog. I didn't know what to make of what had just happened. I knew I should have felt sad or mad or upset in some way, but I felt numb instead. It was as if I needed someone to tell me how to feel.

I put the last plate in the drainboard, snuck past the man I didn't recognize anymore, and waited in my room for my mother to come home.

Chapter 3

My mom told me she didn't believe me. I told her, words sticking in my throat (out of embarrassment? Out of loyalty?) when she came home, three days later. She lay on her bed in clothes that reeked of smoke and body odor. I told her what happened, exactly as it'd happened, and she called me a liar and a slut.

"It's your fault. You wear your hoochie little outfits and bend over all the time. It's no wonder. You're asking for it. Knock that shit off."

"But Mom, I didn't do any of that! He's my *uncle!*"

She narrowed her eyes at me. "I bet you liked it, didn't you? And now you want me to feel sorry for you?"

"I don't want you to feel sorry for me. I just want you to be home more. And maybe for him to leave." I nearly whispered the last part.

She stared at me, lips pursed. "I see. You come up with this crazy story so I could be here more? For what? To give you free stuff? Make you dinner and wipe your ass for you? I work for my money, unlike you. I am out of the house to provide money to feed you. And this is how you repay me?"

I took a deep breath, trying hard to reason with her. She didn't bring in any money, not to her family anyway. We had money from my dad's life insurance, and my uncle did have a job, although he didn't talk about it, and he always seemed to be home, waiting for me. He did keep food on the table for me, I had to give him that. I might have been emotionally and sexually abused, but I was physically healthy.

I watched as she picked a spot on her neck with bony, grey fingers. I shook my head. "Mom, you really don't get it."

"So I'm stupid now? This man practically raised you unlike your low-life father, okay? And you want to accuse him of some nasty shit? What, because he doesn't give you everything you want?" The fact that she called my father a low-life showed that she wasn't herself, that she hadn't been herself for years. I may have been young and my memories distorted, but I know for a fact my parents loved each other with their entirety. The woman on the bed in front of me was the real disappointment. My father never would have tolerated this. If he could see her now, he'd call her weak for letting his death destroy her.

"That's not what I'm saying at all. Mom," I looked closely at her eyes, which she could barely keep open, "are you high right now?"

"Get out!" she yelled. She grabbed a cup off her nightstand and threw it at me. It shattered against the wall far to my left, the drugs in her system messing up her aim.

At the doorway, I turned to face her. "My dad was not a low-life. He was a great man who loved and cared for me. But he's dead and you're not. Goes to show how unfair life is."

After that, I tried to stay away from home as much as possible, but I was still at the age where everyone had curfews and no one had a car. Mostly I just stayed outside at a park down the street until cops started picking me up and bringing me back home.

My uncle would answer and smile, expressing his gratitude for bringing me home safely. "Pre-teens, you know? Never appreciating the roof over their heads," he told them, chuckling the way middle-aged white men do, shoulders bouncing dramatically to each deep bark.

One cop patted me on the shoulder, nudged me inside. I stood next to my uncle, now his turn to rest his hand on my shoulder. My skin crawled. I wanted to scream at the police standing in front of me. *I'm not some stupid pre-teen!* I pleaded with my eyes. *They do horrible things here! Save me!*

If the police tried to read the look on my face, something was lost in translation. They read the face of a rebellious girl who got caught doing something wrong rather than a child who was being molested by her uncle and forgotten about by her mother. "Oh we certainly know. We see girls like this all the time. Have a great night." He answered my uncle's bass guffaws with a couple of his own.

Suddenly, I was a 'this'. I was spoken about, but not to. I was nothing to the men on the doorstep. The men who were supposed to be my protectors. Once again, altogether disappointing.

Uncle Glen brought me inside and sat me on the couch. "You can't keep getting yourself into trouble, little girl." He peeked out of the window, waited until the cops drove away, closed the curtains more tightly. "You can't be bringing people like that around here. They don't like people like us."

I rolled my eyes. "What? Perverts and teenagers?"

The back of his hand connected with my cheek with enough force to knock me over. I cried out, curled up on the couch, surprised he struck me, but also expecting more blows. I closed my eyes as tightly as I could. "Look at me, and apologize." I didn't open my eyes. I was afraid he wanted me to see the next swing as it came. "Look at me, and apologize, dammit!"

I stared at his chest, unable to look at his face. "Sorry," I said through tears.

"Sorry for what?"

"For calling you a pervert," I mumbled.

"Apology accepted." He lifted my head and sat down next to me. He laid my head in his lap, unzipped his pants. "Now, you're going to make it up to me, okay?"

If my mother was home, he wouldn't even look at me. As much as I resented her, I loved when she was there. I could handle her mood swings and her drug-induced ramblings if it meant my uncle was ignoring me.

When she wasn't home, I was irresistible bait. Nights were the worst. He'd come in to my room whenever he was feeling up to it. Sometimes midnight, sometimes four in the morning, any time in between. The first time he forced himself inside me, I screamed. It hurt more than I expected, but that I could handle. What made me scream and cry was the sheer fact that he was taking this from me. My first experience. I'd never have it with a guy I loved. Or even liked, for that matter. It wasn't consensual. It wasn't romantic. It wasn't anything I'd dreamed it would be.

I wanted to be sixteen when I gave someone my virginity. I wanted it to be in a warm bed, or on the beach. At night. I wanted the man I consented with to kiss my neck sweetly. To run his fingertips along my wrists, my hips, the insides of my thighs, so lightly it would bring goosebumps to my skin. I would kiss him full on the mouth, our tongues gliding across each other. My heart would pound through my ribs and against his chest in excitement and nervousness; his would beat against mine in reply. We'd take one another's clothes off, slowly at first, then more quickly as passion arose. He'd ask me before entering me if I was ready. I'd nod, smiling, and give myself over to him completely. He'd kiss me the entire time and our rhythms would align. Afterward, he'd hold me against him, kissing me every so often, lacing his fingers with mine.

But this, this was completely different. It was forceful, and all business. There was nothing tender about it. He shoved his way in, and seemed to like it even more after I cried out. Afterward, he wiped my tears away with the pad of his thumb and told me I was so sexy. Then he told me this was our little secret.

He stayed away for the most part, but at least once a week, he'd be back in my room. Sometimes after school he'd shove my hand down his pants or push my head down. Often, he would hold my face in his hands afterward, semen burning the back of my throat, and tell me that he loved me. "You know I love you, right?" I was his special little girl.

Sometimes, on the days he was sober, he'd wrap his clammy fingers around my neck until I saw black spots, like a film burning through on the screen. Those were the nights he'd pat my face and laugh afterward, telling me I did a great job.

Those were the nights I wished he'd squeeze my windpipe a little too long.

Chapter 4

As soon a s I could, I joined every after school club. I became a swimmer. I did yearbook. Track. Photography. All of it. My principal pulled me into her office multiple times telling me I was taking on too much. I batted my eyelashes and turned on my innocence. "Mrs. Tompkins, I assure you, I'm just trying to get the most out of my experience here. I need to take advantage of what I'm offered. I'll never have these opportunities again."

This always pleased her. She smiled an understanding smile, tilting her head toward me and nodding slightly. "Okay, dear, but if it gets to be too much, no one will be upset with you if you drop one or two."

"Okay, Mrs. Tompkins, I'll be sure to keep that in mind." I doubted if she had that conversation with the valedictorian. That girl was ivy league bound; I was lucky to head to the community college.

I wasn't very good at any of the activities. I came in last place in swim team all the time. I was actually afraid of water, but I wanted to overcome that fear. I tried so hard in that club, but I couldn't keep up with the rest of the team. When the swim coach asked me if I really wanted to stay on the team, I told him that I would like to sit out at competitions and meets, but I would greatly appreciate staying for the practices. "I know I'm not a good swimmer, but I want to get better. I know myself and if I don't have a class to take, I won't go on my own." The coach told me it was perfectly doable. I made a mental note to talk to him a little extra.

I never did well in my photography class either. The teacher tried helping me, but I didn't retain any of the information. He just started letting me do whatever I was going to do. I couldn't focus on what he was saying, and I didn't actually care about technique. I liked trying new things and learning by trial and error, which meant my composition was all wrong and the majority of my pictures were blurry. If the teacher wasn't a balding, bearded, bouncy-ball of a man, I probably would have tried harder. I simply didn't care about impressing him.

Yearbook and track were surprisingly okay. I wasn't the worst at either of those. Certainly wasn't the best, but the teachers didn't pull me aside to see if I wanted to stop participating. Neither of them even noticed that I existed.

Of course, with all this physical activity, I was getting toned. If guys thought I was attractive before, well, my legs and arms had definition that even fewer boys and men could ignore.

I was asked out around every corner. I had a boyfriend or two, but none that I could really stand for long. They were all such children. All awkward invites and slobbery kisses. Girls all tried being my friend. If they hung out with me, maybe boys would notice them.

I went to every sleepover I could. I didn't connect with many of the girls, but some of them had alcohol, which was fine. There was one girl I grew to love, though. Ashley Hale. I could tell she had secrets too, and she thought all the boys we went to school with were wastes of time. The best part was that she had a beautiful home with loving parents. I stayed there as many nights as I could.

"Why don't you ever want to go home?" she asked one night as we painted our toenails and shared a beer. She was beautiful. I thought she was way prettier than me, but she thought I was prettier than her. It's funny how girls are like that. Her hair was long and rich auburn with natural waves. She had big straight teeth, and her mom let her pluck her eyebrows. I asked her to shape mine. My skin around my brows was red and swollen, but I couldn't stop staring at them. I loved them so much.

"It's not a very good situation there. That's all."

"Well, like what?"

I bit my lip and stared at the pink polish drying on my toes. I wasn't sure I could trust her yet, but I so badly wanted to. "It's just bad."

"If I tell you something really bad in my family, will you tell me? I won't tell anyone. I promise."

"Okay. Tell me."

"My brother had to go away for a while. My parents say it was to boot camp because he didn't behave, but," she dropped her voice to a whisper, like she was gossiping, "I think he got sent to the psych ward."

"Wow, okay. Um, really? What for?"

"Yeah, I was really little so I don't really remember it. Plus my parents still try to cover it up. But yeah. People at school said that my brother and his friend were like sixteen and my brother just freaked. I don't know what set him off but I guess he stabbed his friend."

She was so nonchalant about it all. I didn't know how to react. "Is he going to get out any time soon?"

She carefully applied her top coat. "I don't really know. Like I said, my parents still tell me he's at boot camp. Honestly I don't know if he is crazy or if he stabbed anyone, but no one will tell me anything, and I'm not supposed to talk about it, but now I have you. I haven't told anyone else." She looked into my eyes. Hers were a gray-blue that went on forever.

"You have really pretty eyes, you know that?"

"Thanks, I made them myself."

Sweat prickled on my palms. I wished I hadn't changed the subject like that. It made me seem aloof, and that's the last thing I wanted her to think. "Sorry about your brother. And thanks for trusting me with your story. You can tell me anything, you know."

She smiled, nodded. "Tell me about you."

This was the closest I'd felt to anyone, yet I still struggled to find the words. I didn't know if she'd believe me, or if she'd call me a slut like my mother did.

"Okay. My mother does drugs. Hard drugs. I don't know which ones, but I'm guessing heroin. Maybe meth. She's pretty much never home. My dad died when I was little and his brother came to live with us like six years ago or something. Anyway, he's started making me...do things. Sexual things."

She leaned forward, her eyes piercing into me. It wasn't scary or judgmental or even disbelieving. "Paige, that's horrible. What does he make you do?"

"Everything."

"Like, *everything*?" She raised her eyebrows and motioned with her head toward my crotch.

"Yeah." I looked back at my toes, ashamed.

She leaned over and embraced me. "I am so *sorry*. That's awful. I won't tell anyone." She held my shoulders and looked at me. "You can talk to me. Okay? Any time. I don't care if it's the middle of dinner and my grandparents are visiting. You can just talk to me. We should have a secret word."

I laughed. "Like what? Coconuts?"

"Yeah! Exactly. If you're ever feeling super sad about it and want to talk, just say something about coconuts and we'll talk about it. If we can't get away, we'll just have to talk in code."

"My coconuts are really hairy."

She laughed and pushed me. "You'd better start shaving. Boys won't like you if you have hairy coconuts."

"Or probably if I have coconuts in the first place."

She let out a snort and covered her mouth. I laughed harder. I hugged her.

"Thank you so much," I whispered. It was so nice having someone to tell.

That summer her parents took us both on vacation. Three weeks at a cabin away from my house. Away from my mother. Away from my uncle.

We hiked and swam in the lake. We sunbathed and drank beer when her parents were out. They probably knew; there was no way they thought someone was breaking into the cabin stealing a couple beers every few nights. Then again, they probably knew they couldn't stop it and at least we weren't taking body shots with college kids every night and blacking out. Being in that cabin not worrying about anything at my house made me feel safe. It felt like I had a real family. A sister and parents who loved me.

I don't know if Ashley told her parents about my uncle, but I'm sure they knew something was bad about my home life. They never asked why we didn't have sleepovers at my house and they always offered to let me stay with them. They took me to and from

school. They tucked me in at night.
I was in heaven with them.

Chapter 5

For three years, I lived like that. I actually got good at various sports, even the ones I'd never played before.

Ashley's parents pulled strings to get me on the team for some games, like basketball, despite failing miserably during tryouts. I was the best benchwarmer that school ever saw, but it was nice. I loved cheering on my team and not having to be home. I liked the adrenaline of running up and down the court and the feeling of pride when I (rarely) made a basket.

Of course, her parents didn't have everything to do with me getting on the basketball team. I pumped my chest out -- perfect full C cups now -- and tossed my hair at all the right moments. I pleaded with my doe eyes and said, "I just really want to play. I don't have to play during the actual games. I don't care about that. I just want to be a part of something that matters. And it's good for my health, both mental and physical. Isn't the whole point to play and have fun?" Voila, I had them hooked.

"Okay, Harper, but don't complain if I don't put you in any games."

I did my best Marilyn Monroe impression. "Oh, of course not, coach."

"Shouldn't you be a cheerleader? You look more like a cheerleader than a basketball player."

"That is sexist and has homophobic undertones."

He stared at me, blinking. His double chin quivered as he

chewed a morsel of leftover food dislodged from his teeth. I never understood how coaches had double chins. Shouldn't they be fit like the athletes they're teaching? He spun on his heel and walked away.

Well, got him to like you, then trapped him in a corner. Great job, Paige.

Softball was better, though. That was a game I could actually play. I loved the moment when the ball cracked on the bat. I could feel it running through my fingertips, up my arms, and down my spine. It gave me almost as much satisfaction as seeing guys drop for me. That the was the one sport I played all year long. A group of us played during off-season, which the coach loved; it really "showed devotion and drive."

My dad had a Louisville Slugger when I was little. It was broken in and lovely, like old leather. He told me we'd play one day, but we never got the chance. Now the bat sits in a hall closet, patiently waiting for someone to hold it once again.

No one ever came to my games except Ashley. Sometimes her parents, or another of her friends. Never my mother. Never my uncle.

Not that I really cared. It just reminded me why I needed the distraction after school.

Of course, *in* school there was a new distraction. Mr. Owens: history teacher. He was like all the best things you've ever seen personified. Like chocolate cake and lazy days at the beach and your favorite song all wrapped up into one tall, built, intelligent man.

He took an interest in me one day after school when our game was canceled due to rain. I had his class sixth period - the last one of the day - and he noticed me hovering after the bell rang. I didn't want to go home, and without practice, I had nothing to do. Ashley had ballet and I just had a house that might have been empty, but also might not have been.

"Paige, can I talk to you?" His voice was velvet and cream. Deep, resounding. I could never get enough of his voice. And the mouth it came from. Gorgeous white teeth, big and straight, surrounded by kissable lips I couldn't take my eyes off of.

"Yeah, sure. What's up?" I moved my hair behind my ear slowly.

"Do you have anything you need to talk about?"

"What do you mean?" I traced his face with my eyes. Despite being at least forty, he had no lines in his rich skin. His hair was black, no sign of gray.

"Well, when your games are canceled or you don't have one, you linger. Usually the kids who linger have … troubles, at home or with their peers."

I hid a smile. He cared about my well being. I welcomed the butterflies. "Oh, no, no troubles."

"No one's teasing you for playing softball?"

I saw where he was going with this. He hadn't had some beautiful insight into my home life. He hadn't read my mind and discovered I needed help. So, I gave him what he wanted. "It's weird how when you play sports as a girl, the rumors start that you're a lesbian. Not that I have anything against being a lesbian. As far as I know, I'm straight, but I mean, I'm still just a teenager. You never know what could happen in the many years ahead of me. All that bothers me is that people pick up a stereotype and never let it go. There's only one girl on the softball team who might be, but she's not even sure herself yet. Then you get all of the high school population making fun of her and it just makes it even more confusing for her. They make fun of all the other girls too, but they know deep down that they're not, especially when the whole softball team and the whole football team gets together at a house party."

He raised his eyebrows. He'd never heard me string more than three words together and here I was rambling about sex of all things. I continued without pausing. "Then there's me. I'm labeled a lesbian because I play softball and basketball. I'm labeled a slut because I'm above average in the looks department and I have confidence. I don't date guys my own age so I'm a prude. I'm the most popular girl in high school, yet I don't talk to anyone except Ashley. High school is a box dripping with hormones and angst. Contradictions and all this crap that doesn't matter once you get into the real world."

He stared at me blankly. I hadn't given him an answer and he didn't know how to continue. "So, you are having trouble with your peers? Do you need to talk to someone?"

Someone. Not *I'm here for you. You can talk to me.* I stopped myself from rolling my eyes. Instead, I zeroed in. "I don't have issues like my hair having split ends. No, my hair does have split ends, of course. I style and dye the shit out of it. It feels like hay but looks like the girls on the shampoo commercials. That's not what I mean, though. What I mean is that I don't care about the things these girls care about, like split ends and who made it to the cheer team and if Bobby slept with Stacy. I care about real world issues. I know there's life outside high school and none of the stuff that happens here really matters. Once it's over, it's over.

"And this is why I don't date guys my own age. They can't see past their lockers or Stacy's boobs. This is why I like older men. They have careers, homes, stability." I raised my eyebrows and leaned closer to him over the table.

He coughed, rubbed the bridge of his nose. He wasn't fazed. "Okay, well, I'm not sure what your romantic life has to do with struggling with your peers, but I'm going to have to assume you're not having trouble if you're not saying you are. But you know you're more than welcome to stay after school. There are counselors and people here who stay late just for that sort of thing. If you are. Having trouble. With your peers."

"Thanks, Mr. Owens." I smiled like I had a secret.

"You're welcome. Um." He looked at the door.

"See you tomorrow." I nearly skipped out of his class, hoping his eyes were on my ass as I wiggled it for him.

The next week I obsessed over Mr. Owens. In the healthiest way possible, I assure you. Like any other teenage dream. That seductive voice whispering my name in my ear. His strong, midnight hands massaging my pearly breasts. The two of us alone in his locked office, the adrenaline of possibly being caught coursing through our veins.

"Paige," he said, breaking me from my daze, "could you remind the class why Stonewall Jackson was called Stonewall Jackson?"

I sighed. He was calling me out. He did it all the time to other students, but never to me. I finally realized what all the other girls were spacing out about in class. "Because. He… was like a stone wall, always stoic and never to crumble." I did my best impression of a strong army man.

"Okay, Paige. Try to focus a little here, alright?" The class

24

giggled. I went straight back into daydreaming.

I couldn't move my legs fast enough on the way home that afternoon. I had forgotten my home life. I had forgotten my fear, my anger, my resentment. All I had was sheer infatuation.

I'd never felt this before. Of all the men I wanted to be attracted to me, I never felt attracted to them. I didn't understand this new feeling. A crush. I wanted a man to like me not just for the attention, but because I actually liked him.

My heart stopped fluttering happily and plummeted straight down to the bottom of my stomach when I saw my house. I didn't know what to expect when I got inside, but I crossed my fingers that I found nothing. I opened the door as quickly and quietly as I possibly could. There was a creak if you opened it more than halfway, so I slid in before it made noise. The click of the latch boomed in my ears. I stopped dead, heart in my throat, praying I wasn't heard. I was like a child hitting a squeaky step on Christmas morning, sneaking downstairs before their parents wake up. No one came out. I still held my breath as I crept to my bedroom. I stopped when I saw him, laying on his bed, napping, a beer still sweating on the nightstand.

Pure loathing boiled up inside me. Years of my life wasted. I could have been building strong relationships with people my own age. I could have had this feeling of a crush long before I turned sixteen. Instead, I was too worried about not going home to focus on experiences most young girls have.

I glared at him from the hallway, knowing full well that he wouldn't see it. It would never effect him, but it made me feel a little better. I closed the door to my bedroom as silently as I could, curled up on my bed, and waited for Ashley to get home so I could tell her all about my new crush.

Chapter 6

I paused. We were halfway through my third actual session with my therapist and foster care director. I say "actual session" since the first few sessions consisted of the three of us making small talk and staring at each other. I'd been able to speak about all that had happened so easily once I got going. It felt absolutely amazing to get it all out. I cried consistently during the part about my uncle coming into my room at night, which cut my session short. They let me cry it out, but when I couldn't say any more, I left, went back to my dorm to work on a self-help exercise they gave me. I was supposed to write out in detail exactly what he had done to me. Step by step. Then I was to burn it.

I filled a whole notebook.

The next session, I carried on. The exercise had been the most wonderful thing I'd ever done. As much as I loved softball, it didn't come close to the experience of filling and burning that notebook. I talked and talked and talked, never stopping. I felt myself getting lighter, happier.

But then I reached this part of my story. This was the hard part. The part I'd pushed down deep inside me to forget forever. I couldn't *not* talk about it. It was crucial to my story, to my development. I thought talking about the rape would be the hardest part, but that part was cake compared to this.

The doctor looked at me expectantly. He still wore his poker face, as he had throughout all my sessions, even the ones where I didn't cooperate, but he raised his eyebrows, just slightly, encouraging me to go on.

The director didn't have a poker face, which I honestly appreciated just as much as the doctor's ability not to reveal emotions. The doctor was my rock; the director, someone to gossip with. She teared up when I cried, made little gasping sounds periodically, put her hand over her heart. While it was her disinterest at the beginning that made me start talking, it was her personal interest that made me want to continue. Yet here I was, completely blocked by my own mind.

Finally, the doctor spoke. "Miss Harper?" was all he said.

"I-- I don't know." They already knew what happened. It was in the police report, which they both could probably recite from memory with how many times they'd gone over it. I looked at my hands, picked at my pink polish.

"It's alright. Let's take a break this session and talk about what you've already told us. We'll take a deeper look into all of it, okay? Then next session we'll pick up where you left off. Does that sound like a good plan?"

I nodded.

"So. Let's look at your relationships with your peers. Did you have friends your own age when you were little? Before your father died?"

I tried to think back. It seemed so long ago. After a while, I said, "Yeah. Yeah, I did. I remember having playdates and stuff with other kids."

"Girls or boys?"

"Mostly girls. Sometimes there would be boys, but boys always had cooties." I giggled.

He laughed with me. "I do remember having a lot of cooties when I was a boy."

I struggled to imagine this old man in front of me as a kid. Definitely couldn't.

"What happened to these friends of yours?" he asked.

"I don't know. I guess just the normal stuff that happens with kids. You end up in different classes and stop talking to each other. It's not like I hated any of them or anything."

"When do you recall not having friends your own age? Other than Ashley, of course."

I thought for a while. I didn't really like the quizzing. I felt like

I had to have the right answer, but that was stupid. There was no right or wrong answer. This was my development. It was important I tried my hardest. "Maybe when I got to middle school."

"When you noticed your uncle starting to notice you in inappropriate ways." It was a statement, not a question. He already knew what I was going to say before I even said it.

"Yeah, that sounds about right."

"Why do you think that is?"

I sighed. I wanted him to tell me so I didn't have to think so hard about it. He already knew the answer. "Um, because I was forced to grow up too fast? So I started experiencing adult things before I was an adult."

"He spent more and more time with you, and let you spend less time with your peers, is that correct?"

"I guess so. I don't really remember. I thought that was normal though, like spending time with your dad. But I do remember him not letting me go to sleepovers a few times because he wanted to have dinner with me."

The doctor nodded slowly. "You spent time around an older man, talking about things adults talk about instead of the normal things pre-teens talk about. Now, it is completely normal for people to be attracted to traits they see in their parents. That's the way they were raised, so they find people like that. You've heard the phrase that every man marries his mother? Well, this is why that phrase exists."

"Definitely thought that had some weird meaning before. But now that makes sense." I could feel myself turn red when he laughed.

"No, not quite like that. In addition to finding traits in other people like your guardian's, it is completely normal for women to find older men attractive. It's biology. Women look for emotional and financial stability. 'Can this person take care of me and my family?' Men develop emotionally slower than women. Women are ready to settle down and start families far before men are."

"Makes sense."

"What makes your situation different, in your opinion?"

I started shutting down. "I don't know. My uncle fucked me up I guess. What else do you want?" He stared at me patiently. I took a deep breath. "God, I don't know. I only find older men attractive, not guys my own age. I want the attention from men, not boys. Aren't you supposed to be giving me answers?"

"I'm here to help you discover answers yourself."

"You're not helping very much," I grumbled.

He continued, undaunted. "Would you say that the loss of your father played a role in this attraction to older men?"

I thought for a minute. "Yes? Maybe it's like I'm trying to replace him. No, not replace him. But like, fill the void, so to speak."

He nodded and smiled ever so slightly. "And what about your uncle and his actions?"

"Well, I was trying to have him take the place of my dad, but then it got weird."

"He was also taking the place of a lover."

I scoffed. "So loving."

"Yes, his aggression is what squashes your own attraction toward the men you want attention from. You seek the comfort and the solace from your father, but you've become confused about healthy adult-youth relationships, sexualizing them because it's what you've been taught."

Looking at my hands, I answered, "I think so, yeah."

My words hung in the air. "That's all the time for today," he said, leaning back in his chair. "I want you to think on what we discussed today. Just explore the pieces of the puzzle. Come back next time with any revelations and then we'll pick up your story where we left off."

He stopped me when I reached the office door. "Oh, Paige?"

I rolled my eyes, getting ready for him to give me more homework. I turned slowly toward him, my hand on the door handle. "Hm?"

"I know these upcoming parts of your experience are going to be especially difficult, but I need you to be completely honest with me." He stared at me meaningfully; he was the sweet old man who caught the cat with a feather in its mouth.

I put on my most convincing smile before I turned the knob and went back to my room.

I laid on my bed thinking about what he had said. It's not my fault I'm the way I am. There's nothing *wrong* with me; I've just been nurtured differently than most people. People just need to accept me the way I am.

Chapter 7

The day it happened, I was feeling especially flirty with Mr. Owens. I'd worn just a touch of new makeup I'd treated myself to during one of my walks away from the house. I've heard that people tend to act completely differently when they wear masks. Something about how they're not going to suffer repercussions because their faces can't be seen. They can't be identified and the Id part of their brain takes over.

Makeup seems to work the same way. Girls put it on, and the confidence takes over. Even if they're like me and don't need or generally wear makeup. I love it just to play. My winged eyeliner and hint of blush certainly made me feel playful.
I batted my eyelashes at Mr. Owens. When we made eye contact, I slid my eyes down his chest, settling just below his belt for a moment before sliding back up to his eyes, so dark and immense they were almost black. I smirked, flicked up an eyebrow.

He cleared his throat uncomfortably, losing his train of thought.

"So, the events leading up to the Civil War." He paused, attempting to remember his lecture, eyes pointed toward the ceiling. "Ah, yes. We had Dred Scott. I'm sure you've all heard his name, at least I'm hoping you have." Blank stares; he avoided looking at me. He'd see the fire behind my eyes and lose his thought again. Sweet satisfaction. "Seriously? None of you have heard of Dred Scott? Well, you're about to get an ear full. He was a slave back in the 1800s. That's not newsworthy. What is, though, is that he sued for his and his family's freedom. 'But Mr. Owens?' you say, 'how can you sue for your freedom?'"

I giggled to myself. Not because of the subject, but because he was so nerdy. I loved it. Like, who teaches like that? He's just up there, making up conversations and saying it out loud. Probably only like three people were even paying attention in the first place. I tried, I really did, but he was just so goddamn beautiful.

He avoided my eyes the rest of the class. After the bell rang and the class herded themselves out, Mr. Owens called me into his office. My heart leapt.

"Yes, Mr. Owens?" I said, honey dripping from my lips.

He sighed and rubbed his eyebrows with his slender, strong fingers. "I'm not sure how to approach this." I blinked and smiled, willing for him to continue. His eyes wandered around his office. "Um," he faltered again. Finally, he looked me dead in the eye. "Look, I don't know what's going on, but it needs to stop."

"What do you mean?" I asked, being completely honest.

He took a deep breath and blew air out slowly, filling his cheeks. I smiled affectionately. Little things like that made him so irresistible. "I don't know how to put this. Remember how a little while ago, I asked you about why you stayed here and I wondered if you were having troubles?" I nodded. "Tell me if I'm wrong or being too forward, but it seems like after school you wait around here until everyone leaves so you can be alone with me."

"How did you jump from troubles at home to wanting to be with you specifically?" There wasn't a drop of bitterness in my voice; if anything, I sounded defensive and I wanted to shake myself.

"I don't want you to take it the wrong way." Now he sounded defensive. "Girls tend to do that, especially at this age. I've seen it before. They tend to latch onto their male teachers. Sadly, sometimes it's even reciprocated. Not in this case, of course. This is what I mean by 'trouble'. It isn't the trouble I meant then, but situations change with new information."

"Maybe it just takes me a long time to pack up."

"Don't you have basketball or softball anymore? What happened with that?"

"I quit."

"The girls were rude?" Genuine concern crept into his voice.

There was no point in lying. "No, I wanted to see you more." I winked. I'd been practicing my winking just for him.

He sat up straight and immediately built a wall between us. "Paige, your body language, comments, and gestures toward me in class are inappropriate and I'd like for them to stop, please."

My smile dropped. "You just said! It's not like I'm the only one --"

"Yes, I see the other girls. It's something that happens. But they're just daydreaming and whatnot. They're not making rude comments."

"My comments are not meant to be rude. I'm sorry if they came across that way. I'm trying to flatter you."

"By wolf-whistling around your friend when I walk by during lunch? By telling me I've got a great body so the whole class can hear?"

"It's true," I mumbled.

"It's one step away from feeling like I'm walking past a construction zone."

"You're right, Mr. Owens. I'm sorry. I'll be more subtle and respectful of our relationship. I understand that you want to keep things private. Thank you for being so forward with me. Have a wonderful day." I smiled politely and skipped out of class before he could object.

I pranced home, humming happily to myself. The man of my dreams was finally coming around. I shook my head. How could I have been so stupid? Of course he wanted me to keep things hush-hush. I was a minor and a student. He'd be fired and probably lose his teaching license altogether. He was risking a lot to solidify our relationship, and here I was, announcing it to the world.

We'd have to take it slow. Secret meetings at first: simple stuff, like talking after class and maybe meeting him during lunch to "do homework." Then we'd have covert rendezvous' under the cover of night. Maybe we'd meet at his house, or in a secluded park. Somewhere romantic. We could take trips together. I would take the bus to the other end of town and he'd pick me up, to ensure that nosy neighbors wouldn't see us drive away together. Then we'd just drive, wherever the road took us. We'd wake up next to each other, roll in the sand at the beach together, spend all our time together. Our relationship would be that much more special because it would be something no one else knew about.

My tummy flitted with excitement. Our future together would be beautiful.

I cruised into my house without thinking; about my mom, about my uncle, about sneaking around. I just waltzed right in like any normal teenager would. That was my mistake.

"Hey, little girl, you happy to see me?" Uncle Glen slouched on the couch watching the game, legs spread, straining the fabric of his sweats. He was smiling. From his tone, he sounded like he legitimately thought I was happy to see him.

I tried to bring back the happiness I had felt seconds before, so as to not upset him, but it wouldn't come.

"What? Cat got your tongue?" He laughed heartily.

I forced the corners of my mouth upward. "Yeah, sorry, it's just, um, I don't know --" I grasped for the words swimming just ahead of me, trying to find the right ones that wouldn't offend him, ones that would please him but not imply that I wanted him to touch me. I prayed that this was a night he wasn't in the mood.

He laughed again and stuttered rudely. "I–uh–ih–ah. All that school and can't talk straight. Boy, if your dad could see you now. He'd have a field day."

Mentioning my dad twinged on something deep down within me. "My dad wouldn't make fun of me."

"Oh, relax. He liked joking. You probably don't remember, but he'd just have a little fun with you is all. Nothing bad, promise." He put his hands up in surrender, still clutching his beer. "How was your day at school?"

"Since when do you ask me about school?" I sneered. Since when did I talk to him like that?

He seemed slightly taken aback but recovered quickly. "That's what fathers do, right? Ask about school and boys and all that normal stuff."

"You're not my father."

He chuckled. "No, of course not, no one could replace him. I just figure I'm the prominent male in your life, which is normally a father. Therefore, I'm your father figure. See?"

I nodded, inching toward the hall. "School was fine. Good. Same as always. May I go to my room?"

"Don't you want to know about my day?"

"Normally daughters don't ask."

He raised his eyebrows and nodded, considering my answer. "Right. Off you go. Be ready for dinner at six. I'm getting take-out."

I ambled to my room, in a fog. I wondered if my uncle had always been this person. If instead of being that loving man who raised me, he really was molding me to his plaything, and I was a dumb blind child who fell for it.

A calmness had come over me. From where I didn't know, but I welcomed it. I closed my door softly, took off my backpack and shoes, and laid on my bed, phone in hand. I dialed Ashley.

"Hey, boo, what's up? You okay? Aren't you supposed to be at practice?" The panic in her voice made me laugh.

"No, I'm fine, promise. I quit the team."

"Wh--why? You love softball! Not to mention what it keeps you away from."

"I don't know. I think I found a new after school hobby. Plus, lately he's been showing up when I'm sleeping anyway, so there's no reason to stay away after school. It's like the night makes him crazy."

"Shit," she breathed, "sorry." She left enough pause for me to talk about my feelings. When I didn't, she asked, "What hobby, if I may be so bold?" I could hear a half-smile spreading across her beautiful face.

"Mr. Owens," I whispered, not wanting my uncle to hear.

"No, shit! Such a babe."

We broke into a fit of giggles. "I know, right? His perfect jaw line…"

"And his big, strong…shoulders."

We giggled again; I nearly let myself outright laugh, but I remembered my uncle would be able to hear me.

"What do you think it'd be like to actually, you know, have sex with him?" she asked.

"Oh my god, it'd be like heaven. He'd treat you right. Massages and tender kisses and he'd talk about how beautiful you were. And you'd always finish first. More than once." I giggled again.

"Or maybe," she said slyly, "he'd push you against a wall and show you who's boss. He'd let out the wild side I know he has." I could almost see her bouncing her eyebrows up and down.

"I'm pretty sure I'd be the boss, not him."

"Ooh girl. Of course you would be. Sometimes it's nice just to let someone take you though, you know?"

I didn't know. It was different for her than it was for me, I guess. I needed to be in control at all times because I so easily lost it with my uncle. I wanted passion but I know if I were really in that situation, I'd panic. "Well," I sighed, "I have to go. I just wanted to inform you of my new sport."

"Go get 'em, tiger. Keep me updated on that. Maybe this weekend we can hang out. It's been so busy I wish I could hang out before that, but you know how it goes."

"Don't even worry about it, but yeah, definitely. Let me know when you're free. And I'll let you know when I'm not getting up close and personal with Mr. Owens' big, strong muscles."

"Just one in particular. Hey, Paige? Um, try to stay safe tonight, okay?"

"You know I can handle myself."

"I just always worry about you."

"Thank you," I said sincerely. To lighten the mood, I called her *Mom* in the most nasally, obnoxious voice I could muster. "Love you, boo."

"Love you too."

When we hung up, I had the empty, lost feeling I always get when I'm left alone again, like I wasn't sure what to do with myself. So I stared at my wall and sighed a lot, trying to gather the strength to do anything productive at all. My homework mocked me, and I couldn't ignore it any longer.

I drew hearts on my history essay, all along the margins and by my name. I decided that was way too noticeable. Anyone walking by would see them and would catch on immediately to what Mr. Owens and I had. I crumpled the paper and started over. I wanted to send him coded messages within the essay, but I wasn't sure how to let him know just what I was saying. I'd seen on TV coded notes that spelled things out if they were folded in just the right way, but I couldn't figure out how to convey that, and I certainly didn't know if he knew how to make an origami flower.

I decided to write love notes weaved within my essay. That way, if anyone wanted to look over his shoulder, nothing would jump out at them, but he'd also wouldn't be left alone to decipher a code. "Harriet Tubman was an amazing woman," it read. "She was fearless, risking her life to save others from a terrible life of slavery. You're the most handsome man I've ever seen. She was born into slavery, but successfully escaped. She aided seventy slaves in escaping as well, then went on to be an advocate for women's suffrage. I can't wait to see you again tomorrow. Maybe this weekend we can meet. Let me know." The essay requirement was only a page, but I filled three with my notes. Plus I really did admire Harriet Tubman.

Dinner was different that night. There was a charge in the air. Not like the one I felt around Mr. Owens. This was more like a comfort within myself and who I was. I was sure of myself rather than scared and weak. I sat up straighter. I didn't indulge the man sitting at the table across from me. The man who noisily slurped up his chicken chow mein and picked out the peas like a child. The man who couldn't go a day without drinking a beer. The man who suddenly claimed to be my father when he was anything but.

"You look very nice," he said, a creepy sweetness oozing from his words.

"Okay," I answered curtly. I readjusted my chopsticks, subtly reminding him of his embarrassment at having to use a fork. I embodied Harriet Tubman, gathering the strength within myself to fight against this man who thought he owned me and my body.

He coughed. "That's not a good way to answer a compliment. Usually the polite thing to say would be 'thank you.'"

I stared at my food, swallowing the *thank you* that was quickly building up in my throat. I refused to say it. Harriet Tubman didn't speak for women's rights by doing whatever men said. I'd followed what he said for so many years. Anything he told me to do, I'd do it without hesitating. Today, that stopped. I finally realized I have my own life. I'm my own person and I can do whatever the hell I want. I was tired of living in fear. I demanded to get my life back.

"Well," he said when I didn't answer, "is there a reason? A boy you like maybe?" He smiled tauntingly, cabbage stuck next to his short canines. Jealousy dripped from his lips. He tried to hide it, but I remembered the last time I had a boyfriend. My uncle found his number, called him, and threatened him with his life.

"Maybe I just like to dress this way."

His smile dropped. He coughed again, fiddled with his food.

A lightness filled me. He was insecure. I fought back a smile. This man I've feared for so many years was just an insecure little worm. Show any resistance and he crumbled.

"You seem different today. You okay?" he said after a few minutes, his mouth a tight line.

I shrugged. "Just normal changes, I guess."

"You on your period or something?"

My head snapped up involuntarily. My narrowed eyes met his empty ones. I glared so hard and with so much hatred I truly thought he would be physically injured. Instead, he blinked, expecting an answer but mocking me at the same time. He had to get a dig in because of that insecurity nagging him at the base of his brain.

I stood, flipping my hair at him. "For your information, not that it's any of your business, I'm not. I'm just not taking your shit anymore."

He smirked. "Glad you're not on the rag. It would make things tonight a little messier."

I threw my food in the trash as hard as I could and stormed out of the dining room. Maybe I wasn't ready to stand up against him. I fought back hot tears, hoping he didn't hear me sniffling. I wondered how many nights Harriet Tubman cried herself to sleep before she made her move.

That night, after hours of mindlessly watching TV and half-heartedly doing homework, I tried to sleep but sleep wouldn't come. I stared at the ceiling. Spots and squiggles played across my sight, my eyes trying to see through the darkness.
I rolled over to look at the clock. Just after midnight. I'd have to be up and ready for school in less than six hours.

I flopped onto my stomach in frustration, nearly smothering myself in my pillow. I counted sheep. I tried to focus on the blackness of my eyelids. I listened to my breathing, keeping it steady and rhythmic.

My mind wandered back to Harriet Tubman. She'd probably beat me senseless if she heard some white girl comparing her problems to the horrors thousands of people suffered. I'd like to think maybe she'd be happy to know she was still inspiring people years later, even if in small ways.

Suddenly, I felt like a giant disrespectful idiot. I forced myself to think of the man who first introduced me to her. Mr. Owens, with his vast intelligence. I'd have to ask him more about her the next day in class. Picturing him talking to me, educating me, led my mind further astray. I relaxed enough, imagining us holding each other, his lips brushing against mine.

My beautiful half-dream was rudely interrupted by a creak in the hallway. I jerked into reality, unsure of my surrounding and why my heart was pounding. When it finally dawned on me what the sound was, he was already in my room.

"Hey, little girl," he whispered. "Can't sleep, huh? I can hear you in here, tossing and turning. It's okay. I'll wear you out."

"Get the fuck away from me."

He stopped at the edge of my bed. "Ooh, little girl's got a little fight to her, huh? I like that. You're growing up. Getting some womanly defense to you."

"What the hell is that supposed to mean? I grow up and get *womanly defense*?" I spat. I'd never talked to him this way. It was both liberating and terrifying.

He was still a little drunk and in a relatively good mood because of it. I probably could have gotten away with enduring a few seconds of him flopping around at half-mast before he would have wandered back to his room. He would have slept soundly, snoring the entire night, completely without remorse.

Instead, because of my newfound voice, he lunged at me. "What'd you say, little bitch?"

His drunkenness made him slower than usual. My reflexes were strong and quick from sports and I rolled off the bed into a push-up position on the floor before he could reach me. The bedsprings whined as he flopped face-first on the bed where he thought I should have been. He growled in frustration as his hands searched for me, still not realizing I wasn't there.

I stood, attempted to run, but the sheets twisted around my leg and I tripped over them, landing hard back onto the floor. A grunt escaped my lips, alerting him to my whereabouts, but I'd already untangled myself and started running before he could right himself. By the time he figured out which way was up, I'd already opened the door to the hall closet.

I grabbed my dad's beautiful old Louisville Slugger.

"Oh, my little girl's got some fight in her, huh?" he said, lunging at me again. "I'll give you something to fight –"

I spun around, knuckles white as I gripped the bat. I looked him dead in the eye before I heard the gorgeous crack of his skull against solid maple.

Chapter 8

Here lies dear Uncle Glen, to be remembered for his selfless act of caring for his late brother's daughter in a time of need.

As I stared at his motionless body, I cringed thinking of what people would say about him. *Never speak ill of the deceased.*

I spat on him, right in his face. I held the bat up ready to swing in case he woke up, but he didn't move, even after my saliva slapped wetly against his cheek.

I dropped my arm, bat still in hand. My heartbeat slowed. I took a moment to take in the aftermath of what had just happened. Thick, nearly-black blood oozed from his temple, seeping into the worn carpet. His left eye was swelling and turning purple. His right one stayed half open, staring at the wall behind me. His pinky finger twitched.

I expected to panic, to faint, to be weighed down by the guilt of what I had just done. Yet there was none of that. No guilt whatsoever, although it didn't really feel good either. I just felt accomplished, like completing a long math problem. I'd finished a difficult part of my life and it was time to move on.

I called the police. I'd watched enough law shows with Ashley to know that disposing of a body always looks bad, no matter the circumstances. Plus, he was a very heavy man, and yes, I was strong, but I don't know that I could carry him out of the house.

"Nine-one-one what is your emergency?"

I made my voice shake. "A man tried to hurt me and I hit him in the head and now he's bleeding and I don't know what to do he's not moving!"

"Take a deep breath, Miss, and tell me your location."

I gave her our address. She told me to stay on the line, but I hung up anyway. *Ding dong, the witch is dead* was all I could think; I worried I was going to say it out loud.

Also from watching TV, I knew not to wash my hands, walk around, move the body, call anyone, or pretty much do anything. All I wanted to do was call Ashley and let her know the news, but she'd have to find out later.

So, I sat outside and patiently awaited the police.

In the ten minutes it took the cops to get to my house, I did feel a strange mix of emotions. I couldn't stop fidgeting, probably from adrenaline, but it made me giddy. I almost felt *bad* for what just happened. After all, he was my uncle. He was family. He raised me. I hated him, but I'd spent so much time with him, I guess I related to him. I never understood when Mr. Owens talked about Stockholm Syndrome, yet here it was, hitting me over the head.

Above every other subtle emotion, there was emptiness. Like when you watch an amazing movie and you fall in love with all the characters. Then something happens and you know nothing can go back to the way it was. This, right here, was the turning point of my life.

I heard the sirens on the main road getting closer. The police and paramedics turned them off when they pulled into the neighborhood but kept their lights flashing. I stood to meet them in my driveway.

There were so many cars and so many people. It seemed completely unnecessary. It wasn't like he was going anywhere anytime soon. They didn't have to worry about chasing him down.

Police ran inside before the paramedics. That seemed so backwards. If anyone was hurt, they could bleed out while paramedics waited for the police. (*What if he bled out before the paramedics could reach him?*) Later I learned it was to make sure no one was a threat inside. Clearly the threat was outside, standing in her pajamas, shivering every time the cool nighttime breeze picked up. She was the one who played t-ball with people's heads.

An officer approached me, all business. He didn't crack a smile or try to make me feel relaxed in the least. "Hello, ma'am."

Ma'am? What, am I forty? "I'm officer Hernandez. This is officer Nolan." His partner nodded at me. "Are you the one who placed the call?"

I swallowed. I had legitimately started shaking. I thought I'd have to fake it, but here I was, truly going into shock and freaking out. "Yes," I squeaked.

"Are you hurt?"

"No."

"Is there anyone in the home?"

"Just my uncle but he's…"

He looked at Nolan and nodded. The paramedics trotted inside with a stretcher, Nolan falling in step with them. Hernandez watched until they crossed the threshold, then turned back to me. "Ma'am, would you like to tell me exactly what happened?"

"He was trying to attack me. In my bed. He broke into my room and tried to rape me. I got away because he was drunk and I ran to the closet and got my dad's old bat. He followed me and tried again but I hit him in the head with the bat as hard as I could. Then I called you guys and waited out here."

"Mm," he said, writing in a little notepad. His face gave away nothing. I didn't know if I was in trouble or if he believed me or what. "Was your uncle your guardian?"

I didn't know the answer to that. I couldn't say whether or not he'd adopted me. I was so young when he moved in. I gave a non-committal shrug and said, "He's lived here since I was ten."

"Where's your mom and dad?"

"My dad's dead but my mom is at work. She works late." I'd said it so many times I almost believed the lie myself.

He didn't blink at the "dad's dead" comment. Usually people feel bad for mentioning a dead family member even though they couldn't have known in the first place. I respected that. Saying sorry wasn't going to bring him back. "You should probably call her and tell her to come down here."

He watched as I dialed my mother. My heart thudded wildly against my sternum. I hadn't called my mom in so long, I wasn't even sure she had the same number.

After four rings, it went to voicemail. *You've reached Kitty, leave a message.* "Hi, Mom, it's, um, it's me. Something happened and I need you to come home as soon as you can. It's Uncle Glen.

Um, just come back as soon as possible. Thanks. Bye."

The officer stared at me, clearly amused by my impersonal message to my own mother. He'd already decided I was a moody teenager and my mother was an angel working two jobs to support me. I lost respect for him just as quickly as I'd gained it.

The officer's partner came back out to talk to me, following behind the stretcher carrying my uncle. "He's unresponsive. He's going to Higgin's Regional."

"Can they bring him out of it?" The worry in my voice stemmed from the hope he wouldn't ever wake up.

"They're not sure at this point. You'll be able to visit him soon."

For what felt like hours, officials scanned my house. They took photos, samples, examined locks and door knobs. They combed through every inch of every room. They scraped under my nails, examined my body for any sort of wounds. They took my dad's bat. That was the only time I cried, when they took it. "You'll get it back, don't worry," one of the officers said, smiling thinly. I didn't believe him.

"Am I in trouble?" I asked dumbly.

Officer Nolan sighed. "No, but I'll be honest with you, you could be. You'd better hope that you aren't tried for attempted murder. Even worse if he dies."

My stomach churned. Attempted murder? I think that was a little far off. Clearly it was self-defense, but getting raped tends to be the victim's fault, so who knew which way they would rule.

I watched them all leave, a few telling me they thought I should come with them to do a rape kit. I didn't think it would help me at all, considering he hadn't actually done it that time. Lawyers would say I made the whole thing up and I was a cold-blooded killer.

I couldn't go back inside. Going in alone, seeing the dark stain on the carpet in the hallway, knowing my mother would be home soon. I just couldn't face it.

Which was odd. So many nights I wished I would get the guts to kill him, and when I finally did, I felt guilty. I wanted to apologize to him, to make it up to him.

Chapter 9

I paused my story, lost in thought, something dawning on me.

"What is it, Paige?" the shrink asked me.

"It's just, do I -- do you think I love him?"

His eyes, paled with age, met mine. "Do you think you love him?"

I fought back a biting laugh. "This isn't a game! You don't need to answer my question with another question! Believe it or not, you can actually *answer* me with a real answer." I crossed my arms, refusing to look at him.

He sighed. We sat in a standstill for minutes. I looked at all the books on his shelves, all about psychiatry and how to help others as well as yourself. I wondered if he'd actually read them all or if they were there merely for show.

Even though I wasn't looking at them, I could feel the director and my doctor motioning to one another. She wanted him to answer me, since I was clearly not going to break anytime soon, and he wanted to wait it out to let me figure it out on my own.

I couldn't tell if I loved him or not. What would it mean if I did? Or if I didn't?

He was family. You're supposed to love your family, no matter what. You don't choose them, but fate put them there for a reason.

Then again, if your family is wrong, as mine clearly is, are you given permission not to love them?

If I loved him, it would be absolutely insane, and I'm not crazy.

Here was a man who hurt me countless times and felt no remorse, yet here I was, hurting him only once in my defense, bouncing between the unbearable weight of guilt and the ethereality of sweet freedom.

I couldn't think of another explanation. I must have loved him in some way. Looking back to that night, I went easy on him while I filled out the police report. I put all the blame on myself. I skimmed over the attempted rape, over the years of successful rape and abuse, yet filled out all the details of putting him in a coma.

Or maybe I only wanted to relive parts of my life with that man.

"It's okay if you don't," the director said, bringing me out of my trance. "Love him, that is."

My doctor stifled a grumble, clearly upset this woman with no psych degree would interrupt my train of thought.

"Thank you," I said, relief swelling in my chest. Someone had said it. Someone gave me exactly what I needed: permission not to love him no matter how thick blood is compared to water.

"Maybe you should think more on that, Paige, and we'll pick up where we left off next time," the doctor said.

I nodded and walked, nearly catatonic, back to my room.

I was happy to see my roommate wasn't at her desk. She was off somewhere else in the facility, probably seeing a foster family or, somewhat sadly and more likely, she was sitting in the library trying to avoid all social interaction.

Here, in our shared room, I was doing the same.

Yes, it was dislike that I felt. Hell, I think it was actual, bone-deep hatred for the man. He may have been good to me when I was growing up, but people change. I couldn't base my feelings of him on how he used to be, only on how he was now. There was no forgiving him for how he hurt me.

All regret rushed from my body in a single moment. He got what he deserved; he was even let off easy.

Chapter 10

I'd been texting Ashley. She responded sporadically, sleeping over at a boy's house. I told her not to call me, that we'd talk later. I didn't want to interrupt her night.

I didn't tell her I thought I killed my uncle. I only told her everything was crazy and my mom was coming home.

The idea of my best friend finding someone to date surprised me, but also thrilled me. Good for her. She'd have to tell me all about this new boy when we talked. Maybe I'd let her start the conversation. My side would kind of be a buzz kill.

A couple hours later, well after the police had left and the ambulance took my uncle's body to the hospital, my mother's car swerved up the street. She came to a stop, parking halfway on our poor excuse for a lawn.

"What the actual *fuck* did you do?" She came stomping toward me, heels in hand, completely unfazed by the rocks and dirt beneath her bare feet.

I stood, arms up, defending myself against a barrage of punches. "Mom! I was defending myself! Stop!"

"You little slut! Where is he? What did you do?"

Each swing missed, or was more of a gentle tap than anything that would leave a mark. I easily pushed her away from me. Legs buckling, she dropped to the ground. She stared up at me, wide-eyed, like I'd betrayed her.

Red spider webs covered the whites of her eyes. She could

hardly keep her swollen eyelids open. Her face reminded me of the meat of an oyster; shiny, rubbery, the unidentifiable color between white and grey. Her once-beautiful hair was matted on one side, her roots desperately in need of color. "Mom?" Her face contorted. She let out a sob. "Mom, what did you do to yourself?"

I bent down next to her. I put my hand on her arm, my heart pounding. She swatted me away, scratching my forearm with her nails. "Get away from me! Where is he? I want to see him!"

I didn't know how to handle her. She acted like a crazed mother who was told her child had been killed. Except that her child was right in front of her and the person she worried about was anything but innocent. "He'll be fine," I consoled her, although I wasn't all too sure. "We can go and see him tomorrow. Come inside and get some sleep. Please." I walked inside, glad she followed me, and hoping she wouldn't attack me from behind.

I didn't want her to see the dried blood on the carpet in her state. I guided her to the couch without touching her. She flopped facedown, telling me what a slut I was until she fell asleep. I set water down on the coffee table, encouraging her to hydrate, to flush whatever was in her system out. I dug a bucket out of the garage and set it next to the couch too, just to be safe. I laid on the loveseat across from her. I didn't like being that vulnerable around her, sleeping in the same cage as a hungry beast, but if she woke up before me and wandered down the hall to my room, she'd see the crusty blackness in the carpet.

What felt like minutes after closing my eyes, I woke to the symphony of slamming bowls and cupboards. I blinked, the sunlight stabbing my eyes. I squinted over the top of the loveseat into the kitchen. "What are you doing?" I croaked.

My mother popped out from behind a cupboard. "Making breakfast. You have no food in this place. Wow, you look like hell."

I groaned. I could definitely say the same about her. Dark circles cradled her sunken-in eyes. Her cheeks were sallow. I couldn't yet tell if she had all her teeth still, but by the way she talked -- with her lips taught and a slight whistle -- I had a feeling at least a couple were missing. I tried to picture her old self, but it was too far gone.

This woman was not my mother.

She set a bowl of cold cereal in front of my face. I sat up and took it from her. "What is going on? Last night you were hitting me and now you're feeding me?"

She forced a laugh. "Oh, sweetie, I wasn't myself last night. But now I'm right as rain. Now, eat up. We need to go to the hospital to visit your uncle."

How could she possibly be this chipper? When I woke up hungover, I thought death wasn't such a bad thing. This woman had been doing a lot more than drinking booze last night. She should feel like a steaming pile. Maybe she had taken something else this morning to take the edge off, so to speak.

I wish I had some of what she had, whatever it was. Sober felt awful and terrifying.

She watched me eat, but didn't even nibble on anything the entire morning. She rushed me, a bright smile on her lips, still covering the potential holes in her gums.

She wore the same outfit she came home in, slept in. She told me I needed to hurry and there wasn't time for a shower.

The drive to the hospital was silent. There was so much tension, it was almost visible. She stared at the road with a small upturn of her lips, while I stared out of the passenger side window. She weaved in and out of the lane, confirming my suspicions, making me fume even more.

All that bravery I felt the night before was gone. Today, I was freaking out. I didn't know if Glen would live or die, I didn't know if my mother would kill me in my sleep, or if she'd kill me driving. I didn't know what would happen to me.

When my mother saw Glen hooked up to machines, tubes coming out of his nose and arms, head wrapped to twice its original size, a shadow passed over her face. Had we not been in public, she would have come after me again, I just knew it.

She turned to the nurse. "I want to press charges."

The nurse glanced at me, her thick eyebrows knitted. "Excuse me?"

"You heard me. I want to press charges, in his name. He is a victim and he can't speak and I have to speak for him." She tilted her chin up and pushed her shoulders back. Her voice shook, unable to hold back her anger.

"Are -- are you sure? It was self-defense. It's your own

daughter."

My mother cut her off. "Are you stupid? Deaf? Get me the police, right now. I. Want. To. Press. Charges," she said through tight lips.

The nurse scurried out of the room, pointedly leaving the door open. I overheard her talking to an intern in the hall. "Just, go fluff his pillows or something." She was as worried for my well-being as I was.

I texted Ashley. *This is such a shit-show. Please tell me I can come over tonight for dinner or something.*

I hoped it would be a quick process. That the detectives would see my mother was a raving lunatic so I could get on with my life.

"I want you out of this room! Away from him!" my mother screamed at me. I ignored her and stared at my phone, waiting for an answer from Ashley. I was used to dear old Mom's violent mood swings. By the way the intern scuttled around, unsure of how to calm her or to even be heard above her screeching voice, he wasn't used to any sort of scene. He'd have to learn if he was going to work in a hospital. Emotions are high when loved ones are hurt. Granted, this would probably be a special case. Might as well let this be a teaching moment.

Yeah, come over whenever. I want to hear all about it. Ashley's beautiful words lit up the screen. I put it back in my pocket, waiting for someone with some semblance of authority I respected to tell me what to do.

I stared at the pea-green paint on the walls, wondering why they decided to make hospitals even less appealing. At least traditional white has a sterility to it; the green only made people feel more sick, I'm sure.

My mother screamed more at me, threatening me. She pushed me a little, nudging me toward the door. I sighed, knowing she wouldn't outright attack me in a building full of strangers.

The little nurse scurried back into the room, putting on her best calming smile. "Maybe it's best if you wait outside," she cooed in my ear after she phoned the police.

I sat on the hard bench set up in the hallway. I heard the nurse speaking sweetly yet urgently to my mother. "Ma'am, please. They're on their way. They'll be here shortly. Try to keep your voice down. There are patients trying to sleep and recover."

"Oh, yes, of course," she said, as if she'd forgotten herself. "So sorry. It's just -- I can hardly stand to be in the same room with the monster who did that to this dear man. He took care of us. Of her! And this is how she repays him? I can hardly control myself."

I heard her voice quivering. I tried not to gag. I couldn't believe I'd once admired her. She was just a slave. To men, to drugs. I was heading down the same path. I didn't realize it then, but that's exactly what was happening. I needed men the way I needed water to survive. I wish I'd come to that realization then, right there on that bench.

Instead, Detective William Harrington walked into my life.

Chapter 11

The detective and his partner strode down the hall toward Glen's room with a purpose. I didn't know which detective to stare at. She was tall, fit, dark-skinned and absolutely flawless. Her nearly-black hair flowed elegantly behind her, like she had a fan blowing on her at all times. She had a look in her whiskey-colored eyes like she could tie your spine in a knot and hang you with it while still looking smokin' hot.

Then there was him. He was tan, but naturally so, not that fake orange shit I've seen on so many people. Tan like he worked with his hands outside, sweat glistening on his shoulders. His dark hair was peppered with grey, and the sexiest faint creases surrounded his eyes. Just like his partner, he had a presence about him. Unlike her, though, he had a fatherly streak in him, like he'd nurse your wounds after he beat the shit out of you.

"Are you Paige Harper?" the female detective asked. Her silky voice caressed my ears. I gulped.

"Um, yes?" Was I serious? Where was the distance from the situation I had five minutes ago? My aloof attitude? All gone.

"I'm Detective DiPascua, and this is my partner Detective Harrington." I didn't know if the tug in my groin was caused by her or by him. I didn't know if I wanted to run and hide or if I wanted to jump their bones. At the same time. All I could do was stand there, my eyes bulging out of my head. "We're going to need to ask you a few questions, okay?"

I nodded aggressively.

My mother came out of the room. "Finally! Took you guys long enough! I want her out of here!" She pointed at me, foam glistening at the corners of her mouth.

Detective DiPascua turned to her. "Ma'am, she's going to stay right here and answer our questions."

"No, I want her as far away from my Glen as possible. She's a monster!"

The detectives looked at each other. Detective Harrington sat next to me on the bench while Detective DiPascua approached my mom. DiPascua squared her shoulders, widened her stance, and lifted her jaw. "Ma'am, she's going to stay right here with my partner and answer some questions." She kept her voice low. It was soothing, stern, and terrifying all at the same time. "We have gone over her statement and we have been briefed on the case. Because you clearly can't control your anger, I'm going to ask a nurse to stay with them to act as the adult since she is a minor. You and I are going to go take a walk, alright?"

The detective turned on her heel and my mother followed like a hurt puppy.

"Wow," I said, staring after them. "I want to be that powerful."

Detective Harrington laughed. "Yeah, she's something, alright. Usually in the male-female partnerships, the guy takes all the crazies. In our case, it's the opposite." He snapped his head toward me. "Not that, you know, your mom is crazy or anything. I didn't mean that."

"Oh, no, she definitely is. Total whack job."

He stared at me, analyzing my features, maybe memorizing them. I felt an old feeling bubble up within me. The one that reminds me I can make men turn to jelly.

"So, Detective," I said in my most sultry voice, "how can I help you?" There was that confidence I'd lost earlier.

He looked at the nurse who sat dutifully on the bench on my other side. Detective Harrington cleared his throat. "Well, firstly, you are not under arrest and you are free to go at any time. Do you understand?"

I nodded.

He nodded back. "Your mother is making a lot of accusations

about you and what happened with the man in that room. Would you tell me, in your own words, what happened last night?"

I smirked, flirting. "Why did I give my statement to two different police *and* write it down if you were just going to ask again?"

He shrugged, smirking back. "I want to hear it from you personally, not from them."

I nodded. Made sense. "I was sleeping and he broke into my room. He attacked me physically and I ran out of my room to the hall. I grabbed my dad's bat out of the closet and swung as hard as I could. I ran outside and called the police."

"What do you mean by 'broke into your room'? Was the door locked?"

"No, just closed. So I guess he came in, but I didn't invite him."

"I see. Did you go back into the room to hit him with the bat?"

"No, he followed me out of the room."

"How many times did you hit him?"

"Just once."

"Would you show me how you swung the bat please?"

"Um sure?" I pretended to hold a bat and swing.

When I raised my eyebrow at him, he said, "Just making sure your swing matched the evidence. See, if you were left-handed, it would have hit the other side. Do you know the man who attacked you?"

"Why does it matter how I swung the bat?" I wasn't flirting anymore.

"Maybe you were covering for someone." I may have dropped the coyness, but he certainly hadn't. "Now, do you? Know the man who attacked you?"

"He's my uncle."

"If he's your uncle, why did you automatically assume he was attacking you? Would it be odd for your uncle to visit?"

"Does she need a lawyer?" the nurse chimed in, panic laced in her voice as if she really cared about me. More than I'd heard from my own mother.

"No, Ma'am," Detective Harrington said across me. "As I have said, she is not under arrest. She has a right to one, of course, and," he looked at me, "if you don't want to say another word unless one is present, that is your right, but," he looked back at the nurse, "I'm on her side here. Just trying to clear everything up." He winked at me, and my heart fluttered.

The nurse put her hand lovingly on my knee. "Do you want a lawyer, sweetie?"

I shook my head. "It was self-defense. He was attacking me. I don't think I need one."

She sat up straight again. She nodded almost imperceptibly toward the detective for him to go on.

"Right, so, Miss Harper. Was it strange for him to be in your room?"

"Well, yeah, he shouldn't have been in there. I definitely wasn't expecting him in the middle of the night. Then he just lunged at me."

"Did he say anything to you? Or you to him?"

"No, he just came in. I woke up and there he was, about to attack."

"When you say 'about to attack,' how do you mean?"

Before I could stop, I embarrassed the hell out of myself by getting into a half-crouching position and making a snarling face. "Like that."

I felt my face burning, but the detective wasn't fazed. "You said he lunged at you?"

"Yeah, like he was going for my throat."

"You told the officers last night it was attempted rape. Why would you assume he was going to rape you? Has he done that before?"

My mind went blank. I'd forgotten I told them he was going to rape me. Why did I feel bad for him? Why did I want to cover up all the horrible things he did to me? I chewed the inside of my cheek. "I – I don't know why I said that. That was just my gut instinct I guess."

"So you lied?"

I stared at the floor. "About that part, yeah."

"Paige, it's very serious to lie to the police, you understand that, right?"

I nodded, staring at the floor.

"Paige, look at me." Detective Harrington leaned toward me and lowered his voice. His face was so close to mine, I could smell his aftershave. "Do we need a rape kit?"

And that's exactly why I regretted saying the word *rape*. I didn't want to have strangers poking and prodding my entire body. Even the idea shot an icicle down my spine. Sitting in court having everyone judge me, saying I asked for it. That I was a liar.

I stared into his soul, silently pleading with him. "No, I'm sorry I said that. I don't need a rape kit."

Detective Harrington sat up straight again. He wrote in his notebook, but didn't press the matter. "How did you get away?"

"It happened so fast. I don't know. I guess I just kind of rolled out from under him and I got caught in my blankets. But then I got away and made it to the closet before he could catch me again."

"He made physical contact with you on the bed?"

I paused. Would he have? I didn't know what the evidence said, or if they had even processed my uncle for evidence since he wasn't dead. "Yes. A little bit. But I managed to get away before he could put his whole weight on me."

"Hm. Saliva was found on his face. If we test it, will it be yours?"

"Are you sure she doesn't need a lawyer?" the nurse said.

I ignored her. "Yes, it will be mine. I spit on him in the struggle."

"At which point? Before or after you hit him with the baseball bat?"

The nurse huffed and fidgeted. "Before," I said.

"When exactly? If there was a struggle, wasn't it hard to find time to spit in his face?"

He had me. I emulated his partner and squared my shoulders, tipped my chin toward the water-damaged ceiling. "I don't remember."

He smiled, stood. "Well, Miss Harper, I think that'll do it for the day." He held his hand out to me. I took it. It was strong, calloused. It could crush mine with minimal effort. "Go on home and try to get some rest." He let my hand drop.

He nodded to the nurse before turning away to join his partner in dealing with my mother.

"Come on, dear," the nurse said, putting her hands protectively on my shoulders. "Would you like something to eat? Do you need to call someone to take you home?"

I faked my best smile. "Thank you so much, but I'm okay. I'll just take the bus."

Her mouth tightened. "Are you sure? It doesn't seem safe, a young, pretty girl like you taking the bus."

I shrugged. "Wasn't safe in my own home either, though."

Her mouth opened and closed like a fish.

"Thank you again," I said, trying my best to save her from wanting to dig herself a grave. "I'll probably be back soon, to see how he's doing."

I walked out of the hospital past the two detectives and my crumpled, crying mother. Detective Harrington smiled and nodded at me.

Chapter 12

At dinner that night, I was a nightmare. One second I was giddy and barely able to sit still. The next, I was overcome with deep, troubled sadness.

Ashley's parents noticed my mood swings, my fidgetiness. In retrospect, they probably thought I was on drugs.

"Paige, honey, are you alright?" Mrs. Hale asked, her mousy-brown eyebrows knitted. She cocked her head toward me. Her eyes were the color of the ocean, sometimes on stormy days, sometimes on clear days, depending on what was on her mind. Today, they were the Atlantic during a hurricane. I always loved them, and now that they showed genuine concern for me, I loved them even more.

"Yes, thank you. I just had a little bit of a rough day."

"Do you want to talk about it? You know this is a safe place."

She sensed some of the things going on in my home life, and I'm sure Ashley told both her parents at least a little bit of what was going on, just so they wouldn't question my need to be there. Telling me it was a safe place was her way of letting me know that she knew and she wouldn't do anything unless I asked her to, in which case she would do everything in her power to help me.

"My uncle's in a coma," I said.

Both Mr. and Mrs. Hale stared blankly at me. They were reading me for how to react. Normally it would be a tragedy. In my case, it was actually a blessing.

"It was kinda my fault," I added.

Their poker faces broke. "Oh, honey," Mrs. Hale said while Mr. Hale reached for my hand. "It's okay. Whatever happened needed to happen."

I broke.

I couldn't stop it. The tears poured from my eyes like a hot, heavy rain. My shoulders shook with each embarrassingly loud gasp for air. Stupidly, I worried I would literally drown.

Ashley hugged me and her parents told me to just let it out. I was thankful for them, not telling me that I was too pretty to cry or that only the weak broke down. When I finally regained my composure, I said, "I'm sorry. I don't know where that came from. He was an awful man. I shouldn't be crying about it."

I looked at Mrs. Hale. Her face was serene, quiet. The monsoon that had spilled from my eyes seemed to have cleared hers. I relaxed.

"It's shock," Mr. Hale said matter-of-factly in his deep, loving voice. "And now things are very different. But trust me, you'll be okay. Things will go up from here."

I nodded, sniffling. Ashley grabbed dessert from the fridge. "We're eating this in my room," she said, pulling me into her room.

We shed our clothes down to our underwear and flopped on the bed. She turned the TV on, flipped to a cooking show, and turned the volume up. She gave me first bite of Ben and Jerry's Funky Monkey, sliding the spoon easily between my lips.

This was a safe place.

The next day, things were definitely going up, just as Mr. Hale said they would.

Ashley and I were sitting in the courtyard eating our usual crappy school lunch of cardboard and grease when the breathtaking detectives showed up. The front desk secretary pointed them in our direction. How she knew me was beyond me. I had no idea what her name was and I'd only ever seen her when I passed the office to go to fifth period.

I nudged Ashley's shoulder. "Heaven is real," I said.

She nearly choked on her bite. "Holy shit," she said, sputtering, "is that them? You weren't exaggerating."

"You want him or her?"

"Seriously, dude, I want either. Both. Damn."

"Miss Harper," Detective Harrington said when he reached us.

I stood up to shake their hands. "Detectives."

They both looked at Ashley, either expecting an introduction or for her to leave, I couldn't tell. I followed their gazes. There she sat, cheeks bulging, eyes straining in their sockets, hunched over like a gremlin. "Um, this is my best friend, Ashley."

She crashed back to earth and swallowed everything in her mouth. I doubted if she'd chewed it; I swear I could see it chugging down her throat. "Hi," she croaked.

The detectives nodded at her. "Miss Harper, we wanted to ask you some follow up questions," Detective DiPascua said. "Is now a good time?"

"Oh, of course. Is here okay? I mean, it's closed campus but I'm sure you could talk to someone and they'd let me out."

"Terrance Owens has been kind enough to offer up his classroom during the lunch hour for some privacy, although I'm sure it won't take that long." She stared at me while I stared at nothing in particular. "If you'd like to follow us."

I jumped, finally getting the hint. "Oh, um…"

I looked at Ashley. She nodded earnestly. "Yeah, I'll talk to you after school." She turned to the detectives. "Really nice meeting you."

I sat in my normal seat in Mr. Owens' empty classroom with my new objects of infatuation. It felt a little naughty, like I was cheating on my husband with the gardener.

Detective DiPascua pulled up a chair and sat facing me while Harrington wandered around the room. "So, Paige, would you like to tell me your story? I know you already told my partner here, but I was hoping to hear it for myself."

Butterflies bypassed my stomach and slapped against my throat. The first time I tried to speak, only a squeak came out. I tried again. "Um, yeah. That's – that's fine."

She looked at me, smiling encouragingly. Big, white teeth surrounded by blush-pink lips.

I blinked, realizing I was staring. "Oh, right. Let's see." Dear, sweet mind of mine. Usually so calculating, so precise, so clear, now just a blank, shivering screen.

I looked at Harrington, who stood with his back toward us, thumbing through our books. My eyes locked on his ass, perfectly contoured in his khakis. Pictures fluttered back onto the screen.

"So I was in bed, sleeping," I said, all my confidence back. I rehashed the story, exactly as I'd told Harrington, never taking my eyes off him. If I looked at her, I couldn't function.

When I finished my story, she leaned into my line of sight. "Thanks, Paige. Now I'm in the loop. Did your uncle like to hurt you?"

I shrugged. I didn't know if I could tell her. I still didn't want my uncle to get into trouble. Even after spending hours thinking about how stupid it was to protect him, I didn't want to see him go to prison.

"It's okay to tell me." She leaned forward. "This is a safe place. We're here to help you."

I shrugged again. Interesting, how often people use that term "safe place". This classroom felt nothing like Ashley's sheets. I looked back at Harrington. I knew he was paying attention, even if he was pretending not to, by the way he peeked over in my direction every so often.

"Okay, we'll come back to that when you're ready. Paige, I'd like to talk about your mom. Is she at home?"

My shoulders were getting a workout. "She works a lot so maybe, but maybe not."

"Have you talked to her recently? Did you see her this morning?"

"I don't see her very often. She usually leaves before I get up."

"Right. I only ask because we're trying to carry out this investigation that she requested, but now she's completely unavailable."

"I'm sure she'll get a hold of you guys. She's a very busy woman."

"I don't doubt it. It's just that when someone is as ... passionate about getting justice as your mother was, they usually don't just drop off the face of the planet. In fact, we usually can't get them out of the station. I just wonder if you think maybe something happened to her."

My eyes snapped to hers. Was she accusing me of hurting my mom? As much as I resented the woman, I'd never do anything to her. "Do you want me to call her? I'm sure she's fine." I pulled out my phone and dialed her number before the detective could answer.

"It isn't necessary, I'm sure she is too. I just had to ask."

I turned away from her as the phone rang. My heart pounded in my chest at the prospect of ignoring the goddess in front of me, but I stayed on the line, determined to prove I wasn't a violent person. On the fourth ring, I heard my mother's voice. "Yeah?" The first time she'd ever answered when I called.

"Um, wow, you answered. Hi." I couldn't hide the shock, even in front of the detectives.

"What's up?"

I handed the phone to DiPascua. If I'd told her the police wanted to talk to her, she would have hung up.

"Mrs. Harper? This is Detective DiPascua. Is everything okay?"

A moment passed before I heard the little buzz of her voice. DiPascua nodded. "Okay, yes, I understand. Would you be willing to come to the station and make that official? I –" she looked at the phone. My mother had hung up on her. She could be such a bitch sometimes.

I took my phone back. "Told you she was fine."

The detectives looked at each other. Harrington raised his brows. DiPascua stood. "Thanks so much for your time, Miss Harper." She extended her hand. "We'll be in touch."

I led the way out of the room. Mr. Owens stood talking to another teacher in the hallway. He waved at the detectives who thanked him for letting us use his room. I blew a kiss in his direction.

Ashley texted me during sixth period. *They asked me if he raped you. I didn't know how to answer.*

So they questioned her too. I felt bad, dragging her into this mess. I hoped if there was a trial, they wouldn't make her testify. Hopefully she didn't have enough information to be important to the case, whatever case this was. Self-defense, manslaughter, attempted murder.

I just told them something wasn't right with him and you didn't ever want to talk about him. I hope that's okay.

Sounded perfect to me. Noncommittal but also implying the truth. I was thankful for that girl.

I called Ashley at 5 o'clock that night. I told her I wanted to go on an adventure.

"I can't drive by myself yet. My parents would never let me

take the car."

"Are they home?" Her parents found it to be very important to have a date night once a week, away from home.

"No, they're at the movies but they'll know."

"No, they won't. Just don't get caught. We won't be gone for long, promise."

Finally, she caved. She always caved.

She pulled up to my house in her mother's silver SUV fifteen minutes later. I'd been waiting, pacing in front of my living room window.

I slid into the passenger side, slipping a little on the cream leather. I wondered if I'd ever be able to afford something so luxurious for myself before I snapped at her, "Jesus, you live like two seconds away! What took you so long!"

She put up her walls. "At least I'm here. I almost backed out. Be thankful for that."

I smiled at her, knowing that was an empty threat. She rolled her eyes, letting a breathy laugh escape. "Shut up. I hate you," she teased. I smiled wider.

I made her drive to the station to wait for the detective. The clock crept closer and closer to six, and Ashley's whines reached an unnatural pitch. At ten after, when I was about three seconds away from tearing my hair out, that beautiful man walked down the steps to the parking lot. A leftover smile sat on his lips. I wondered if DiPascua had put it there, and if I'd ever do that.

He got into his sedan and drove slowly out of the lot. I made Ashley follow him. She did, despite all her protests.

In movies, the person being followed always leads the follower to some dark lair, some really messed up secret place full of drugs or women or a death chamber.

Real life was not the movies.

Detective Harrington went to the grocery store. He was in there for ten minutes and came out with a bottle of wine peaking over a paper bag.

Ashley complained more.

I made her follow him.

He stopped at a mailbox. Ashley glared at me. "Oh wow, he has something to *send*? Getting wild and crazy now, huh?"

"Fine, if you're not going to let it go, just take me home."

"Finally. Thank you."

Every turn we took, though, my detective had taken first. "Ugh, I don't want to follow him and now I can't get away from him. Oh, the irony," Ashley said dramatically, hand at her forehead.

A knife twisted in my gut. What if he knew? But how would he know? Images of him waiting for me at my house ready to arrest me for stalking ran through my head.

Then again, so did images of him waiting at my house, ready to take me.

Ashley stopped the car in the middle of the street. "What the hell are you doing? He's going to see us!" I yelled.

"No, Paige, look!"

He had pulled over in front of my house. The car was still running. He didn't get out. *He knew.*

I frantically told Ashley to pull into a driveway and prayed that he hadn't actually seen us. "What is he doing?" she asked, hunched down so only her eyes showed through the window.

"I can't tell." My heart pounded in my ears; my entire body trembled. My nervous stomach considered vomiting. I held my breath to keep it down.

After what felt like hours, he drove away. Just like that. Ashley dropped me off in my own driveway. She threw the car in park and turned toward me. "I think he was checking up on you. I wonder what would have happened if you had been home." Her voice trailed. She gave me a sideways glance and raised her eyebrow. We both broke into giggles.

"I seriously can't believe that!" she said, excitement spewing from every pore. "Like, that's a big deal. Paige has a boyfriend! A silver fox."

I punched her arm. "Maybe he was just checking to see if my mom was home. They can't track her down."

"Bitch, he's off the clock! I don't care how much you love your job, you don't go run errands and then go check on a drugged-up psycho just for fun. What if she had been home? He wouldn't have questioned her. That's not protocol. No, he was there for you."

My lips curved in a Cheshire grin. If I sat there any longer, I *would* puke, just from excitement. I hopped out of the car and leaned in to say my farewells.

"Welp, that was fun. Don't get pulled over on the way home.

See you tomorrow. Love you." I nearly skipped up my driveway.

"We're not done talking about this!" Ashley yelled after me as she backed out onto the street.

I took a deep breath while I fished for my keys. The ghosts of my dark house tried to take me down, but even they couldn't get to me that night.

Chapter 13

Mrs. Quinn, algebra teacher. She sure knew how to drone on and on about absolutely nothing. Day fourteen of the Pythagorean Theorem. A^2 plus B^2 still freaking equals C^2. We get it.

The door opened and a freshman on an adventure handed Mrs. Quinn a pink slip. There was a shift in the room; students coming out of their trances to revel in the disturbance.

"Ms. Harper," Mrs. Quinn said in her nasally voice. "The principal would like to see you."

"Me? Now?" I raised my eyebrows. My heart did a little jig. My first irrational thought was that my mother was there about to do something humiliating, stupid, and possibly really bad for me, like accusing me of murder.

Our teacher sighed. "Yes, unfortunately." She looked at the freshman. "Doesn't he know better than to take students away from learning time?" The freshman both shook and nodded her head. "You can go now, dear. She'll be in the office in a moment." The girl scampered out of the classroom.

I packed up my notes (doodles, to be more accurate) and walked the lonely halls to the office. It's weird, just how different high school looks when no one's around. It seemed so big, impersonal, unnervingly quiet.

I handed the secretary the pink slip. She waved me into Mr. Hall's office.

Mr. Hall was a gentle man. He'd replaced Mrs. Tompkins at the beginning of the year after she'd had what all the students were calling a mental break. He hadn't yet found his footing, still ignorant of just how awful teenagers could be.

He was the type of man you want to be your husband in the sense of security. He would cook your favorite meals and rub your feet, tell you you're pretty. He wasn't the type of man to ignite passion within you. He reminded me of a puppy, but with opposable thumbs.

He stood when I came in. "Hello, Miss Harper. Please, have a seat."

I sat in the hard plastic chair across from him. His desk took up most of the room; it felt like an ocean between us. The chair was too low. I was a little girl drowning beneath the waves. It was probably intentional, left over from Mrs. Tompkins who always made sure students knew their place.

"How are you? Everything going all right?" he asked.

Small talk before bringing down the hammer. I immediately bristled. I felt myself slouching, making myself even smaller. "Yeah, it's okay."

When I didn't offer up more information, he continued, even though both of us knew it'd be a mostly one-sided conversation. "The detectives called this morning. They said the case is likely to be dropped. Your uncle is stable and probably going to make it."

I checked my phone. Two missed calls and two messages from the station. I smiled. "I always knew everything would be fine with that."

"Good, good. Your classes going okay?"

"Yeah."

"Good. How are you feeling after everything, you know, with your mom and your uncle? Are you able to focus okay on your schoolwork?"

"Yeah."

"If you need to see the counselor, know that it's perfectly acceptable. No one even needs to know, not that your friends would judge you for going. You have good friends. Ashley, the people on your sports teams?"

I had no idea he knew who I was, or who Ashley was. I don't think he ever said one word to her. It made me feel icky – there's really no better word for it – knowing he had eyes everywhere.

"No, they wouldn't care."

"Anyone making you uncomfortable? Kids can be pretty brutal, especially in high school. You're so vulnerable at this age. Figuring out what to do with your life, who you are, what you like. Hormones are going crazy."

"No, everyone's acted like normal."

"That's good. Teachers? They've been okay?"

I fidgeted. I just wanted to get this conversation over with. I didn't realize getting out of class would be worse than sitting through a lecture. "Yeah. Nothing different."

He sighed, laced his fingers together. "Miss Harper. I'm not really sure how to go about telling you this."

Here it was, the moment we'd all been waiting for.

"Just tell me," I said, shrugging.

He sucked air in through his teeth. He slouched. This time, he was losing power. I pulled my shoulders back in response.

"Well," he said, "something's been brought to my attention, from a teacher. He feels you are too…you're making him uncomfortable."

What the hell? I was expecting something more along the lines of, "Your uncle is coming home and your mom is putting you up for adoption." I definitely didn't have to pretend I was shocked. "Uncomfortable? How? Who?"

"He says you're making lewd comments to him well within earshot of the other students. He says you're staring."

It all clicked. Another man who couldn't handle what I had to offer. Instead of seducing my way out of this, I raised my voice, imitating a squawking bird. "What else do teachers expect? They're talking at the front of the class. They always complain we're not paying attention but then we look at them and pay attention and all of a sudden it's uncomfortable staring? And as far as comments go, I don't know what they would be. Everyone makes comments in every class. I can't think of anything I've said that's *lewd*."

"He says you wait for him after class." Mr. Hall shifted in his seat. The leather squealed, and color rose in his cheeks. Just as I expected. I would bet my last penny Mr. Hall had a screeching wife at home, leaving him battered and scared.

I amped up my acting.

"Because I don't want to go home! You might have noticed, or maybe you haven't heard, but I have a shitty home life. My mom accused me of trying to murder my uncle. My dad's dead. My house is always empty. I hang around for a few minutes after school because I can't handle going to that house!" Tears pooled in my eyes. My voice cracked. Man, I was good. "*That's* the reason I joined so many clubs and sports. Does that not make sense? I finally decided I didn't want to be a part of any of them anymore but I still didn't want to go home, so I hung out in Mr. Owens' class. Is there really any harm in that?" The tears spilled over.

Mr. Hall sputtered. "I didn't mean to – I'm sorry. I never intended for you... Here, have a tissue. It was just brought to my attention so I had to address it. I will speak to your teacher about all of this. This is such poor timing."

I sniffled, regained my composure. "It's okay, I understand. I'm sorry I got a little crazy. It all just came out at once."

"No need to be sorry. You need to let it all out."

"Thank you. Is there anything else you need from me?"

"No, no that's all. I'll figure it out."

As I started to leave, Mr. Hall stopped me. "Paige? How did you know I was talking about Mr. Owens?"

"You said he complained about me waiting for him after class."

"Yes, but every class ends, and there are ten minutes between classes. It could have been any one of your male teachers."

"Weird. Didn't you ask me why I don't go home after school?" I really dug myself deep that time. I didn't know how to get out of it. Other than by making him think he's losing it in his age.

He cocked his head to the right. "No, Miss Harper, I don't believe so."

"Huh, you must have mentioned his name. I don't know. Have a good day."

I skittered out of there, back to algebra.

I couldn't turn my mind off for the rest of my classes. How could Mr. Owens say those things? We had something. I felt it.

Unless I was wrong. Maybe he didn't really feel anything for me. But I was only flirting. Harmless. There was nothing *lewd* about our conversations. I never did anything to him. Only complimented him, let him know I thought he was attractive. Certainly nothing inappropriate. None of it was even half as inappropriate or alarming as the catcalls directed at me when I walked down the street.

Or maybe I was out of line. I never really heard anyone else say those types of things to their teachers. They definitely said those things *about* their teachers in their own group of friends though. I mean, every day I was hearing how hot Ms. Edgerton was, and the things the boys would do to her. Ashley and I talked about Mr. Owens all the time. She liked her dance coach and talked about him all the time. ("I mean, probably he's gay because every other dance coach I've come across has been, but really he doesn't seem like it." "Or maybe," I'd tell her, "he's straight and really likes younger girls like you.") I wasn't that different from them. All I was doing was letting my teacher know my eyeballs appreciated him, and that the rest of my body would like to appreciate him too.

Unless.

Unless he was feeling guilty about his feelings toward me. That must be the reason he went to the principal. He knew he couldn't be with his student, much less a sixteen-year-old, but he had desires. All men do. I learned this very quickly. They have needs and desires that they can't always control. Here he was, brimming with these needs, but he knew it was forbidden.

My heart fluttered. Forbidden love. He felt guilty and wanted to confess his guilt, just like at church. He needed to free himself, but he couldn't outright say that he was attracted to me. He wanted to bring attention to it without saying, "I have feelings for Paige Harper, please relieve me of my sins!"

I bet it didn't work though, admitting guilt without actually admitting guilt. I bet he still has his desires, gnawing at him. He'd have to give in eventually.

At lunch, I told Ashley all about my trip to the principal's office, and about my revelation. "I dunno, dude. That sounds a little crazy," she said.

"What do you mean?"

"Like, Owens is really hot, and I know it would be the best thing if you were right about all that, but do you honestly feel that way? Why would he do that? He wouldn't go to Mr. Hall with a problem like that. He could pull you out of class. If he wanted to be with you, wouldn't he want it to be a secret and not draw attention to it?"

I rolled my eyes. "You just don't get it."

"I guess not, but seriously, that is such a stretch."

I looked at the wall, fuming.

"Paige! Don't get weird on me. It's just gone too far."

"Whatever."

She got the hint and changed the subject. Something about her dance recital. I only half-listened until lunch was over. I filed Mr. Owens under the folder of the few things I couldn't talk to her about.

Butterflies fluttered along the lining of my stomach before I walked into history class. I was more confused than ever after talking to Ashley. Had it gone too far? I mean, what would *really* happen if he and I started something? When I saw him standing at the front of the class, writing the day's lesson on the board, all I could imagine were long walks on the beach and happily ever after.

He didn't seem to notice me when I walked in. I took my seat near his office door, my heart racing. I couldn't keep myself from smiling. I suddenly didn't know what to do with my hands. I fiddled with a pen, flipped through my textbook.

The bell rang and he began class as always: "Good afternoon, class. The sign-in sheet is going around." He jumped right into the lesson, his delectable voice washing over me.

Halfway through class, I noticed he hadn't even looked at me. He didn't call on me to read or to answer questions. They were answers I actually knew, too. My heart sank, squeezing itself next to the dead butterflies in my stomach.

After class, I waited for him. He wouldn't look at me. "The homework is just to read through chapter six, right?" I squeaked.

"Yes, through chapter six."

"No worksheet?"

"No worksheet."

"Okay then. See you tomorrow."

He didn't answer me. I trudged outside, barely picking up my feet. A wet, heavy sadness wrapped itself around me. I just couldn't believe he'd treat me that way. I understand acting like he didn't have feelings for me to his coworkers and his boss, but to my face? When we're alone with no one in the world to judge? It baffled me.

I sighed and listened to the messages from the detectives. The first was from DiPascua. "Hello, Paige, this is Detective DiPascua calling. I just wanted to let you know that the investigation can no longer continue until your uncle wakes up. Give us a call back at the station when you can and we'll explain more. Thanks."

The next one was from Harrington. "Paige, it's Will Harrington. Trying to get a hold of you but you're probably at school. Call back at the station or on my cell phone." He left his number. I put it into my phone under *Det. Studmuffin.* I laughed at myself, embarrassed even though no one was around.

I wandered into the neighborhood next to mine. Sometimes I liked to go there, to see all the perfect houses with their perfect yards. Not that my neighborhood wasn't nice. It certainly was, but my house tended to ruin the aesthetic. It could be cute, would be cute, if my dad were alive. Green grass, big climbing trees, no chipped paint. Instead, the trees and grass were dead, speckled with mounds of dog shit, and the outside of the house looked like it belonged in a ghost story.

The neighborhood next to mine was quiet, sweet. Every single person was friendly to each other. Everyone of different backgrounds, religions, races, they all greeted each other throughout the day. Their kids played in the street together. There was no prejudice, no broken homes, no white trash like what my family had become.

There was a small park, more of a little cluster of trees and patch of grass overlooking the city, that I liked to sit at. Unlike most people, I kept my back to downtown and faced the homes.

I laid on my side, twirling a blade of grass around my fingers. The sunlight stretched my shadow nearly to the sidewalk. Goosebumps rose on my arms. A familiar sedan drove slowly up the street. I squinted, trying to see the driver. He turned just before the park and I glimpsed the side of Detective Will Harrington's face.

I grabbed my backpack and half-jogged down the street. I looked at the sign. Benjamin Franklin Drive. What an unnecessarily long street name.

The blue sedan pulled into a driveway about halfway down the street. I slowed to a normal walking speed.

He was dragging the trash and recycling to the edge of the

sidewalk by the time I walked by him. I kept my gaze ahead of me, avoiding eye contact with him until I was just the perfect distance away from him. I didn't want to look at him from thirty feet away and awkwardly fill time until we passed each other.

I smiled when he saw me. Sweet, neighborly, innocent. He smiled back and waved, sweet, neighborly, innocent. Then it registered.

"Paige Harper?" he said, half a wave still in the air.

I feigned a double-take. "Oh! Detective! Hi."

"What are you doing around here?" Genuine interest, not a threat.

I crossed the street. "Just taking a walk. I don't want to go home. No one's there."

"I can understand that. Did you get our messages? We didn't get a call back."

"Oh, yeah, I've been busy, sorry. Good news, right?" He'd invited me into conversation and I refused to let it drop.

"Yeah, pretty good news. We'll know more when he wakes up. Hopefully he won't press charges and then you'll be home-free. If he doesn't wake up soon, well, then it gets a bit more convoluted." He smiled, a little sadly, then shook his head. A breeze picked up his day-old cologne and a hint of sweat. I breathed deeply. "You walk around here a lot?" he asked. He had more to tell me about the case, but clearly he was trying to spare me. I took his bait instead of prodding him about my legal future.

"Sometimes. I usually hang out at school, but I didn't feel like it today."

"How come?"

I shrugged. "I feel like teachers get annoyed with me hanging around all the time."

"No, I'm sure that's not true. You're a nice girl. Helpful. I'm sure they enjoy having you around."

"Maybe sometimes, but they have their own lives and everything."

"What happened to doing sports?" Detective Harrington asked.

"I got sick of them. I had other interests. How did you know I played sports?"

"Well," his breathy laugh rippled through the air, "by the swing you took at his head, I just kind of assumed." He looked me in the eye. "Also I'm a detective. It's my job to look into people."

"Makes sense." I saw a flash in the window. The white curtains fluttered closed. Someone had been peeking out at us. "Well, I'll let you get back to your evening. Have a good one."

"Yeah, you too."

I snuck a look over my shoulder. A curvy woman hugged the detective, reaching up on her tippy toes. She pulled back. He shook his head. She put her hands up, pointed in my direction. I snapped my head back forward. I smiled. They were talking about me.

William Harrington. Will. I felt his name on my tongue, and I loved the way it tasted.

I circled the block, succumbing to giggles and resurrected butterflies. I slowed down when Will's house came into view. It felt nearly impossible to keep my legs from running. They shook with each step I took. I stayed across the street, so it would seem like I was just taking my regular walk, not hoping he'd still be outside.

My stupid grin dropped a little more with each step as I passed the house. He wasn't waiting for me. Just like Ashley said. I was taking things too far again.

Two houses down from Will's and I heard a screen door slam. It took everything I had to keep up my slow, steady pace and not to turn around.

"Paige?" A woman's voice, one I didn't recognize. I turned.

The woman stood at the end of her driveway. She still had the day's makeup on, still wearing a modest dress, crinkled a little at the waist, but she wore little blue slippers. I walked toward her, plastering a smile on my face. When I reached her, I stuck out my hand. "Hi, nice to meet you."

She shook my hand. Hers was cold and small. "Nice to meet you too. I'm Eva, Will's wife." We dropped hands. "Do you have anywhere to eat tonight? Will said you were just out here until your mom got home, but it's getting late."

"Oh, it's okay. I'll figure something out. I always do." I smiled brightly, mentally kicking myself in the teeth for not saying the exact opposite.

"When does your mom get home?"

"Um, it depends."

"Why don't you just come inside and have dinner with us. Then

Will can give you a ride home. A young girl like you walking around at night." She put her arm around my shoulder. She had a slight accent; soft Ts and Ds. Subtle, but I made a mental note to ask her where she was from later. I wanted to show interest in her, like she was my friend and I wasn't threatened by her at all.

The best thing to do was to get in good graces with the wife. Then she'd never suspect anything.

She held the door open for me and as I stepped over the threshold, I was enveloped in warmth. The smell of dinner cooking on the stove, the sound of a sauce bubbling, the gentle *click-whoosh* of a gas oven kicking on. Memories of childhood and love flooded my brain. The memories before my father died, before my mother turned to drugs, before my uncle turned to me. This was a home full of love, just like ours had once been.

"Here, honey, have a seat. I'll just go set the table. Will's in the shower, but he'll be out soon."

I sat in the family room, hidden from the kitchen. *Will's in the shower.* I couldn't stop my mind from wandering, imagining hot water washing over his naked body.

Mrs. Harrington talked to me, snapping me out of my trance, raising her voice just a touch to be heard around the wall. "I hope you're not a vegetarian."

"No, I'm not, don't worry."

"Okay, good, because we've got pork shoulder cuchifritos."

I had no idea what a cuchifrito was, but considering how delicious everything smelled, I wasn't lying when I said it sounded perfect.

I let my eyes wander around the room. There was no TV, just a beautiful built-in bookcase filled with books, maps, family photos. All smiles. A boy in his terrible twos, smiling broadly over his new plaything: a baby sister. A missing front tooth. Braces at the Grand Canyon. High school graduation, both the girl and the boy. My heart tugged when I saw the portraits of their children. I wasn't sure what type of jealousy it was: the kind where you have a broken family and someone else doesn't, or the kind where the man you're falling for has so much that he would never want you.

On the coffee table were travel books. I shuffled through them. Puerto Rico, Italy, the States.

"Have you traveled much?" I jumped and slammed the book

closed when I heard Will's voice. "Sorry," he laughed. "Didn't mean to sneak up on you." He sat on the cream-colored couch next to me.

"No. I went on a Ferry in Seattle once. I can't remember why we were there, but that's about it."

"Hopefully you get to see the world. It's too big a place to be kept in one spot your whole life. We always take a trip every year. These last couple years have been a little harder, since we're paying for two college educations now, but Eva took up a job in the morning at channel four."

"Is she on the news?"

"No, she's behind the scenes. But she has to get up just as early as the newscasters."

"What did she used to do?"

"She stayed home with the kids. Raising a family is a full-time job, you know?"

I didn't. I pretty much raised myself. He started to apologize after realizing what he had said when Mrs. Harrington called us to the table for dinner.

She said a prayer in Spanish before we could eat. Will leaned over to me. "She's religious. I never really was."

I looked at her. "Where are you from?" It came out sharper than I intended.

"New York," she said.

I nodded and looked hard at my food. A wave of acid from my gut lapped the base of my throat. My skin prickled. I doubted if she was the type of woman who found ignorance endearing.

"But my parents were from Puerto Rico," she continued. I loved the way she trilled her Rs. She playfully pushed Will on the shoulder. "You told me I don't have an accent anymore."

"I don't hear it!" He was cute when he was defensive.

"You can't really hear it," I said. "It's really subtle. Plus you were speaking Spanish when you were praying."

She tapped herself on the head. "Oh right, duh. I forgot. I never say it in English because he doesn't listen anyway. We only spoke Spanish in the home, but at school everyone spoke English. So I just have just a little accent." She held up her forefinger and thumb to show me just how small her accent was.

She looked so perfect. A mix of sexy and cute. Heartbreakingly, *they* looked so perfect. I heard Ashley's voice again, telling me I was taking it too far. I pushed her away and pulled my hair around to one side, showing Will my neck. Boys always turned to putty when you exposed such a kissable spot to them.

I was determined not to give up. I wanted to make Will come to me, but I'd underestimated Eva. She noticed right away what I was doing. Of course she did. She was a woman. We're intuitive, even more so when our husbands or children are involved. I'd have to reign it back in. I covered my neck with my hand, pretending I had an itch. I glimpsed at Eva, hoping my cover worked.

She took a bite and put her hand on Will's leg. My whole body shook.

Will cleared his throat. "So, Paige, you're our guest. Tell us a little about you."

I laughed modestly. "I don't know where to start."

"What do you like to do for fun?" Eva asked.

Make men crumble, but I couldn't say that. What would sound impressive and smart? "I love to read. And paint. Acrylics."

"Oh, wow, a little Picasso! I'd love to see some of your works," Eva said. Was she being genuine? I couldn't tell. Either way, I hoped she wouldn't push the matter. I think I painted (poorly) once in kindergarten.

"They're definitely not like Picasso, but I'm pretty proud of them."

"What do you like to read?" Will asked, unknowingly saving me from myself.

"Pretty much whatever comes my way."

"So you like to keep to yourself," Eva said. It was not a question.

"Well, I guess." When she put it that way, I sounded like a loner.

"I liked to keep to myself when I was your age," Will said. "Still do."

Eva looked at him. "Really? Hm, something I never knew about you. I always thought you were the popular football player."

"I was, but that doesn't mean I didn't like being by myself. The best company is yourself, once you learn to love yourself."

"Oh, I doubt if she has any trouble loving herself." There it was. She was so open and accepting of me before, but a woman can sense a threat. She'd been hot and cold through all the small talk, trying to decide if I was one or not. After that statement, I knew exactly what she thought of me.

Will cleared his throat again. It seemed to be his go-to in uncomfortable situations.

"Dinner is absolutely amazing, Mrs. Harrington. If I become even half the cook you are, I'd be happy," I said, smiling. I did mean it too. Ashley's parents were good cooks, but this was the best meal I'd ever had.

"Do you have family meals at home?"

"Eva," Will said sternly.

"It's okay," I said through a smile. "I don't. My dad's dead and my mom's never home. So this meal is something I really appreciate."

She swallowed, looked down at the remains of her food. Her tone softened. "You're welcome, honey. I'm glad we can be here for you. And I'm sorry, I didn't realize it was a touchy subject."

"Apology accepted. You didn't know." I peeked over at Will. He was nodding to himself. That's right, admire me for forgiving your snarky wife.

The rest of the dinner passed in uninteresting conversations peppered with uncomfortable silences. Eva touched Will's arm often, like she was claiming him, marking her territory.

I helped clear the dishes. I wanted them both to see me as helpful and responsible. Eva seemed genuinely impressed, surprisingly. "Oh, honey, you're so sweet!" she cooed. "If we could get our own kids to help clean up, it'd be a miracle."

"You made such a lovely meal, you shouldn't have to clean up too."

She raised her eyebrows at Will. "You hear that? She said I shouldn't have to cook *and* clean. Godsend, this one is."

I could not tell how she felt about me. One minute she thought I was going to jump her husband's bones (which would be correct) and the next she was calling me a Godsend (also correct, but she probably wouldn't feel that way after I jumped her man's bones). I had to admire her for keeping me on my toes.

"Okay, okay," Will surrendered. "I'll clean up. But to be fair," he said to me, "I do the cooking and cleaning every other night, *and* the crock pot did most of the work, so don't let her fool you."

She laughed. "I'm not fooling her! She's too smart. Well, then, I'm off to bed. Maybe I'll get some reading done with all my extra time not having to clean. Paige, honey, is it time for you to go home?"

Will answered for me. "She can help me clean up. I'll give her a ride home after."

A shadow crossed Eva's face. "I thought she didn't live far."

"Come on, babe, you were the one saying you didn't want a young, pretty girl like her walking alone after dark."

Pretty? He called me pretty! I'd been told that all my life but hearing it from his lips was just something entirely different.

"Of course. Your mom will be home soon, right?" she asked me. Her tone was dark, bitter.

"Right." I had no idea what time it was, but it was rare for my mom to keep a schedule anyway.

She hugged Will, then kissed him hard and deep. "Goodnight, love." She raised an eyebrow at me before turning to head upstairs.

I rolled my eyes at her back. Got it, lady, he's yours. For now, anyway.

"That's all fake, isn't it?" I said after I heard the master bedroom door click.

"What is?" Will asked, picking up a plate to rinse off.

"The whole thing. Her affection toward you. This perfect little life. I can tell. It's all an act because I'm here."

"Maybe I should take you home now," he said.

"I'm sorry. I didn't mean to upset you."

"Oh, you didn't. I'm just going to be cleaning up and you shouldn't have to."

I was going to argue with him, that he had just told his wife I was staying to clean, but I didn't want to push him. And I sincerely did not want to do dishes. At home, we'd usually use paper plates or eat out of the take-out cartons.

We went to the car without speaking. He opened the passenger door and I flopped into the sedan. "Why don't you ever talk about stuff?" I asked when he sat in the driver's side.

"What?"

"Like right now. I'm calling you out and you're avoiding it. At dinner you avoided everything. Why don't you face things?"

His eyes widened, taken aback. "I guess I never really realized I did that. What do you want to know?"

"About you and your wife."

Will's mouth tightened into a thin line as he reversed out of the driveway. "That's a little personal. I've had plenty of people over for dinner and not half of them know about my love life. It's not polite to pry."

"There's no better way to get to know someone," I said, dripping with innocence. I batted my eyelashes.

"I guess that's true. Yeah, dinner was different than normal. She's really very supportive. I work long hours and I'm usually in a bad mood. She's understanding. She lets me vent or whatever whenever I need to. We really only ever see each other for dinner, if I'm not working late. Dinner's usually pretty quiet though, unless we're talking about work. But then there's only so much to say. She goes to bed really early, as you saw. She leaves before I get up. It's not traditional, but it works for us."

"She seemed very protective of you. Like she saw me as a threat."

"She doesn't have any room to talk."

He was bitter. I knew it was a slip said out of suppressed anger and not an invitation to pry, but I asked anyway. "What do you mean?"

"No," he shook his head. "Maybe next time. It's too late to get into it now."

I turned on the radio. By the time I found a good song, we'd already pulled up in front of my house. "Well, thank you so much for letting me hang out. My mom should be back soon. I'll talk to you later."

He waited until I unlocked the front door. We waved at each other and I scurried inside to call Ashley.

I dialed her number as I ran from room to room, turning on every light. "Hey, babe, it's me," I said when she picked up. I flopped on the couch, taking full advantage of having the house to myself, but also a little uncomfortable with the idea of walking down that hall again. I'd have to face it eventually. Any time I needed to go to my room, I stared at the ceiling or just flat out closed my eyes.

"Hey, what are you up to?"

"Oh my god, you'll never guess. I just got back from Detective

William Harrington's house." I said his name in my best pompous British accent.

"No shit? Really? How'd you manage that one?"

"I was just taking a walk in the neighborhood and Will just happened to see me and invite me in."

"That's so crazy! Was it just you two?"

"No, sadly. His wife was there. Total bitch. She made awesome food though."

She laughed. "As long as she's got something going for her."

"I think I might take a stroll around the neighborhood again soon."

"He's so hot. I can't believe you got to eat dinner with him. Speaking of hot boys, actually, I found one myself."

"Who is it? Do I know him?"

"Maybe, but considering he's not a hundred years old, probably not."

"Oh shut up. I'm not that bad. I'd never date a hundred-year-old dude. My limit is ninety-eight." I had a small moment where I imagined what it would be like if I actually stayed with a man like Will. I'd reach a point where I'd be looking like a super hot MILF but I'd be stuck with the burden of changing his old man diapers. I shook the thought away.

"His name is Jake. He goes to Redfield. He's a senior. Super cute. I met him at dance. He's one of the girls' brothers."

"So you can be best friends with her and get to know him, right?"

"Yeah basically. She's kinda weird, but I'll just have to make a sacrifice for love."

We talked for another hour before I fell asleep on the couch, my future looking bright for once.

Chapter 14

Harrington took the scenic route home after dropping off Paige at her run-down little house. His heart raced. He'd gone too far with the girl. He was the lead detective on her case. Even if the case was in a standstill, it was still open. If the captain found out he'd had her over for dinner and had driven her home, alone, he'd have another heart attack.

Harrington couldn't help feeling bad for the girl though. She had no family, at least none worth mentioning. She only seemed to have one friend, which was odd since all the students he and his partner had talked to said she was one of the popular girls. The students admired her and thought it was just difficult to get in with her clique, despite the clear reality being that she had antisocial tendencies.

Understandable, considering her home life. Lucky thing, being a beautiful blonde in high school.

Eva sensed it too. It *was* her idea to have her over for dinner, and Harrington *did* try to protest. He told her no multiple times, saying it was against protocol and he could get in serious trouble for it. She went and did it anyway.

"What was I supposed to do? Drag my wife back inside before she could invite Harper to dinner?" Harrington's words hung in the empty car, an imagined argument with the captain if he were to get caught.

Eva sure did seem strange at dinner. She was never that

attentive. Had she actually been flirting with him? He laughed aloud, shaking his head. Maybe she was feeling randy.

A flash of a thought, less than a second, passed through his mind. Eva, Paige, and him, wrestling in the sheets together.

He shifted in his seat, swallowing hard, wishing he hadn't seen what his own mind had created.

He paused outside his home, slowly putting his car into park. He sighed. Maybe Eva would know what to say. She usually did. He could turn to her for anything.

Upstairs, he brushed his teeth and slipped into bed next to his wife. His side of the sheets was cold against his naked legs and torso. He shivered, sliding closer to the warmth of the woman beside him.

She was awake. She pretended to sleep, but twenty years sleeping next to the same person every night left no secrets. "What's the matter?" he whispered to her. It was odd, how people whispered when sleep hung in the air, as if not talking at full volume made any difference as to level of wakefulness.

"I don't know about that girl," she said, speaking normally, almost forcefully, like she'd spent the minutes he was gone rehearsing what she would say when he got back.

"I was just thinking that. If the captain found out we had her over for dinner during an open investigation, I'd be in big trouble."

"That's not what I meant."

The gears turned slowly in Harrington's mind. He stared at her, his beautiful, angry wife, until it finally clicked. "Oh, honey, no," he cooed, pulling her toward him. Her body was rigid, unwilling to relax into him. "That's not happening. Nothing like that is happening, I promise." He kissed behind her ear. She melted, albeit slightly.

"Sure as hell what it looked like to me at dinner. She was flirting with you, you know."

He ran his fingertips along her slender neck. Goosebumps rose on her skin. "Is that what all that was about? Of course she's going to flirt. She's a sixteen-year-old girl. They don't know how to interact any other way. There's no need to feel territorial. I'm all yours."

Finally, she relaxed completely. She stretched her neck for him, hinting for him to continue kissing her. He obliged, thankful the evening hadn't delved up unpleasant memories.

Chapter 15

A week later, Will and Eva invited me over again. Mostly Will. I saw the look she gave him when he beckoned me over as I walked past the house two nights later, and again two days after that. Daggers, swords, and the hate of a thousand suns.

Maybe I'm overreacting, but she was pissed nonetheless.

At dinner, she jabbed at her food with her fork. "Isn't it interesting? We've never seen you in this neighborhood before, and now all of a sudden we see you almost every night. And somehow you ended up in my house again. Hm, imagine that." She smirked.

"Eva!" Will whispered. "We talked about this."

"What? It's true."

I stabbed a piece of grilled chicken. "Maybe you just never noticed me before. I've walked this neighborhood for years. Now that you know who I am, you're starting to notice me." I bit the piece of chicken, scraping my teeth along my fork.

We sat in tense silence, Will punctuating it with poor attempts at light-hearted conversation. Eva would laugh, open-mouthed, at everything he said. "Oh, babe, you're hilarious!" she'd cry every so often. I managed to hold back most eye rolls, but a few slipped. She kept her hand on his. I let her have her moment. Because later, when she wasn't there, I could work him over uninterrupted.

Unlike last time, Eva refused to leave us to clean up. She asked me to help her clean while Will sat on the couch. "Just relax, baby.

We'll get the mess this time." She kissed him on the forehead and took his plate.

Looking at him from the sink, he looked anything but relaxed. He stared at the corner above the TV, mind clearly racing, probably wondering how much trouble he was going to be in. His leg jolted up and down uncontrollably. He kept his spine straight, and I could hardly tell if he was breathing.

Eva washed while I dried. She slammed dishes around, most likely wishing they were my face.

Afterward, she headed upstairs to get ready for bed. Also unlike last time, she left the door open. So much mistrust after only a few days.

I really couldn't blame her.

I sat next to Will on the brown leather couch, maybe a foot of heavy, tense space between us. I slouched, curling up into myself, completely unsure of what to do or say, both of us knowing full well Eva could hear us. "Thank you so much for letting me hang out here til my mom gets home," I finally said, not looking at him.

"Oh, of course." He cleared his throat. "You've been through a lot. It's completely understandable."

"You won't get in trouble for having me here, will you? With work?" In those cop shows Ashley and I watched, there were always serious repercussions when the detective got 'too close' with a victim.

He coughed again. This stupid coughing thing he did was already starting to grate on my nerves. "It's not exactly…protocol, but you don't really have anywhere else to go, so there's no harm in it."

"Okay good. I just -- I just really appreciate it."

He looked at me then, smiled. Not awkward that time, but warm. Sincere. "What do you want to watch?"

I told him I didn't care. I truly didn't. I didn't plan on watching anything anyway. I told him I was tired and I'd probably be falling asleep soon so we could watch whatever he wanted. He flipped it to some reality show he thought I'd like and fidgeted with the remote.

We sat in silence until the commercial. I flopped over and laid across the couch, my feet toward him. I'd made sure to wear my shortest fabric shorts and a loose crop top. When I laid down, I maneuvered my top to show just a hint of the under side of my breasts. I closed my eyes, but left them open just enough so I could fuzzily see him. In the darkness of the room, I doubted if he could see the flutter of my lashes as I blinked.

Not that he was looking at my eyes anyway. He did just as I wanted, and I felt the thrill in my stomach of being noticed. At first, he just glanced. Purely out of curiosity to see just why I was moving. Then he stared straight ahead, like he was transfixed by the commercials. When the show came back on, I dropped my mouth open, just slightly, and breathed heavily with a little catch at the top: a dainty, girly snore.

I watched him turn his head then. Subtly and slowly. I arched my back, almost imperceptibly, but it caught him. He was hooked, moving his eyes along my legs, stopping for a minute at the sweet spot -- the half-moons where my legs meet my perfect, round ass. He took a breath, sucked on the side of his lip. Up his eyes moved, so carefully, until they hovered at the swell under my top.

He looked back at the TV and laced his fingers in his lap. Basically, the exact opposite of what I wanted. Frustration swelled in my chest. I was offering myself up to him to take full advantage of me and he wasn't taking the bait like I needed him to.

I laid there completely still for another half hour, bored and annoyed with him. I couldn't understand why he wouldn't at least touch me. All I wanted was for him to want me. Finally, my phone vibrated, saving me from straining so hard mentally. Telling him telepathically to rub my legs was exhausting.

"That's my mom. She's home now." I stood up, stretched. I checked my phone. Ashley texted me pretending to be my mom, just like I asked.

Will hopped up, clearly thankful for the reason to leave. "I'll take you home. Or, I'm sure Eva will take you if you want."

"I'd like for you to take me," I said, a bit too eagerly, a bit too meaningfully. "You know, I'd just feel safer. Having a man with me."

He blinked rapidly before saying, "Yeah, of course. Let me go get my shoes." Men loved feeling like the hero.

I spent the two-minute car ride home trying to get him to open up to me. I needed to be a person to him if this was going to work, not another case, open or otherwise. "So, how are things at work?"

I asked cheerfully. Last time he clammed up about his wife. I remembered to keep things casual and to come on less strongly this time, even though all I wanted to do was shake him and yell that he deserved better than her. Specifically, he deserved me.

He laughed. "You really want to know about my job?" I blinked and smiled, encouraging him. "I thought girls your age just talked about makeup and boys."

"First of all, that's sexist and second, girls my age should be given a little credit. We do have more than air between our ears. Most of us, anyway."

"Alright, alright. Sorry. I withdraw my sexist remark." He smirked. Already he was loosening up, maybe even flirting a little. "Work is fine. I'm behind on a lot of paperwork, but that's pretty normal."

"Paperwork? I thought you were supposed to catch bad guys? You can't really do that if you're writing at a desk all day."

"Well, true. But that's a part of it. Boring and thankless, but an essential part nonetheless."

I waited, sat with him in silence for a minute. He looked at me out of the corner of his eye and smiled a little. I couldn't help myself. I had to ask the burning question, but I had to do it carefully, innocently. Like I was just making small talk. "How are things with Eva?"

His smile dropped. "What do you mean?"

I winced. I could only hope this car ride was salvageable. I put on my most innocent voice. "Oh, nothing! Sorry, I was just wondering like with work and everything. You spend a lot of time there or whatever, so I don't know. And like we talked about last time. Maybe you guys talked or something. I didn't mean anything by it."

He laughed uncomfortably. "No need to get defensive. We're okay. Same as two days ago." He shook his head. "I don't know why I'm discussing my marriage with you."

I gave him my biggest smile. "Guess I'm just easy to talk to."

As we pulled into my driveway, he leaned back in his seat and looked me in the eyes. "You're holding up pretty well, for what you've been through. Most people can hardly function normally this soon after an attack, let alone be cracking jokes and laughing."

I looked at my knees, brushed my hair behind my ears. "Well, you've helped a lot. Having you and your partner so open about explaining how it all works really makes a difference."

He took a breath. "You know? This may sound weird, but maybe you can be our unofficial, unpaid intern in the office. Just on the days you need somewhere to go. And until your uncle wakes up, of course."

I pretended to mull it over. I didn't want to seem too eager despite feeling like I would throw up out of pure excitement. "I accept. Let me know when I start, boss." I raised my eyebrow with the word *boss,* hinting.

"Tomorrow, after school. Bring your homework, though. It's a part of the job description." He smiled, but was completely neutral, like a dad joking with a stranger in line at the grocery store.

I rolled my eyes and got out of the car. I slammed the door, a little too forcefully, my frustrations from the night clearly making themselves known. I took a breath and smiled. "Thanks again," I said, leaning down to look at him through the open window. I crossed my arms under my boobs, pushing up my cleavage.

I saw it. Just a flicker of a glance. My smile turned genuine. I still had him.

Chapter 16

Detective Harrington watched as Paige swung her hips while she walked up the driveway. He willed himself not to stare at her legs, not to want to feel them wrapped around his waist. Jesus, she was only sixteen. Yet he couldn't help but notice those feelings of desire bubbling up within him anyway. While he could force away the thoughts two days before, it was nearly impossible now.

He had invited her to dinner to calm Eva down, to reassure her that nothing was going on, that this wasn't like last time. He thought maybe Eva could be a surrogate mother to Paige.

He now knew that was idiotic.

She waved at him when she unlocked the door, the universal motion signifying that she was safe. He drove around the corner and dialed Doctor Woods, the psychiatrist on staff at the station.

"Hey," the detective said, "You remember the girl we brought in a couple days ago? The one who bashed in her uncle's head? I think she's hurting more than she's letting on. I told her she could unofficially intern at the station starting tomorrow just to get her in. I'm hoping maybe you'll get a chance to get close to her, maybe see what's going on in her head?"

"Sure, if she'll already be there." He paused. "Isn't this out of your hands now?"

Harrington could tell the doctor was trying to tell him he thought spending so much effort on this girl was an issue without actually saying it. There were plenty of missing kids and other crimes more pressing than this one. "Yeah, but she's really shaken up. She doesn't want to go home until her mom's there. Can't say I blame the kid. This will give her something to do in an environment where she can feel safe. Just until she can finally feel comfortable alone again."

Doctor Woods sighed. "Whatever you say, detective."

Harrington laughed as he hung up. Woods only called him "detective" when he completely disagreed with him, but this is what Paige really needed. She wouldn't see someone outright, but if Doctor Woods was subtle enough, he could really get the girl to open up.

Plus, as much as he hated to admit it, even to himself, he wanted to see her again. There was something about her. She seemed older to him. More mature, although that could be because she lost her childhood to that monster. At the same time, she needed him. Not in a childish way. In more of a protective way. He liked protecting delicate things. It made him feel important. Strong. Needed.

As he lay next to his wife that night, he thought about holding Paige, feeling her skin against his, the rise and fall of her chest. He no longer fought off his fantasies; it was completely futile to even try. They were perfectly normal to have, he thought. They were more fantasies of protection than sex, anyway. He told himself he wasn't necessarily attracted to her; he just needed to be needed.

He slept peacefully, with half-remembered dreams about forbidden acts with a teenager.

Chapter 17

I sat in my last class of the day, excitedly awaiting the bell at 2:30 that would release me to the police station. I smiled at the irony.

I know Will was only having me come in because I had no where else to go and he wanted me to feel safe, but the truth was, I felt perfectly safe by myself. I was even feeling better about being home, around that spot. I took this as an opportunity to be close to him.

Mr. Owens caught me smiling. He didn't say anything to interrupt his lecture, but he lifted an eyebrow in my direction. Apparently he thought smiling during his lecture about the deaths during the Civil War was out of place.

He passed out worksheets and told us we had fifteen minutes to complete it. We were encouraged to work in groups. I didn't look around and ignored anyone who turned their head my direction. I always worked alone.

I felt his presence the way all teenagers feel the presence of authority before I saw him. I looked up, straightened my posture. "Hi, Mr. Owens."

"Hi, Paige." His beautiful voice, always a lullaby to me. Smooth, deep, calming. "Are you going to be able to fill out that worksheet? From what I could tell, you weren't paying much attention to the lesson today."

"It's hard to pay attention to a lecture about men shooting each other when there's such a beautiful distraction at the front of the room." I gave him my best impression of a doe-eyed beauty. Even I was unimpressed by my efforts. I'd only been half-assing my seduction lately with him.

He narrowed his dark eyes at me, warning me not to push it. I didn't break his gaze, but I also didn't say more.

He turned and walked back to his office. Mentally, I whistled at his perfectly-shaped rear end. Never underestimate the power of a good workout and a pair of well-fitting khakis.

When the bell rang – that sweet, glorious bell – I didn't hover around my desk with the hope Mr. Owens would ask me to stay behind after everyone left. Then he'd lock the door and take me on his desk. That fantasy was pushed aside to make room for the new development involving an even older, more authoritative, more impressive man. Instead, I heaved my bag over my shoulder and nearly ran off of school grounds.

I snuck into the bathroom on the bottom floor of the building. It was warm outside and I was sweating. I rinsed my face, reapplied my makeup, and fluffed my hair. A little spritz of my emergency perfume on my wrists and neck and I was ready to go.

I stepped off the elevator on the fourth floor expecting him to be waiting for me. I don't know why. Looking back, that seems completely unreasonable.

The room was buzzing with people: some who were obviously working hard, and some who were stuck trying to look busy so they could avoid all their paperwork. Will's partner saw me first.

"Hey, Paige!" Detective DiPascua greeted me. She smiled warmly, showing her impeccable teeth. Not veneers, either.

I shook her hand. "Um, Detective Harrington said I could come by after school sometimes. If that's okay. I can get you coffee or something." The words tumbled out of my mouth, one over the other. I felt myself turn red.

She put her arm around my shoulders and led me to Will's empty desk. "He mentioned you'd come by. Don't let these lazy men make you get their coffee though, okay? Everyone can get their own, I promise. Harrington is out getting a late lunch, but he should be back soon. Do you need anything?"

I smiled sweetly and told her I didn't. She said she'd be in the room on the left if I needed her.

I took a deep breath, hoping I hadn't made too much of a fool of myself in front of that goddess. I wondered if they'd had sex. She was very attractive, and powerful. Jealousy twinged in my gut. I pushed the thought aside. He was powerful too, and there would be too much of a struggle if they got together, just like the struggle he has with his wife. Too many headstrong people in one place. Will wanted someone like me, someone willing to do whatever he wanted to make him happy.

I sat in his chair. A hint of his cologne stuck to it. I closed my eyes and breathed deeply. The knot of jealousy in my stomach turned to a flutter of excitement. He'd invited me here. He wanted me.

I opened my eyes. I saw DiPascua standing in the threshold of the room talking to a man in an expensive suit. She motioned toward me and smiled. He looked over his shoulder at me. He waved and I awkwardly waved back, unsure of whether or not I was supposed to know him.

He walked up to the desk. "You're the new unofficial intern Harrington was talking about, huh?"

So he talked about me. Obviously he said good things considering how receptive this man was to me. That was how the boys in my high school talk to the girls their friends like.

He held out his hand to me. "I'm Doctor Woods, but you can call me Brian."

I shook his hand. Pudgy and dry, but his grip was firm. I hate limp handshakes to the point of offense. "Is someone hurt?" I asked stupidly. This time, I wasn't pretending to be dumb for attention.

He stared blankly at me before it registered what I had said. He chuckled. "Oh, no, not that kind of doctor. I'm a psychiatrist here. I help heal mental injuries rather than bodily. I have an office upstairs, but I spend most of my time around here."

"Oh." I laughed at myself and hit my head with my palm. "Duh. Don't you usually see people in private offices though?"

Doctor Woods stood with his hands relaxed in his pockets, his posture straight. Not in an uptight way, but like he was comfortable with where he was in life. I straightened my spine a little. "Well, I work with the victims as well as the perpetrators in ongoing cases. I'm here to help the victims and figure out the inner workings of the bad guys."

"To make them confess."

"Yes, if they're guilty."

"Well, yeah, I guess that's important." He was watching me, analyzing me. My palms prickled with sweat. I wasn't used to someone trying so hard to see through me. "How often do you get crazies who confess to something they didn't do?"

"I don't know if 'crazies' is the right way to describe them, but not all too often. It does happen though."

I bristled at him scolding me for my word choice. I looked past him, through his thinning hair, to the back of the room, no longer interested in what he had to say.

I think he got the hint and changed the subject. "DiPascua says I'm not allowed to hassle you for coffee, but isn't that what interns are for?"

The corner of my mouth twitched. Not a smile, but I didn't want to be entirely rude to this guy if he was friends with Will.

"Alright," he said, looking down, his confidence not quite broken, but banged up a bit, "it was good to meet you. I look forward to seeing you again if you stick around."

"Yeah, you too."

I waited until he rounded the corner before I moved. I pulled my book and notebook out of my bag, stacking them neatly on the desk. I opened each to the page we left off on in history class. I hadn't taken notes, and I hadn't even written my name on the worksheet we were supposed to have turned in at the end of class. I'd fill it out today and turn it in tomorrow, acting like I forgot to turn it in even though it was done all along.

But I couldn't focus. There were so many things to learn about this man before he came back from lunch. Here I was, at his desk. His home away from home. I searched in my bag for a pen. I had plenty, of course, but I pretended I didn't. It gave me a chance to dig through his drawers. I had to take stock of what was in there quickly so it didn't look like I was snooping.

I checked the bottom drawer first. Pens are always in the top drawer and I would probably find a pen very quickly if I started there, leaving me with no reason to search lower. It only held files, probably for work, nothing personal. I moved to the middle drawer. A clipboard, a gun holster, an iPod and headphones, and one pen which I pretended not to see. Not a drawer he used often.

I opened the top drawer quickly. No pens. Highlighters and notepads scribbled over with names and addresses. A bottle of aspirin. Loose change. A cigarette he might have been saving for a particularly stressful case. And his wallet. I looked through the glass at his partner. She was on the phone, her back toward me. Everyone else in the office was focused on their work. I opened the wallet while it was still in the desk, in case I needed to close the drawer abruptly.

I looked at his ID. I tried not to laugh at his picture. It wasn't horrible, but his eyes were wide and he was caught in a half-smile, like the guy taking his picture told him "On three" and only counted to two. He was an organ donor. That resonated with me. Meant he cared about other people. He turned forty-seven last month.

I flipped to his pictures. His wife. Two school pictures of kids, a boy and a girl. The last one was a family portrait. It looked recent - Will had the same amount of grayness around the temples and Eva's hairstyle was current. Their kids were all grown up. The son had a beard, and the daughter had laugh lines around her eyes. College-aged, but still older than me.

My heart sank. People were always saying stuff like, "He's old enough to be your dad," and this time it was true. He'd definitely consider that every time he looked at me.

"What are you looking for?"

I jumped, slamming my knee into the corner of the drawer. "Ow, shit. Um, nothing. A pen."

Will stood there smirking at me. He didn't look mad, just amused. He raised an eyebrow and pointed to a mug on his desk full of pens and pencils.

Right next to a picture of his wife.

"Oh," I laughed guiltily. "Duh."

"You're not going to make a very good detective if you can't even find pens in a logical place."

"I never said I wanted to be one."

"Then why are you interning?"

"Because you told me to!"

He held his hands up in surrender. "Alright, alright. Whatever you say."

The flutter in my gut came back. He was flirting with me. In front of people. He may have photos of his wife and kids, and I may be young, but he was definitely flirting. "So," I said in a seductive voice, "what do you need me to do for you?"

Will took a breath, looked at his hands. Oh no, I overdid it. "Well, you can just hang out while I do paperwork. I'll pull up another chair."

This is where the excitement ended. We worked in silence (although I had trouble focusing and really didn't get any work done). He didn't glance at me or even brush up against me. Instead, he stared intently at files with a furrowed brow and made marks every so often. Then he'd move to the computer and type. Then back to the files. I scooted subtly toward him, rested my leg against his. He pulled away. "Oops, sorry," he said and laughed.

Frustration boiled inside me. A lump formed in my throat where a scream tried to escape. I shoved it down and waited until it was acceptable to head home.

"Alright, well, my mom's probably home now. I'd better get back."

He stood. "Do you want a ride?"

Finally. Progress. "Sure, I'd love that."

"Okay, yeah, one second." He stood up and yelled toward his partner. "Hey, Di. Want to give our girl here a ride home?"

I felt like I was going to vomit. "Oh, no, actually, it's totally fine," I said hurriedly.

He smiled and looked down the hallway. "No, it's not a problem. I'm sure she won't mind. Di!"

"No, really. It's okay. I want the fresh air anyway. I'll be fine. I'll see you later. Thanks for letting me hang out here. Bye!"

I nearly ran out the front doors. I couldn't believe I actually thought he'd like me. I was so stupid and ignorant. Just a little girl. He was thirty years older than me with a wife and kids. What would he possibly see in me? I wiped hot tears out of my eyes.

I don't remember the walk home, but it felt like I'd made it there instantly. I flopped on the couch and tried not to cry.

Chapter 18

Detective Harrington stared at the doors as they slammed behind Paige. "Huh," he said to no one in particular.

His partner walked up and stood beside him. "I thought she wanted a ride?"

"She wanted fresh air."

"Or maybe," she said meaningfully, looking straight at him, "she just wanted a ride from you."

Harrington scoffed. "I don't think so. I could be her dad. I'm losing hair off my head as quickly as I'm growing it in my ears. I sprouted a gut. Yes, sprouted," he repeated when she gave him a questioning look, "literally over night. What would she do with someone like me?" Even he could tell he sounded too defensive.

"Just be careful. She was digging through your wallet earlier, you know."

So he had caught her doing something sneaky. He gave her the benefit of the doubt when he startled her earlier, that maybe she really was just looking for a pen. "She's not very trusting. Would you be in her situation?"

DiPascua shrugged as she turned away. "Grab the doc. He talked to her earlier. See what he says. Which, by the way, you should have seen the daggers shooting from that girl's eyes at his back. She certainly is something." She disappeared down the hall.

Harrington sighed. His partner might have been right about this girl. He'd have to get her to the station in a more official way. The ruse of her being an intern didn't prove successful. He told her multiple times to talk to Doctor Woods, but she refused. At least he'd talked to her a little, so maybe he would give it another couple of days.

But he'd definitely have to stop taking her to her house. Then again, if she didn't feel safe walking, an officer would be the best person to help her. He would absolutely have to stop letting her come over to his home. She obviously didn't have anywhere else to go though. She never mentioned friends, and her family was out of the question, except for her mom, but she worked late nearly every night. Plus she was crazy.

Sweat prickled under his arms. He was making excuses to see her. There was no way he could be attracted to a girl younger than his own children, not to mention acting on that desire. She was quite pretty - long honey-colored hair, clear chestnut-colored eyes, full lips, a small button nose - but she was also basically a fetus.

No matter how hard he convinced himself otherwise, there it was, blatantly presenting itself to him. It wasn't a fatherly protection, but rather a sexual interest. There wasn't a way to ignore it anymore. The thing was, he wasn't sure if he wanted to.

He followed the hall to Doctor Woods' office. He rolled his knuckles on the door frame. "Hey, Doc."

Doctor Woods looked up from his computer screen. "Detective," he said cheerily, standing to shake Harrington's hand. "I'm guessing you're here about the girl?"

"You would be right. Paige is her name."

"Right, Paige. Well, I was only able to talk to her for a few minutes before I lost her. She's like a lot of the juveniles I've met with. Think they know everything and easily offended. I think she could warm up to me quickly, but say the wrong thing and I could lose her even faster."

"Like what?"

"For one thing, telling her what to do or telling her she's done something wrong. I suppose not necessarily *wrong* per se, but disagreeing with her. Does that make sense?"

Harrington stared blankly at him. "How are you disagreeing with her already? You just said yourself that you talked to her for five minutes."

The doctor sighed, unable to put his thoughts into words. "For instance," he continued, gathering himself, "when you suggest that someone shouldn't be doing something, like your kids. You say something along the lines of 'If I were you, I wouldn't stick your tongue to the frozen pole' or 'Are you sure you want to call your ex in the middle of the night?' To her, little suggestions such as these sound like chastisement or scolding. She can't be wrong, and she can't feel that she's being told she's wrong. It makes her feel stupid. She needs to be intelligent and all-knowing. She's built up walls to prevent anyone from knowing who she is, where she came from, or what she's thinking. She studies every word, planning her next move, just so other people see her as right."

"So? Maybe she's just guarded. She's got trust issues lately because of what happened."

The doctor stared at him with narrowed eyes.

"What?" Harrington asked uncomfortably.

"Nothing. It's just that people who care about someone else use the phrase 'because of what happened.' People, like detectives, who are unbiased, say exactly what happened. 'Because of the rape. Because of the burglary,' et cetera."

Harrington crossed his arms and planted his feet firmly apart. He tilted his chin up, raised an eyebrow. If the shrink wanted to challenge him, so be it. Harrington wasn't one to lose easily.

"Hey," Doctor Woods said, putting his palms up in surrender, "I'm not suggesting anything. Just observing. It's my job. Anyway, what this means for Paige. It's too soon to tell, of course, but from our little visit, I'd say she wants to be an adult."

Harrington rolled his eyes and scoffed. "Wow, great analysis, Doc. She's sixteen. What sixteen-year-old doesn't want to be an adult?"

"She doesn't let herself be the child she is. She was forced to grow up too quickly. Childhood isn't something she remembers fondly. She needs the approval of adults, and for them to treat her equally. She has issues with authority."

"Hate to burst your bubble, Doc, but none of this seems special or even worth noting. What you're saying fits every other teenager ever. Trust me, I raised two of them."

The doctor ignored Harrington. "She treats men and women differently too. I was noticing the way she talks to Di and the way she talked to me. Di makes her nervous, while the best way for her to talk to me is to flirt."

Harrington scoffed. "Teenagers flirt. That's how they think they can get their way, and usually they do. Do you not remember that? I know it was a long time ago and everything, but still. Plus, Di scares everyone. If you can talk to her without breaking a sweat or feeling like you're going to shit yourself, you're probably a sociopath."

Dr. Woods laughed despite himself. "While that is entirely true, there's something different about the way Ms. Harper acts, though. I can't quite figure it out yet. Give me more time with her."

"Forget it. She already says she refuses to see a shrink."

"Officially. You were the one who wanted me to see her, remember? Now I'm invested. See if she wants to come in more often. I'll casually strike up a conversation with her again, being sure to talk to her like a colleague and not like a victim or a child. Let me know if you find out anything, like little quirks. And if you could, I'd like to see her file as well."

"Whatever you say." Harrington strutted out of the office. He didn't need excuses to see her when he had the doctor's orders.

Back at his desk, Harrington looked over Paige's file. It made him sick to read over all the things that pervert had done to that poor girl.

As a detective in crimes such as these, he had to harden himself to the evils of the world. He had to completely separate himself. But sometimes, a case got to him.

He called his daughter. "Hey, dad," she said in her sing-song voice. He could hear music, chatter, and clanging dishes in the background.

"Hey, champ, what are you up to?"

"Just studying for my O chem test. The internet is out at the apartment so I'm at the coffeeshop, basically wasting my time. I can't even hear myself think here. I don't know how people do this shit."

Harrington laughed. "You're a smart girl. You can figure it out. Just called to say hi. I've been thinking about you lately. How have you been? How's everything going with Johnny?" Johnny was her boyfriend. Tall, health-conscious, and the only one Harrington didn't hate. Disliked, sure, but not hate.

"Um, we broke up? Yeah, like three months ago. I totally told you. Now I'm kind of seeing another guy. He's nice."

"'Kind of seeing'? What does that mean? Who is he?"

"Like we're not necessarily exclusive. We've gone on a couple dates. It's nothing serious. He buys me dinner and stuff."

Harrington felt his heart rate spike. "How old is this guy? If he can afford to buy you dinner, he's definitely not a college kid."

"Okay, first of all, there are plenty of rich boys here. Secondly, he's not that old. He's – it's fine, dad. I promise. I'm a big girl. I can take care of myself. Anyway, I got to go. I have to study. I'll call you later. Love you." *Click.*

His hands shook. He couldn't sit in his seat anymore. He stood up and paced. It wasn't good enough. He needed to hit something.

People stared. The captain made a bee line for him. "Hey," his voice boomed. "Take a walk. Outside."

Harrington stormed through the doors, heeding his captain's unsaid warning.

Was his daughter being taken advantage of? Was it her professor? Men were monsters, preying on the angels of the earth, chewing them up and spitting them out, changed and broken. He raised her to be smarter than that. He raised her to take care of herself, not to allow some dick with legs to cajole her into thinking she needed him, that he was *nice.*

When his breathing returned to normal and his heart rate slowed, he went back to his desk, where Woods was waiting for him.

"Cap said you were upset and I needed to talk to you, make sure you can handle the case," he said, face completely neutral.

Harrington sat on the corner of his desk, facing the doctor. "I can *handle* the case. That was personal. Bad phone call. Glad the captain can *handle* his crew himself," he spat.

"Some people are better with emotional situation than others. Emotions scare him, that's all. Did you get the phone call worked out?"

"No, I didn't, actually."

"Your daughter?"

So the bastard really did have eyes and ears everywhere. "Yeah, with my daughter, so it's none of your business."

"Well, it certainly is if it's affecting your ability to work the case. If you can't be unbiased and only look at the evidence. If you hold Ms. Harper on a pedestal, thinking she's perfect when there might be more to the story. If you can't control your anger. All because you see your daughter in the case. All because you need to protect her."

"Amanda doesn't need protecting. She's a grown woman." The anger in Harrington's voice dropped away, leaving a touch of sadness in its wake.

Woods nodded slowly. "She doesn't need her dad anymore, but Ms. Harper needs someone. She needs protection because she never got it growing up."

"Exactly."

The word hung in the air. Woods stood up. "I'm not going to give my evaluation to the captain just yet. I'm going to let you think on what we've talked about and let you sort yourself out." He walked back to his office, leaving Harrington over-analyzing every word he had spoken. He couldn't for the life of him figure out why he would need to sort himself out.

Chapter 19

I called Ashley. "You want to come over?" she asked. She sounded distracted, like she was doing homework.

"No, it's okay. I just wanted to tell someone."

"That sucks. But you know, I mean, he is married. I know he's super hot and whatever, but he's probably not going to go after you, you know?"

I sighed. "You're supposed to go along with this. What kind of friend are you?" I was joking with her, but I was a little hurt at the same time.

"Paige." She was focused entirely on me now. "It was fun, chasing him. The fantasy was fun. It really was. He did check up on you that one night, I'll give you that, and we can still joke about it or whatever. But I mean, don't cry about it. Go out with Brian or Steve. They're both drooling all over you, and they're seniors. Older men, like you like."

"Not quite old enough."

"Oh, well, excuse me for suggesting you go out with someone who doesn't need Viagra and who doesn't have wrinkly skin flaps that clap in the wind."

My tears turned to ones of laughter. "You're such a bitch. Call me later."

"Kay. Love you."

"Love you. Bye."

I held my phone to my chest. She just didn't understand, and she wouldn't. This wasn't something I could talk to her about. Things were changing between us. Before, I could talk to her about literally anything. Suddenly, Owens and Will were off limits.

The thing was, she didn't know the way he talked to me, the way he looked at me. She'd never seen the connection we had. There wasn't any way she could understand.

I tried to sleep, but I flipped and tossed, unable to keep my eyes shut. My body was cold despite my abundance of blankets. I couldn't get him out of my head. Every conversation we've ever had flew through my brain, as well as my conversation with Ashley.

I made up scenarios. I thought of better responses to her arguments, made up arguments, made her agree with me.

I thought about Will. Of course I thought about Will. I wondered what he was doing, what he was thinking about, as I stared at my ceiling. Did I cross his mind? Did he imagine I was beside him in bed, instead of his wife, as I so often did? Did he masturbate thinking about me? I giggled like a child.

Suddenly, I couldn't handle being in my house all alone. I needed to see him. My body itched beneath my skin.

Maybe his wife wouldn't even be home. Yeah, she would probably be out. She works weird hours. He would like to see me. I could just drop by, no big deal. If she's there, I wouldn't go in. If she's gone, I could go inside, just to talk. I need someone to talk to, someone wiser than any of my friends.

I turned on my light at stared at the clothes on the floor, picking out the best outfit for the occasion. This was the best idea I'd ever had.

Chapter 20

Detective Harrington groaned as he crawled into bed next to his wife.

"Long day?" she asked.

"Oh, the usual."

"Wanna talk about it?"

Usually he liked talking to Eva about his job. He couldn't go too far into detail, of course, but she was always there for him to clear his mind. Sometimes, the things he saw and people he dealt with were too much for him to handle alone. He'd seen plenty of detectives with no healthy outlet deteriorate quickly. He promised himself long ago he'd never let that happen.

This time, he wasn't sure he wanted to mention the events of the past couple days. In a strange way, Harrington wanted to keep Paige to himself. He told himself it wasn't anything inappropriate; he simply didn't want to talk about it. If he didn't talk about it, though, Eva would suspect something when there was clearly nothing going on. Considering she was already suspicious of Paige, and probably hated the girl, he had to balance on a thin rope so she wouldn't figure out just who he was talking about.

"There's this victim and I'm kind of worried about them," he said vaguely.

She rolled her eyes. "Diós mio. You're going to have to give me more than that if you want help."

He sank further into the baby blue sea of down comforters and memory foam. He paused, calculating just how much he could say. "They had a bad home life, right? And they're only sixteen with a dead dad and an absent mom. From the reports and the way they act, the person taking care of them sexually abused them, so the victim pretty much has no one in their life. They only have one friend they trust, but they need more than that. I just don't really know what to do."

"Honey, there isn't much you *can* do. You know that." There was a bitter warning in her words. She sensed it was that little hussy he was so worried about, but wasn't positive. Most kids in the juvenile system were abused in one way or another. She leaned on her elbow to face her husband. Staring at him, she looked for his telltale signs of lying -- he rubbed his nose, or sometimes had a slight twitch at the right corner of his mouth.

He stared at his hands above the covers. "I'm a little worried too because I want them to see Woods, but they won't. So I kind of told them to come in as an 'unofficial intern,' whatever that means. That way Woods can talk to them without there being pressure. I just wanted them to have some structure or something. It didn't really work out too well."

Eva knew. Her breath caught in her throat. "Is this about that little whore who was here the other night? Paige or whatever her name is?" Her tone soured.

Harrington grimaced. "Eva! What the hell?"

"She was all over you and you know it. I'm just telling you the truth."

"She's a *victim*. Jesus, Eva. Show a little respect."

"First of all, I'm just warning you not to go back down that rabbit hole, not that I *officially* know who you're talking about anyway. But that is so sad for that person, whoever she is. You've already tried to do something before, but if she's not accepting the help, what else is there?"

Harrington did his best to ignore the sarcasm dripping from her voice. "I suppose that's true. I just hate that there's no justice in this supposed justice system. Girls are getting hurt and sent back home with nothing. I just want her to be able to talk to someone. She'll never be right again unless she gets help. She's been completely abandoned."

Eva leaned deeper into her pillows and stared bewildered at her husband. "Why is this case hitting you so hard?"

"I don't know. Sometimes they just do. Maybe it's because I'm getting old. I've just seen too much of all of it to not be affected by it."

"Ah, your paternal instincts are kicking in again. That's so sweet, baby." She leaned over to kiss him. "*Paternal*. Because you're old enough to be her dad."

Harrington ignored her. "If the captain finds out about her 'internship,' I'm going to be in so much trouble. Woods did get to talk to her a little bit. Unsuccessfully. She shut him out."

She laughed. "Well of course she did. He's a stranger trying to get her to talk about a traumatic event in her life. Remember when Amanda was sixteen? You couldn't even get her to tell us what she wanted for breakfast in the morning, let alone anything personal, and we're her parents. Just give it time. Maybe just let her figure it out herself. She's still so *young* and irrational. And if she's had such a traumatic life as she claims, it's going to be so hard to help her. You've already got so much on your plate. Maybe it would be better to actually bring her into the station on official terms. Have an officer take her out of school and bring her in. Sit her down in an interrogation room and actually interrogate her, just like every other messed up kid you've ever dealt with. Clearly 'unofficially' isn't working."

"Do you think it's unorthodox to bring her back here again? Maybe for dinner?"

Eva rolled her eyes at the ceiling. Rage bubbled inside her. Sweetly --and not so sweetly -- dancing around her feelings about the girl wasn't working. She'd have to bring facts and logic into it to get through to her husband. "Yes, it's fucking *unorthodox*. She could be seriously unstable, Will. You could probably get fired over this, or at least taken off the case. She shouldn't have even come over the last two times. And yes, that was my fault, the first time. I totally saw how you want to help her. I just don't know that it's a good idea." She counted to three to calm herself. "Keep two things in mind, *amor*. First, she bashed a guy's head in with a bat. We don't know one hundred percent that what she says is true. No, Will," she said, holding her hand up to stop him from protesting, "that's the facts. No one except the two of them knows what happened. She might have just gotten tired of him and took a swing.

"Second, keep your history in mind. Remember who and what is important in your life," she pointed at herself, "and don't mess that up."

He turned to face her, propping himself up on his elbow. He hadn't thought about the repercussions of getting involved with a victim, especially one that young. He was so caught up in protecting Paige and in wanting to see her again, that he forgot the reasoning behind not getting personal with the victim. They're at their most fragile and vulnerable when the detectives find them. It makes it easy for them to snap at any given moment, or for them to latch onto the detective to absolve what happened.

He definitely didn't think that Paige had lied. He'd seen the inside of that house -- a complete disaster -- and he'd seen the way she acted when they first questioned her. This wasn't a crime of passion or anything of the sort. No, this was self defense. He didn't see any problem with Paige. She was strong. "I guess you're right. Like always," he said, kissing his wife's lips again.

She kissed him harder, encouraging him. The shock of his wife initiating sex wore off quickly. He lifted himself onto her. He wanted her, and he wanted to satisfy her. He kissed her jaw line, her ears, her neck. He massaged her breasts.

She sighed impatiently, laid there unmoving. She had noticed he hadn't mentioned her second blatant warning, and she was trying her hardest to keep the wrath subdued. He, oblivious to her anger, upped his efforts, kissing her collar bones, running his tongue over her nipples.

When she sighed again, he looked at her. "Do you not want to? I thought --"

"Oh!" she said, like she thought he was completely silly for even suggesting that she wasn't interested. "No, it's fine. Go ahead."

He almost gave up, but refused to go yet another night without being intimate with the woman he married. He couldn't remember the last time they'd touched each other like this. Somehow, though, she didn't feel any passion or lust. It was simply a wifely duty. Maybe he had read her wrong. Maybe a kiss was just a kiss.

Harrington kissed her again, whispered that he loved her. She didn't answer.

Her lack of enthusiasm nearly made him go flaccid.

A thought of Paige flashed across his mind. He instantly felt that familiar sweet tug at his groin. He closed his eyes as he entered his wife. He allowed himself to imagine Paige beneath him.

When he rolled off her, his wife looked at him. "Wow. Where in the world did that come from?"

"Did you actually enjoy that?" he asked, clearly irritable.

"Yeah, I mean, it was nice."

"*Nice?* You just laid there like a dead fish while I tried to spice things up a little. Do you even want to be with me romantically anymore?"

She turned away from him. "Of course I do. Don't start. I'm just tired. Goodnight."

Harrington dropped it and turned opposite of his wife, allowing himself to reflect on what had just happened.

His wife didn't want him anymore apparently. Somehow, though, he wasn't hurt by it. He'd thought he wanted her, until Paige walked into his life. All of a sudden, he was imagining having sex with another girl. Her case was still technically open. She was damaged and underage. If he acted on his desires, he'd lose his job and his wife. Not to mention the jail time he'd most likely face.

His own children were older than this girl, for God's sake. He nearly flew into a rage at the thought of his daughter with an older man earlier that afternoon, yet here he was.

He hated himself for thinking it, but if Eva didn't want him anymore (and hadn't seemed to want him in the last few years), it would make things easier for him to be with Paige.

For some reason, thoughts about her naked body pressed against his wouldn't leave his mind. He loved the woman snoring lightly next to him. She was there for him every time he needed her. Even tonight she was there for him.

Kind of. Her advice was pockmarked with insinuations, allegations, bitterness. She still didn't trust him after all these years. There needed to be trust and love and passion. Otherwise it wasn't a marriage.

For yet another night, he fell asleep still thinking about Paige. But this time, there was no guilt.

Chapter 21

I dressed in all black that night. You're supposed to wear reflective colors and bring a flash light when you go out after dark, but I wanted to blend in. I knew my way around the neighborhood perfectly well. I'd walked these streets hundreds of times.

The nights when Ashley wasn't available, I'd wander around the neighborhood next to my own. If only I'd known then that this street so close to mine was home to Detective William Harrington.

Patience pays off, right? Now here he and I were, fate bringing us together. I stopped across the street from his home. I'd never taken the time to notice this particular house before I knew he lived there. I sat on the curb to absorb it, to commit it to memory.

The house was quaint, similar to the others on the street, but not an exact replica. A little two-story with an arched doorway, a light burning in the front window. The lawn had been recently mowed. I wondered if Will had done it, mowed it on his off-time, shirt off, skin glistening in the setting sun. Or if his wife had done it. Her husband worked long hours. I'm sure a strong woman like her would know how to rev up a mower. With only a detective's salary, a part-time job on her side and two kids in college, I doubted if they'd hired someone. When their kids were still living at home, they probably did all that dirty work. Scrutinizing the stucco building in front of me, I wasn't sure how long they'd lived in such a small house. It seemed too tiny for a family. Maybe their old house seemed oversized for them when the kids left for school.

This was their little retreat.

A pang of jealousy struck me right in my gut.

I wanted a little retreat with him. This woman didn't deserve a man like him. He was strong, caring, protective. She was bitter and flat. She was a woman with her own agenda, and no need for someone else. He had to settle for her because he hadn't met me yet. I was someone he could nurture. He needed that.

Now he'd be figuring out a way to get rid of her and be with me.

I breathed deeply to calm myself down. Of course he'd leave her. They had no chemistry. We did.

I stood, feeling a rush of confidence. I looked around me. When I didn't see anyone, I headed over to the house.

I walked normally, with a purpose, in case nosy neighbors happened to be looking out their windows. That way it would look like I belonged there rather than someone creeping around at eleven at night in the suburbs.

I walked onto the porch, then shimmied behind the bushes in the front to peek in the front window. My heart thudded in my throat. I really hoped no one chose to close the blinds at that moment to see my face peering in. Luckily, the living room was empty. There was the couch Will and I had sat on together the other day. I wanted so desperately to be back on that sofa with him, our arms wrapped around one another.

I crept around the house, still hiding behind the bushes. I nearly ran into the fence leading to the back yard. The gate was locked, which was stupid because it was a low fence. I hopped over it easily. I paused in case a concerned neighbor wanted to check out the movement on the side of the house, but I didn't hear a sound. If they'd called the police, well, hopefully it was a busy night and they'd take their time getting there.

The side of the house was home to an adorable little garden. It was hard to distinguish what plants they had in the dark, but I could see for sure they had crowns of broccoli, almost ready for picking. I'd always wanted a garden. My dad always talked about starting one with me once he had the time.

I carefully stepped over and around the leafy greens. There was no light in the kitchen, so I continued around to the back. A blue flicker came from the master. They were watching TV. Unwinding from the day, snuggling under the covers.

I had to stop myself from gagging.

I didn't know how to get up high enough to see inside. I half-ran to the back of the yard and stood on the little fence, completely forgetting I was supposed to be inconspicuous. I was so set on seeing inside that it didn't matter if anyone saw me.

I could hardly make out anything. They had those sheer fabric blinds that let in light but block the view. Of course he would close the bedroom blinds. I couldn't be so lucky to see right in. I tried to maneuver myself to see through the cracks in the side, but it was useless.

I climbed down and trudged back up to the house. I laid in the grass under the window, looking up at the few stars that were bright enough to shine through the city's light pollution. It was comfortable there, in that safe back yard. A good place to play with kids, to have summer barbecues, to set up a hammock and cuddle in. An ache welled up under my ribs. I yearned for a place like that. My own home with my own yard. Such a lovely idea. I couldn't wait to build a home with Will in the near future. Something we could be proud of. We'd have dinner parties and everyone would talk about how perfect our lives were.

I must have fallen asleep, though I don't remember drifting off, dreaming about our life together. I woke up shivering with a major cramp in my neck. The window was dark and the first rays of the sun peeked over the hill, casting a sleepy gray light over the neighborhood.

"Shit," I grumbled as I unfolded myself from the ground. My ribs ached and my left leg was pins and needles. I looked up at the bedroom window one last time. The blinds were shut tight.

I wandered back home, trying to decide if I cared that I'd most likely be late for school, or if I cared about anything.

I jumped in the shower, attempting to hurry, but the warm water rolling down my cold skin was too sweet to rush. It caressed me out of my apathy. I closed my eyes and imagined Will running his hands along my body, sharing that cramped shower with me.

The water turned lukewarm and I willed myself to leave my fantasy. I stepped out of the shower – my lonely shower made just for one – and wiped steam away from the mirror with my towel. I looked myself over. Yeah, I decided, I was attractive. My boobs and hips were getting bigger, my waist slim. Not quite my mother's perfect hourglass, but I was certainly nowhere near boyish. My soft, pouty lips begged to be kissed. My thick lashes didn't need mascara, and my skin didn't have a flaw. My teeth were a little crooked because my mother never opted to get me braces, and I had that button nose from my dad's side, but I think those added character.

I rolled and blow-dried my hair into big waves. I dressed in a flowy floral skirt with tights and little Oxfords. I tucked in a form-fitting V-neck tee and topped it all off with a thick open sweater. A touch of lipgloss and I flounced off to school. My mood was much improved from when I first woke up, and I couldn't control it. I'd decided I would pay Will another visit at the station after school. I reminded myself I could have anyone I wanted, and I had my sights set high.

Chapter 22

When the bell of sweet freedom rang, I waited for Mr. Owens. I didn't think he'd do anything with me, but I wanted to talk to him about something that had been gnawing on my brain for the last few hours.

In third period, it dawned on me that maybe I was making a mistake in pursuing an older man. We had been reading *Lolita,* and instead of reassuring me, it creeped me out. I went back and forth. It was different because Lolita was twelve, hardly a woman yet, unlike me. Then again, would other people look at us the way I looked at those fictional characters?

I was genuinely worried that I was too young for Will. I mean, I knew I wasn't, but what if he thought I was? Mr. Owens was about the same age, maybe a few years younger, and he was around girls my age all the time. He would be able to tell me what I needed to know.

"Mr. Owens?" I said, walking up to his office door. "I have a question for you."

He took a deep breath, probably trying to control himself around me, but I was unfazed. I'd moved on and I wasn't going to regress. "Yes, Paige? What is it?"

"So, there's this guy. And I really like him. But he's older than me and I don't know if it's weird. I mean, I don't think it's weird, of course, but I'm worried he would."

"Is he old enough that *society* would think it's weird? Or better yet, the law?"

"Well, the law, no, because I'm the age of consent in this state, but society, I don't really know. But, like, older men trade in their wives for younger models all the time. Old men always date women who are at least ten years younger than them, sometimes even younger. Some of the most prolific men in our culture publicly date girls less than half their age."

"First of all, the age of consent just means your parents have to approve. It has nothing to do with your feelings. Secondly, if you're questioning society and him and how they would view the relationship, maybe it's best not to pursue it."

"But I really like him. Like, I can't stop thinking about him. He's so strong and soothing. He makes me feel safe."

He leaned back in his chair and sighed. "Paige, look, you're very young, by anyone's standards. As a teenager, you have a ton of hormones and everything else running rampant in your body. You see older men, and for young girls, that's stability. They see someone who can provide for them, and who will take them places. Show them the world. But look at it from the other side. A middle-aged man seeing a teenager is not normal. You're still a child, even with makeup and your hair done and push-up bras. An older man who would date a girl as young as you is a predator. He'd be taking advantage of your naïveté, of your innocence. He'd be controlling you. Yes, young girls are pretty and promiscuous and can be very tempting to older men, especially older men feeling nostalgic for that time in their lives when they had no responsibilities, but that doesn't excuse their behavior. It just doesn't."

A weight collapsed my lungs. "But, he likes me too," I squeaked.

He looked at the ceiling. "Did he actually tell you that? Is this thing consensual? Actually consensual?"

"Yeah, I mean, I'd totally be down."

"Consent goes both ways."

"What are you saying?"

"From the way you're talking and the way I've seen you act, you can be very … persistent. You come on very strong and you live in your own head. Is this man actually giving you attention, or is he just being nice to you and you're taking it the wrong way?"

"That's a silly question. Of course he actually does like me."

"Because everyone likes you, right?" He raised an eyebrow.

"No, well, yeah, but I really feel it. I think he would do it. Haven't you ever thought about it?"

"About what, Paige?" He crossed his arms and legs.

"About having sex with one of your students?"

He fumbled with his words. "Are you -- do you mean..." he pointed to him, and then to me. He hung his head. "Paige get out," he whispered.

"No, but I'm serious! There are a lot of attractive girls. I can't be the only person wondering it. And this guy, I'm sure he would want to have sex with me. I just need to get his wife out of the way."

He looked at his wedding ring, then back at me. "Get out, I said!" he yelled. "I don't want to see you back in here again, do you hear me?" He was standing now, pointing at the door.

"What -- why?"

"Your inappropriate comments are not welcome here. This is a learning environment. This is where people who want to learn, can. It is a safe zone, for both student and teacher. I am not here to feed into your little fantasy world."

I took a step back. He honestly thought I was talking about the two of us. I scoffed. "You're a little late, buddy. This time, I wasn't asking you to be a part of any of my worlds, real or fake. I was simply asking a legitimate question."

Mr. Owens squeezed the bridge of his nose between his thumb and index finger. "Please leave."

"Fine, nice talking to you," I spat. I turned on my heel, grabbed my backpack, and walked as calmly as I could out of the school. I refused to let him make me feel embarrassed for being curious.

I wandered to the station, paying the bathroom mirror a visit. My curls flattened a little and my eyes were bloodshot from the day, but I still looked presentable.

I lifted my chin and walked out into the main office area of the station. I tossed my hair when I saw him. I tried not to look too eager, yet happy to be there. Just as he turned around, a voice behind me said, "Oh, Paige. Is that you? How are you?"

I turned around. The doctor waddled toward me, tiny beads of sweat forming just along his thin hairline.

"Um, hi. Fine, thanks." I turned back around and headed for Will again.

"Say, do you think you have a minute to talk? Just a little."

I looked at Will, pleading with my eyes for him to save me. He didn't get the hint. His eyes grazed right past me and settled on the doctor. "Sure thing, Doc. I'll go grab us something to drink. Will that be enough time?" The doctor nodded and Will smiled at me. What, the male doctor had to ask the other male in the room if he could talk to me? He couldn't have asked *me* because, what? I don't have control over myself?

This had to be a joke.

The doctor put his hand on my shoulder and guided me to Will's desk. I plopped down and pulled out my homework.

"Paige, how are you holding up?"

"Fine," I said.

"Nothing bubbling up to the surface? Now that you've had time to process what happened, that is."

"Nope."

He nodded, looking down at nothing in particular. "What about school?" His eyes flicked up to mine.

"It's fine."

"Who's your favorite teacher?"

My heart jumped. Did he know? I shrugged. "I like my history teacher. And my English teacher."

"Yeah? Are you good at those subjects?"

He must not know. "I'm okay. I have As in them."

"Oh, good. Good grades are so hard to achieve. I was never an A student. I tried, but I just couldn't keep them up. Flunked all the tests." He chuckled to himself.

I looked over my shoulder to see if I could see Will. Getting drinks couldn't take that long.

When I sat forward again, the doctor narrowed his eyes at me. "How's it been coming here after school?" he asked.

"Good."

"It's nice having somewhere you can feel safe, right?"

"Yeah, I don't really get that at home."

"Does Will make you feel safe?"

I couldn't stop the grin from betraying me. "Yeah, definitely." I chewed on the skin next to my thumbnail.

"He's a good guy. He really cares. Sometimes too much."

I stared at him, trying to figure out what he was getting at. His pudgy face revealed nothing. "Maybe that's not such a bad flaw."

"Maybe not, but sometimes he has trouble focusing on the task at hand. Sometimes he gets too involved in a case. Makes it too personal."

I thought back to dinner. "Like with me?"

Doctor Woods leaned back in his chair, played with a paper clip. "No, not like with you."

At first, I didn't understand what he could possibly mean. I stared at him, and he stared back, until the cogs locked together in my mind. "With another girl?" I whispered.

He nodded slightly. My heart lurched. My eyes traced over every detail of his face, trying to read if he was lying. I looked at his mouth for a curve of betrayal, at his eyes for a twitch, at his hands for a tremor. I was good at reading men, but yet again, he gave me nothing. "Well, I mean, I don't see any other girls here after school."

"Not right now." He dragged out the sentence, implying there were other times.

"He's done this for other girls?" He shrugged. I moved to my other thumb to chew on. I sat for a second before I decided he was lying. I flipped my hair back. "I doubt it. He's not that type of person."

"Not what type of person?" The shrink looked me dead in the eyes. When I didn't answer, he went on, not breaking my gaze. "Not the type of person to treat just anyone as special? Only you because he sees something in you. Something he hasn't seen in other girls, right?"

"Exactly."

He blinked at me. "Of course, my mistake. So how long do you think you'll be coming around the station?"

"Until I feel safe at home without my mom around, I guess."

"Uh-huh. I thought you said you were holding up just fine though?"

I rolled my eyes. "Maybe I just don't want to talk about it."

"Your mom is gone a lot. What does she do?"

"She works."

"Ah, yes, but where?"

I'd never been asked where she worked before. I didn't have an answer ready and I stumbled. I drew a blank thinking of what places had long hours. "Um, she's, a nurse."

"Oh, smart with a good heart, huh? That's how I always feel about nurses. Which hospital?"

"Over at Foothills."

"Where your uncle is? Hm. Tough job. Now, forgive me if I'm wrong, but didn't your mom press charges against you? I mean, you never would have even been in this whole thing if it weren't for her. It probably would have been an open and shut self-defense case."

"She had a lapse in judgment."

"Pretty difficult lady to get a hold of too, your mom."

"I don't know." My cheeks burned. I caught a glimpse of Will walking down the hall toward us. "Can I get back to my homework now?"

The doctor stood up and pulled the chair out for Will. "Of course. Thanks so much for your time. We'll chat again later." He winked at me, nodded at Will and waddled back to his office.

"How are you holding up?" Will asked me.

"God, everyone keeps asking me that exact thing," I replied, irritable.

"Oh, sorry. I don't know, I guess that's just what people say."

I looked at his perfect face, sadness written all over it at having offended me. "No, don't worry about it. I'd probably ask myself the same thing. I'm doing okay though. Getting back into the swing of things."

"Do you think you'll visit him?"

My eyes widened. I never expected him to ask me such a personal question, especially so sweetly. "I don't know. I honestly hadn't thought about it."

"It could be really good for you," he laughed, "or I guess it could be really terrible. I don't know. I'm just rambling. Long day."

"No, I appreciate it. I think it'd be good for me to go, for sure. Probably alone though."

"I could take you, when you're ready. I could just wait outside. It's kind of a far walk for you. Plus then if something happens you have a quick getaway."

"Like if my mom shows up?"

"Or anything. I don't know." He was adorable, fidgeting, so unsure of himself.

"I would really like that. Thank you." I leaned forward, putting my hand on his.

He looked at it for a second, then pulled away. "So, my wife and I will be out the day after tomorrow." He put extra emphasis on *wife*. "I'm taking the day off. You're more than welcome to come here after school if you wanted. Di will be here still."

I didn't know how to respond. "Okay," I said.

"Because, you know, what you said. About me and her not being that close anymore. We're going on a date."

Well, planting the seed that he and his wife weren't getting along certainly backfired on me. "That's awesome." I was completely unconvincing and I didn't try to hide it. "Where are you guys going?"

"I rented a room downtown. We're going to go to dinner at The Cellars and then heading back to the room. They have a spa there." He paused, licked his lips. I looked down at my homework, staring pointedly. "Why do you seem so upset?"

"Oh, nothing. That sounds really nice."

"Paige," he warned, "we talked about this."

I gulped. "About what?"

"About talking about what you're feeling. Even if it's not about what happened, you still need to talk about it."

I wanted to stay calm, mature, reasonable, but my emotions took over. "It's just…she's so controlling. Haven't you noticed? She doesn't want me around even though you're opening your heart to me. You've been so kind to me and she's trying to ruin that. You've helped me heal and she doesn't want that. She wants to make you smaller. It's like she's jealous of what we have."

"Thank you. For talking about it."

The comment hung in the air, thick and tense. I stood up and started shoving my stuff back in my bag. "Okay, well, I'd better get going. Have a great trip. I'll see you later." I left before he could say anything to me, to make me come back to him.

That night, I lay on my couch, a thin blanket covering my legs, and dreamed of Will. I wanted, no, needed him to look at me that special way. Eyes heavy, a smirk tugging at his lips. Every word he spoke would be in a half-whisper, like he was telling me a secret, even if he was just telling me he liked my hair. He'd look me over constantly, running his teeth over his bottom lip, and feed me compliments like chocolate.

I love you, Paige. Let's run away together.

I needed to hear those sweet words. Every nerve in my body strained with frustration. I fought back tears. I stared at his name in my phone, wanting desperately to call him.

I'm leaving her for you, Paige.

He'd say it, I knew he would, if I'd just call him, give him the chance to express himself, just as he told me to do. That woman was corrupting him, keeping him away from me. I had to do something, but I didn't know what.

I pressed the little green telephone button next to his name. The other line rang.

And rang. And rang.

Until the voicemail picked up. *This is Detective Harrington. If this is an emergency, call 911, otherwise, leave a message at the beep. Thanks.*

I listened to the quiet static, trying to figure out what to say. If his wife listened to his messages, he'd be in trouble. She shouldn't anyway, since it was his work phone, but I couldn't trust her not to.

All the things I wanted to tell him, but couldn't, rushed through my mind. *I love you too, Will. Let's run away together.*

Finally, I hung up. I laid there, depressed, anxious. I fell into a fitful sleep, dreaming that I was drowning and Will was there to save me, but I always jolted awake just before he could.

Chapter 23

"Paige? Can I ask you something?" Detective Harrington questioned. He'd been shuffling papers around absent-mindedly for the last fifteen minutes while Paige pretended to do her homework at his desk.

Things were tense between them since he mentioned vacationing with his wife. Paige wouldn't look at him, and she hardly spoke to him. She said more to Woods than to him, and that was extremely rare. He wanted her to talk to him, but he had nothing to talk about except uncomfortable questioning. He asked her anyway, since talking about the weather was getting him nowhere.

The day before, his partner had planted a seed in his mind: why wait for her mom to get home if her mother was the one who turned her in? "I mean, we both saw this bitch," DiPascua said. "Crazy, tweaking out, clearly doesn't love her own daughter. Paige is a smart girl. She doesn't take crap from anyone. Even when we first saw her in the hospital, Paige was completely emotionally severed from her mother."

"Who knows? She's the girl's mother. That counts for something."

"I don't think it does in this case. Something's weird, Harrington. I don't trust her. And you know what? There's no record of her working at that hospital. Paige lied about that. It's pretty obvious that woman can't hold down a job anyway, with the drugs she was on."

He'd scoffed at the time, shook his head and walked away from her. Of course Paige would lie about her mother having a job. You don't tell the cops that your mom does drugs. Yet he was about to ask this victim he'd gotten too close to already more personal questions, instead of leaving it to Woods.

"Sure," Paige said. "Shoot." She set down her pencil, giving him her full attention. She looked straight into his eyes. A coy smirk tugged at her glossed lips. He thought, just a flash, about kissing those supple, shiny lips. He shook his head, determined to stay focused.

"My partner brought up a good point the other day." She stared at him expectantly. He couldn't believe he was selling out his partner instead of just owning up to it. He didn't know what was wrong with him. He could always get answers from the perps, exuding confidence, dripping with testosterone. She was his downfall. She made him lose his train of thought. He didn't want to hurt her feelings. "Why – why are you killing time here?"

"What do you mean?"

"I mean," he paused, sighing, trying to string together something coherent. "Well, I know I asked you to come in and maybe talk to Woods and everything, but you've been here every day. Supposedly waiting until your mom gets home." He mentally punched himself for saying *supposedly*. "It's just, you're always saying how you don't want to go back home alone, which I understand, but if your mom is the one who pressed charges and made such a scene, why do you want to wait until she's home? Do you really feel safe there? With her?"

"Um. I don't –"

"And she never seems to get home at the same time. Sometimes you'll leave here at five, other times at nine. If she works late consistently, why is she never off at the same times? Or even late?" The words spewed out of his mouth now. "You never talk about her or about what happened. Why she would blame you."

She was the one faltering now. "It's complicated."

"Paige," he pulled his chair closer to her, "be honest with me. It's okay."

"I don't know if it…changes things."

"With the investigation?"

"Yeah."

"We can't really do much about it until your uncle wakes up, if he does. Your mom's kind of dropped the whole thing, so until we get a word from him, the case is pending." He felt bad deceiving her like that. He could, and would have to, use whatever she said against her if the situation called for it. They were setting up a court date as they spoke. They just needed a signature. He'd never felt bad before about leading a suspect on through questioning, even telling outright lies to get them to admit their guilt. *You're on shaky ground, Will,* he thought. He pushed aside his personal feelings to get to the root of what really happened.

"Kay, well, here's the thing. I wasn't completely honest with you. My mom is pretty much never home. She's a crazy bitch and I never know where she is. She hates me." Her voice raised an octave or two, defensive, telling him she felt like a kid in trouble rather than a woman who'd attempt to murder a guy out of spite.

His stomach turned. Just a kid afraid of getting grounded. He scooted his chair back an inch. "Whoa, there, it's okay. This is just you and me, just talking. Like friends. Start from the beginning." Finally, she was talking. Finally, she was doing what he had intended to begin with. He hoped Woods or DiPascua stood off in shadows somewhere listening.

She laughed humorlessly. "That's a long beginning. You probably won't believe me anyway. She didn't."

"Try me."

"Dear sweet old Uncle Glen likes to screw younger girls, preferably ones related to him. He's sort of lost his interest in me since I've gotten older and filled out. Now I think it's just more of a tradition. Boredom maybe."

He thought back to that first day he questioned her. He'd known even then that he had raped her, but he couldn't get her to say the words. Tears stung the backs of Harrington's eyes. Sex crimes, especially ones against young kids, always got to him. He could never understand wanting to prey on the innocent. "Paige, he's sick."

She looked at her hands, shrugged bitterly. "Yeah, well, my mother seemed to think it was me that's sick. She thinks I coaxed him and because he's a man, he couldn't resist. He was 'under my spell,' but if he hadn't been blinded by my sluttiness, he would never have done anything."

"No, Paige, she's wrong. So, so wrong." He moved his chair closer to her again. "Rape is about exuding power over someone who is meek, not about wanting sex."

"He definitely wanted sex though, so I don't know about that one."

"Pedophiles are sexually attracted to children, yes, but it's mostly dominance. It isn't you. There's something wrong with him. You just happened to be his target."

"I could have stopped it. I should have said no or something, but I never did."

"No. That's the thing. He knows it too. He's an authority figure. Not to mention his strength and size versus that of a child. Plus, you did stop it, right? Is that what happened? He tried to rape you again and you were fed up with it?"

She nodded. "I should have done it sooner. Or at least hit him harder. You know what's stupid? I actually felt bad after it happened. I've wanted him dead for so long, but then when I thought it did actually happen, I was sad."

He put his hand on hers. He almost pulled away, thinking better about touching a rape victim, but she moved her hand, just slightly, to receive his. "Because you loved him, once."

"Yeah, I guess I did. It's so weird how he flipped like that. From practically being my dad to being my attacker."

The silence hung thick. She sat up straight, pulling her hand away from his. "So, basically," she continued, "he came into my room and I ran out into the hallway. He was drunk. I grabbed my dad's bat and hit him as hard as I could. Then I called the cops. They said to call my mom, so I did, which I kind of regret."

"It actually turned out pretty well for you. If he had died, we'd be conducting a very different investigation."

"He still could die." She sounded morbid, like a part of her wished it to be true despite the knowledge that she'd be in a much more troubling situation if he did.

"He could, yes, but he's stable. The doctors don't seem to think he's going to go anytime soon. That's good news," he added when her face dropped. "You won't get charged with murder or manslaughter."

"I guess that would be pretty shitty."

A bark of laughter escaped from his throat. "To say the least."

"Anyway, the reason I hang out here is because I don't want to be alone. There's nothing in that house but bad memories, you know? My dad dying, my mother never being around, Glen. I mean, I hang out at my friend's house sometimes, but she's busy. And I don't want to be a burden. Here, you can work around me. Plus I'm getting so much stuff done. I'm a pretty good student, but even I usually don't do all my assignments. My teachers are going to think I've been replaced."

He chuckled. "If you ever need anything, the station's always here."

She nodded and buried her nose back in her history book. When she studied, she got a little crease right between her brows and she ran her teeth along her bottom lip. He couldn't hold his smile back. She was adorable.

God, what was he thinking? He just spent ten minutes talking to her about how her uncle was a pedophile and he was sick. He could actually see how her uncle could be attracted to her.

She didn't look like a kid. She looked like a young woman.

Looks didn't really matter in this case. She was younger than his own kids.

Then again, she acted more mature than his kids. Than many other kids her age.

Her age. Which was way too young for him.

He would have to tell DiPascua what Paige had just told him. This case was going to become something entirely different. The prosecution would rip her apart, trigger her PTSD – which she probably didn't realize she had yet – right up on the stand. She'd have to relive every rape down to the smallest detail, then get called a liar. She'd cry in front of everyone, and there would be no one there for her.

Other than him.

"Are you okay?"

He snapped back into reality. Paige was staring at him. "What?"

"Are you okay? You're, like, twitching, and stuff."

Harrington laughed in discomfort. "Wow, I hope it wasn't that bad. I was just thinking."

"Anything you want to share with the class?"

"No, I don't really remember what I was thinking. That happens sometimes, you know?"

"Whatever you say, boss." She smirked and looked back at her book.

Age was just a number anyway.

Chapter 24

I was called into the principal's office yet again the following day right after my last class. "Hello there, Paige," Mr. Hall said cheerily. Maybe he was attempting to make me feel like I wasn't in trouble by being so cheerful, but it didn't work.

"Hi, Mr. Hall. What happened this time?" I didn't try to smile. I was so tired and miserable, I didn't even care.

His voice caught and his eyebrows twitched, unsure why I was being so cold. I doubted if any of the two thousand students there was ever cold toward him. "Well, it's a very serious matter, I'm afraid."

I stared at him. I didn't drop my gaze. I didn't feel shame and I wasn't going to pretend I did. I waited for him to continue.

"Alright. Well." He fumbled about for his words. He looked at his hands, at his knees, at his computer. He could barely glance at me. He shook his head, probably giving himself an internal pep-talk, and finally looked at me. "Miss Harper, Mr. Owens has filed to have you removed from his class."

I clicked my tongue impatiently. "Why?"

"He says you make him uncomfortable, and you take away from the other students' learning."

"'Take away from other students' learning'? Are you kidding me? How?"

Mr. Hall cleared his throat. "He says you make rude comments. You daydream. You don't do your work."

"Okay, my comments are not rude. And I hardly ever say anything in the first place. How is daydreaming taking away from other students' learning? Everyone daydreams. Especially in that class. Not doing my work also doesn't effect anyone else. Except I do my homework. I have an A in that class." I was almost yelling. I tried to calm myself down.

"Miss Harper," he said, his tone comforting, "his request cannot be ignored. This is the third time he's said something."

"Wait, the third? This is only the second time I've talked to you."

"Yes, well, the first time, we decided to wait it out a little, dismissing it as girls being girls. Miss Harper, this is very serious. I've pulled you from his class, and that's all there is to it. I had to do a little rearranging of your schedule, but you have all the same teachers except in history and algebra, so you'll be right on track still." He handed me my new schedule.

I took it from him and stood. "Mr. Owens should know by now I'm not interested in him. I've moved on." I left his office, shaking, before he could wipe the bewildered look off his face and answer me.

I called Ashley. "Hey. Can I come to your recital? I'm out front. I can run around back and meet you. Unless your parents already came to get you."

"No that'd be great! I'd love it if you came. I can show you that I'm the best freaking one and I deserved to have the lead in the play." I had forgotten that she didn't get the lead and was still feeling bitter about it. I hoped her bitterness wouldn't steal the spotlight from my bitterness.

I walked up to her just as her parents pulled up. "Hey, little lady!" her dad said to me. "You coming along? What about softball?"

"Oh, I quit. Just wasn't feeling it anymore. I actually quit a while ago. I can't go to her practices but I remembered her recital was open to family and friends, so here I am."

"Well, that's great. It really means a lot to her." He looked at Ashley. "Not that she's standing right there and could tell you herself or anything." Everyone giggled and I felt my anger subside slightly.

Her family rearranged themselves in the car: Dad in the

passenger side, Mom in the back, and Ashley in the driver's seat. "Whoa, there, am I about to die?" I joked as I slid into the seat beside her mom.

"Oh whatever," Ashley said. "I need to practice like all the time. If I'm going to be a strong independent woman, I need to be able to drive."

"And we want to be strong, independent parents who don't have to cart their daughter around everywhere," her dad said.

"Exactly. Plus then I can come get you and we can go everywhere together," Ashley said, looking at me in the rearview mirror.

"Sounds dangerous to me," I said.

We joked and laughed and caught up with each other on the car ride there. Ashley was all nervous energy right before, fidgeting and breathing heavily. But she looked beautiful dancing, like she was right at home on that stage, twirling and leaping and doing things I couldn't even dream of doing. I could tell it was something she loved. She had a glow about her that couldn't be forced.

I wondered if that's how I looked when I played softball. Now I didn't really have anything to feel passionately about.

"Well, how was it?" Ashley asked after her dance.

I scooped her up in a bear hug. "You were amazing! I'm so proud of you."

"Did I do okay? I don't know. I messed up a couple times."

"Oh my god, I didn't even notice. Don't be so hard on yourself, girl."

I watched as her dance teacher told her he was proud of her, but she needed to remember to point her toes. She forgot a step and it almost ruined the whole thing. I shook my head. I couldn't believe he was chastising her like that, and she was nodding the whole time, not getting upset, just accepting it, absorbing it. I couldn't handle being scolded like that every single day. She was the most beautiful being in the world on stage, yet he hardly seemed to care about the good parts.

I gave her another hug and reminded her how amazing she was after she'd changed, hoping she wouldn't beat herself up. She smiled, calling me a good friend.

At her house, we were bundles of excited chatter. There was no mention of Glen. Honestly, he didn't even cross my mind.

"So how's it going with Detective Studmuffin?" Ashley asked as we ate our dinner. Grilled steaks, potato salad, fresh fruit. ("Why only have 'summer meals' in summer?" her dad said as he served us.)

"Oh, what's that? Studmuffin?" Mrs. Hale said. She raised her eyebrows. "You have a boyfriend, Paige?"

I felt heat rush to my cheeks. Lava right up under my skin. "No -- I -- not yet." I turned my head to Ashley and whispered, "Bitch."

She hardly tried holding back her giggles. "What? Sorry! I thought they weren't listening."

"They? We're sitting right here!" Mr. Hale exclaimed. He laughed too.

"Anyway, what's the deal with him?" Ashley asked.

"Well, shit, now I feel put on the spot. I don't know. He's fine. I'm going to see him tonight probably."

"Already on the third date, eh? You know what happens on the third date, right?" Ashley nudged me meaningfully with her elbow.

"No, I don't know," Mrs. Hale said. "Please enlighten me."

"Yeah, what does it mean?" I asked, passing the heat to her.

"Oh, I definitely don't know. I was just wondering if she did. Obviously she doesn't. We're all innocent here."

The light-hearted feeling continued until it was time for me to head home. I'd nearly forgotten the issue with Mr. Owens and Mr. Hall. I decided to wait until school the next day to mention anything to Ashley. I didn't want to bring her down.

"Are you really going to see him tonight?" Ashley asked as she walked me to the door, parents out of earshot.

"No, he's out."

"Out?" She raised an eyebrow. "Like, on a date?"

"Yeah, something like that."

"With his wife, maybe?"

I shrugged. "Yeah, probably with her."

She shook her head and rolled her eyes before she hugged me. "Just don't do anything stupid, boo."

"I'll try my best. Can't guarantee it."

She laughed and hit my arm. "Whatever. Thanks for coming today. It really means a lot."

"Meh, not like I had anything better to do I guess." I grinned at her.

"Get the fuck out," she said, laughing.

I felt a little guilty, remembering that the only reason I went to see her dance was because I needed to blow off steam from the news about school. Only a little.

I shrugged it off and walked toward my house until I knew she wasn't looking anymore. I took a left and looped around until I made it to Benjamin Franklin Drive. I smiled.

I walked up to the front door like I was supposed to be there. The house was dark, except for that one light they always left on in the living room. To deter intruders, I'm sure.

I looked under the mat for a spare key. I found nothing but built-up dirt and a dead beetle. I checked around the mailbox, under the bushes, on top of the door frame. Nothing. I walked around the back, never looking over my shoulder. I wanted people to think I belonged there if they decided to look out their windows, just like last time.

I checked under the mat to the back door. Nothing. A little ripple of panic coursed over my body. Maybe I couldn't get in easily.

I checked around the plants and didn't find a key. I lifted a little ceramic frog in a pink tutu, and there it was. A squeal of delight nearly burst from my throat.

The key slid in the lock smoothly. The click of the deadbolt slipping into the door was the sweetest sound. I slipped the key into my back pocket to keep safe.

I'd already seen almost all the downstairs area except for a spare bedroom tucked away in the corner. It looked like an office space, though rarely touched. I flipped through some pages left out on the desk, but there was nothing interesting there. More pictures of the family on shelves. Mostly her side, except for one of an older white couple, which must have been his parents.

I made my way upstairs. I hung a right into another spare bedroom. Definitely the daughter's room, kept the same as when she left for school. I walked down a ways to the last bedroom: the son's room. It was kept the same as well, except for big plastic containers marked *scrapbook* in the middle of the floor.

I peeked in the top container. Her most recent scrapbook page sat on top. Summer. In one photo, the son looked to be about twelve, his mop of hair glistening with water from the pool, the rattail all boys get at some point in their lives hanging over his shoulder. In another, the daughter stood at the edge of the pool in a pink one-piece, arm floaties at full capacity.

Part of that photo was cut off. I riffled through the container until I came across the other half. It was crumpled like garbage. It was of Will, smiling at his little girl, encouraging her to jump in. He seemed so young. He was tan and fit. He held himself high, no burdens of life weighing him down yet.

The sick pang of jealousy clenched my gut. I dropped the picture and closed the lid.

I backtracked down the hallway to the master bedroom. There's a certain feeling you get when you go into a parent's bedroom, like it's forbidden to be there. I tiptoed around to find the light switch, as if someone in the empty house might hear me and yell at me for being where I shouldn't.

Everything was in its place in the room. Not a wrinkle in the baby blue comforter. Not a white pillow was out of place. No photos on the nightstands. Only ocean décor. It was almost as if no one had ever lived in this room, like it was a model home. I opened the drawer on the nightstand on the left. Socks, his. Nothing hidden. I checked the other one. A book about raising children. I looked in the dresser. Jeans, pajamas, a drawer for ties. The bottom right drawer held her bras and panties and a vibrator. I stared at it, unsure of whether to panic for having touched it or to laugh because I had found it in the first place.

I tucked it back where I found it and got up to wash my hands. The bathroom was immaculate as well. For two people who worked all the time, they sure found a lot of time to clean. I wasn't nearly as busy as either of them and I couldn't even figure out how to pick my dirty underwear up off the floor.

I squirted *Tropical Sunrise* soap into my hands. I didn't know a sunrise had a smell, but apparently it was fruity. Definitely not Will's scent.

I rifled through all the drawers and the medicine cabinet. Mostly her things. Hair products and makeup. He had one drawer with a razor and a toothbrush. He was almost completely absent from this room as well.

Their closet was more of the same. Three-quarters her clothes, and a tiny corner for his. I felt the dress shirts and suit jackets between my fingers. Soft and worn. I doubted if he got paid enough to afford new work clothes very often. It made him seem even more humble. The space in my heart reserved for him grew a little.

I moved back to the bedroom. A laptop sat on the desk in the corner of the room. They had a perfectly good office downstairs. I don't know why they'd use a cramped area for their work.

I opened the laptop. Password protected. I typed in a few things. *Ihearteva, justice43,* other crap I knew wouldn't be his password. I didn't even know if it was his password or hers. I closed it again, not caring too much to see more family photos. I doubted if he had anything about me. I was his little secret.

I faced the bed again. I pulled my boots off, as well as my jacket. I laid them carefully on the floor. I pulled off my jeans and my top and pushed the decorative pillows onto the floor. I slid between the sheets on his side of the bed, hugging one of his pillows, breathing in his scent. Woody and dark. I'd finally found him.

I woke up from dreams just out of reach around one in the morning. I fixed the bed the best I could, slid back into my clothes, and stumbled out of the house, back to my cold, empty one. I crashed on my couch, still enveloped in his ghost.

Chapter 25

Detective Harrington and his wife got home before eight the next morning. They'd been happy and loving to begin with, but the novelty of the mini staycation wore off as the wine did. Thoughts of Paige Harper slithered into both their minds.

She's a child.

She's so much more than her age.

She's a whore.

She's beautiful, smart, sexy.

She's a home wrecker.

I have a wife, but I can't stop thinking about her.

They drove home in silence. Nothing bitter, just disappointment.

The detective tossed his keys on the kitchen table and stared into the fridge while Eva went upstairs to shower. "Will!" she shrieked.

He ran upstairs, heart pounding. She stood at the foot of the bed, staring at the pillows. "What?" he said irritably, the racket in his chest settling.

"Someone was here."

"What?"

"I said someone was here, in our bed. The pillows are all messed up."

"Oh come on, stop being so paranoid. Those things are always just thrown up there without any rhyme or reason."

She snapped her head toward him. "Actually, no, they're not. I have a very specific order I like them in and they are not like that. They go blue, white, blue, then two white ones in the front. There are two blue ones together in the back and the other ones all just thrown on there. Someone was here!"

"Well, did they take anything?"

They both looked around the room. The laptop and her jewelry were all in their places. "No, but isn't that weird?"

Harrington rubbed his face. "I don't have time for this. I gotta get to work." He grabbed clothes from the closet and left without saying he loved her.

As the front door clicked behind her husband, Eva set to rearrange the bed, thinking maybe she was just being paranoid.

She pulled two long blonde hairs from between two white pillows.

At half past two, Harrington looked at the clock. She'd be getting out of class now. He hoped she'd come by the station. After the last time they talked, he wasn't so sure she'd feel comfortable coming in. Yesterday morning, he thought he wanted her to stop being a part of his life. This morning, though, he wanted her more than ever.

Doctor Woods walked up to Harrington's desk. "Ah, looking at the clock. Anything important happening?" he asked.

"Just checking the time."

"Gets boring sometimes without any perps, right?"

Harrington forced a laugh. "You got it."

"Your girl coming in today?"

"Excuse me?" Harrington's eyes strained against their sockets.

Doctor Woods put his hands up in surrender. "I didn't mean anything by it. I was just asking if Paige was coming in." He took a mental note to look into their relationship more. Harrington had never been so defensive about a victim. Well, except once.

Harrington relaxed, but only to seem like he didn't care. "I don't know. She didn't leave on a very good note last time."

"You hope she does though?"

Harrington glared at his colleague. "In a strictly professional way of caring for a victim, yes."

"I hope she does too. I want to interview her again. There's something very intriguing about the girl." He tapped his fingers on the desk. "I'll be in my office if she comes by. Let her know I want to talk to her. Maybe you should hear what she has to say."

Harrington saluted to him as he walked away. "Sure thing."

He tried in vain to focus on filing the paperwork of a man accused of raping his neighbor. Harrington would fill in a few words, but his thoughts would always meander back to Paige.

He was in the middle of a stretch and a yawn when she walked in, looking perfectly happy, like they'd never had their last conversation. "Hey, boss," she said. He loved the way she called him that in her sweet, innocent little voice.

"Hey, how are you?" He stood up to pull out the chair for her.

"Okay. How about yourself? How was your date night?"

"Oh, it was fine. It didn't quite go the way I'd planned but it could have been worse." Was that a smirk that flicked across her mouth as she gave her condolences? "How'd you do? Did you come into the station?"

"No, I hung out with Ashley. I went to her recital and had dinner at her place."

"Is she in a play?"

"Not yet. She does ballet. She wants a lead at some point. She's had little parts here and there, but never a lead."

"I'm sure she'll get it. From what you've said about her, she can achieve whatever she sets her mind to."

Paige's face fell. She was probably used to being in Ashley's shadow. Ashley was the type who got to have dance recitals if she wanted, or anything she wanted for that matter. Paige was the type who was lucky if she had enough money for lunch. "Yeah, she's pretty amazing like that. Wish I could be more like her."

"You're amazing how you are. Trust me."

They held eye contact for a beat before she blushed and turned away.

"Oh, I forgot," Harrington said, breaking the tension, "Doc wants to see you again. He's really intrigued by you."

A shadow passed over her face. "Do I have to? I don't really like the guy. Sorry, I know he's your friend and all, but I don't like talking to him."

"It's okay, you're entitled to your own opinion. It's because he's a shrink. It's hard to feel comfortable around shrinks, you know? Even now I feel that way and I've worked with him for years. You definitely don't have to see him if you don't want to, but I know he'd appreciate it."

"Would you appreciate it?"

He smiled, bemused. "Well, sure. Here, I'll walk you to his office."

Harrington put his hand on the small of her back, steering her toward the little room down the hallway.

Doctor Woods stood up to shake their hands when they walked in. "So good to see you, Paige. How are you?"

"How am I holding up?" she asked, bitterness dripping from the corners of her mouth.

The doctor didn't falter. "No, no, just how are you?"

The shadow Harrington saw when he first mentioned Woods lifted from Paige's face. "I'm okay, thank you."

"That's good to hear."

They made small talk until Woods asked if they could continue their discussion from earlier. Paige looked to Harrington for her answer. When he nodded, she said, "Yeah, sure. Why not?"

They went to an interrogation room. "Just because it's quiet," Doctor Woods said. "Sometimes I can't focus in my office with all that chatter from the halls. Detectives pretending to work and all." He winked at Paige. She smiled. Before he followed her into the room, he told Harrington to stand behind the glass. "I think you'll be interested in her answers today."

"What's up, Doc?" Paige said when Woods sat across from her.

"I've never heard that one before," the doctor joked. Paige shrugged, smiled. Harrington was surprised to see her smile at him. "So, tell me, how's school going?" Woods continued.

"Fine. Same as always," Paige answered. She was so calm, so serene.

"How's history class? And English?"

Her eyelashes fluttered. "Fine. I'm a little behind in history now, so I'll need to catch up on that here today. But I got an A on my English essay about *East of Eden*."

"That's great news about your essay. Why have you fallen behind in history? I thought you liked it?"

"I had to rearrange my schedule. Something about classes being too full. Me and a few other kids."

"Is that right?" Doctor Woods said noncommittally.

Harrington fidgeted behind the glass. He'd seen Woods work before. He was a genius, and seeing him pick Paige apart made him antsy.

"The thing is," Woods continued, "I called your school and talked to your principal."

"Why?" Paige's entire face dropped.

"It's completely routine. We care very much that everyone who needs our help gets it. Now, Mr. Hall said that you had a request filed against you by your history teacher. Is that right?" Paige stared hard but didn't answer. "Want to tell me your side? Sounds a little extreme to me, personally."

Paige chewed her cheek before answering. "It was ridiculous. He said I made him uncomfortable. Like, what? That's so dumb."

"Uncomfortable how?"

"I don't know, I guess he didn't like the way I talked to him. I didn't conform to his stupid standards." She folded her arms and plopped back in her seat.

"Mr. Hall said he complained of you making overtly sexual comments to him. He said you'd stay after class, not for help with homework, but in a way suggesting that you just wanted to be near him. I don't know, you don't really seem like the type to do that sort of thing though."

"I'm not! Ugh, that's such bullshit!," Paige yelled, snapping forward in her seat again. Color raised on her face. "Okay, I was being raped by my uncle and I didn't want to go home. If algebra was my last class, I would have hung out later around there. Just like I'm here. He's so dumb."

He was surprised she had been so forthcoming about being raped. It took her this long to tell Harrington, Doctor Woods never expected her to just blurt it out. He grazed over it, not wanting to scare her off. "And the comments?"

Paige leaned back again and picked at her nail polish. "I don't really know about that one. The thing is, women are subjected to so much objectification and are over-sexualized almost as a hobby for men, yet someone makes a joke toward a guy and he flips. All of a sudden, he's a blubbering mess and can't handle it. He should have just grown a pair instead of filing a request to have me removed. Now I look like a perv."

"You don't look like a pervert. Things get twisted so easily when humans are involved. That's the real reason your schedule was moved around, isn't it?"

Paige chewed her cheek again, nodded.

"Are you attracted to Mr. Owens?"

Harrington paced. He couldn't see where the questioning was going.

"It's okay if you are," Woods encouraged. "It's perfectly natural for girls to be attracted to older authoritative men."

Paige ran her eyes across the doctor's face, trying to decide if he was to be trusted. "I mean, yeah. But everyone is." A smile tugged at her lips. "There's just something about him."

"Have you ever fantasized about him?"

She laughed. "Yeah, but I'm definitely not the only one."

"Tell me about one of them."

Harrington felt the anger vibrate through him. You don't just ask a teenager about her sexual fantasies! It was rude and inappropriate.

Paige covered her face with her hands, took a breath, set her hands in her lap. "Okay, this is super embarrassing, but whatever. You asked!" she said, flirting, always flirting. Harrington tried to ignore the acidic jealousy bubbling up within him. "Okay, so I always want him to, like, call me into his office or something after class. He'll say something like, 'Paige, can I see you for a moment,' in his super sexy voice. Then I'll walk in there and he'll close the door. Then he'll tell me I'm beautiful and he just can't fight the feeling anymore, or something like that. Then he'll touch me gently behind my legs and pull me onto his lap, kissing me. And then, you know. I don't know, it's dumb."

"No, it's not dumb. It's completely natural to have sexual fantasies." Woods paused, taking a breath, letting Paige revel in her fantasy with half a smile still on her face. "In these fantasies, is he ever aggressive with you?"

"No, he's always very gentle."

"Are you ever in charge?" He placed his hands on the table in front of him. He was showing her he had no hidden weapons. She could trust him.

She sat on the question for a minute. "No, I guess I never really thought about it."

"So he's always making the first move to you?"

"Yeah, I guess." She blushed again.

"Why do you think that is?"

She shrugged.

"Do you ever have these fantasies about other authoritative men?"

"My other teachers are all old women."

Woods laughed. "I guess that makes it difficult. Maybe someone outside of school, then? Like maybe Detective Harrington?"

"Why? Did he say anything about me?" she whispered, like she was about to hear a secret in the schoolyard. She leaned forward, eyes wide, smiling fully.

"No, he hasn't really talked about you to me. I was just wondering about you." Woods' tone turned to aloofness. He always did that when he got what he wanted. Harrington tilted his head back and sighed, unsure of how he felt about what he'd just heard.

Paige knew she'd been another of Woods' victims. She kneaded her hand with her fist, sat up straight, stiff. "Oh, I mean, he's okay. He's nice to me. So is his partner. Is it – can I go do my homework now? I gotta work on that history homework and all."

Woods smiled warmly. He reached for her hand. "Of course. Thanks so much for chatting with me. We'll catch up again another time."

Will hurried to his desk, to act like he hadn't been listening to the entire conversation.

"Here's your girl back, alive and well," Woods said brightly. "We should talk a little later," he murmured to Harrington before strolling away, whistling.

"How'd it go?" Harrington asked Paige, forcing a smile.

"Fine, nothing too exciting. He's just trying to help." She slapped her history book on her desk.

Detective DiPascua and Doctor Woods talked in the hall, just out of earshot. Harrington strained to hear them, but it was no use. DiPascua looked over at them every few seconds. She was rubbing the back of her neck; something she did when she was hearing something she didn't like.

"Yeah, he's a good man," Harrington responded, distant. "Excuse me for a minute." He squeezed her shoulder before joining the doctor and his partner.

Woods led him to his office while DiPascua went to sit with Paige.

"Will, I'm going to be honest with you here," Woods said, offering Harrington a seat.

Harrington declined, too anxious to sit. "What's the deal? She seems like a normal victim."

"I'm not so sure. Will, she's obsessed with you. With older men in general."

Harrington scoffed. "Nice assessment, Doc. We see that in plenty of child abuse cases."

"I'm being completely serious. She needed you to answer for her. She sought out your approval." Harrington rolled his eyes -- his only defense when he knew he was being proven wrong. Woods ignored it and went on. "Did you see the way she reacted when I mentioned you? She lit up. She *needed* for you to have mentioned her. When I said you didn't, she was crushed. When I talked to her the other day, it was the same thing. When I made her feel like she wasn't special in your eyes, she acted as if I'd said something offensive and crude. She doesn't consider other victims to be other humans. They're only threats. Last time, I told her you get too involved sometimes, but not with her. She said 'I don't see other girls here after school' in such a matter-of-fact way, like that made her your one and only. You should have seen the way she looked when we were talking. She literally twitched. Her eyes got this big." He held his hands in circles over his eyes.

"It doesn't mean anything," Harrington said. He wished it'd sounded less whiny. "Look, she's messed up, I get it. Most every person that walks through that door is. You of all people should know that. Of course she needs to feel special. Everyone does at some point, she just does a little more right now."

Woods rubbed his chin. "Will. Have you not heard the things she says to you?"

Harrington narrowed his eyes. "I'm sure you'll reiterate."

Woods took a deep, frustrated breath. "She mentions sex or something to do with it multiple times a day. Just to you. Not to me, not to Di, not to anyone else in the office."

The detective scoffed, asking the doctor to give specifics.

"The last time she was here," Woods answered, "she mentioned how her bra kept riding up, and how she just wanted to take it off. While it may be true – I've heard those things are colossally uncomfortable – and she simply has no filter since she's a teenager, her tone and word choice felt deliberate." When Harrington raised his eyebrows in defiance, he went on. "As she adjusted her bra in front of you rather than modestly turning to the side or doing it slyly, she specifically said, "Jesus, my titties are getting to big for this thing. I can't wait to get home so I can take it off and let the girls free.' Then, later, she talked about maybe selling her underwear online. Then she went into detail about it, backing it up with facts from her own … secretions. Will, she wants you to sexualize her. She wants you to make a move, to take advantage."

"She's like that with everyone. She's an attractive young woman. That's how they all are. Plus girls always say crap like that. They like the attention, even if they're not getting it the right way."

Woods sighed, trying with every atom in his body not to get angry at his friend for being so blind to what was clearly right in front of him. "Tell yourself whatever you need to sleep at night, but just be careful with her. She's unreliable, manipulative. She shows a different part of herself to each and every one of us. The only one I think she's herself around is Di," he added to lighten the mood, "but that's because that woman is a superhero. She can see through anyone's lies, no matter who it is."

Harrington nodded to the doctor, refusing to crack a smile, although he was completely right about his partner. That woman could turn anyone to jelly. "Who is she really then?"

Woods' light tone from seconds before turned serious. "She's an insecure, broken girl who needs years of help to become a functioning member of society. It's not too late to help her, but she's spiraling fast."

Harrington nodded. "That's exactly what I'm trying to do: help her." He made to leave but the doctor stopped him.

"One more thing. Her being here every day needs to stop. It's getting weird. People are asking questions."

Harrington saluted Woods, turned on his heel and nearly stomped back to his desk. DiPascua and Paige were laughing. She could turn anyone to jelly, that is, except for this girl, apparently. He was incredulous, but relieved. Finally, someone Paige connected with.

"Hey, Will," his partner said, the laugh still playing on her lips. "I need to talk to you. Later, of course. I'll let you guys get back to it. Have a good one." She squeezed Paige's hand and looked meaningfully at Harrington.

He sighed and flopped into his chair. Maybe he was wrong. Di was playing Paige, ready to rip her in two whenever the right moment presented itself.

Eva emulated Di when he got home, tearing him a new one about the safety of their home. "I live with a fucking cop and we aren't even safe! What are you good for anyway?"

He tried to convince her she was crazy, that no one broke into their house, but that only made things worse.

Finally, he agreed. "I'll call a locksmith tomorrow." He walked the house, gun in hand, to check for intruders. "Like checking under Amanda's bed for monsters."

"Except these monsters are real, you fucking idiot!"

She yelled at him in the shower, while he brushed his teeth, while he tried to read. Finally, she ran out of steam and let him sleep.

But when he turned over and closed his eyes, he caught the scent of familiar citrus on his sheets.

Chapter 26

At lunch, Ashley blathered on about tests. If she didn't pass her math midterm, she'd get a C in the class, and that just wasn't acceptable. She needed to get into the AP calculus class next year or else her entire college career would implode before she even got there.

People all around the courtyard stared at us. Mostly at me. Word had gotten out about what happened with my uncle. Nothing ever stayed a secret in high school. I could hear their whispers; they hardly tried to stay quiet anyway.

Slut.

I bet she liked it.

I'd rape her. She's super hot.

Ashley took a bite of her sandwich – one her mother made for her when she found out she was eating grease for lunch every day – and I took a bite of cardboard with imitation cheese.

Ashley grunted, tapped her chin, and swallowed her bite quickly. "Dude, you gotta let my mom make you lunches too."

I reached up and felt the throbbing lump on my own chin. I stared at my pizza in sadness.

"I've literally never seen you with a zit," she said, words dripping with amused shock. "It's all that grease. Probably stress too. You're gonna get fat!"

I stared at what my school claimed was food. She was right, of course. I was going to get fat and ugly unless I got some actual nutrients in my body. But I didn't want her mother's charity. "I can take care of myself."

"Sure you can, but will you? I know you. You'll spend an hour wasting away on the computer in the morning instead of making yourself a salad for lunch."

"I can make myself food," I said defiantly.

She rolled her eyes, probably thinking about my fridge. I had mustard, old cheese that was probably green by now, and a few eggs.

I thought about legitimately making myself food, and I knew I wouldn't do it. This morning I was almost late to school because I sat on my couch reading all about myself on a website dedicated to slutty and shady people. *She'll have sex with anything that moves… She slept with her uncle, claiming rape… She totally wanted it… She gets trashed at parties and fucks other girls' boyfriends… She takes pain pills because she can't deal with her own pathetic existence.*

"Yo, earth to Paige," Ashley chimed. "At least let her make you lunch like half the week."

I shrugged. "Yeah, okay." I switched gears, not wanting to think about my pathetic existence. "I still can't believe Mr. Owens kicked me out of his class."

She nodded, swallowing her bite slowly. "Seriously, that was weird. I'd never heard of anyone doing that. I mean, for a day or whatever for disrespecting them, but nothing like that."

She was aloof. She didn't care at all. She was saying the words, but she meant the opposite. "You're lying right now."

She pushed a piece of lettuce into her mouth. "Him kicking you out of class wasn't weird. You were weird. I honestly don't blame him."

I picked at a pepperoni. "Thanks for being honest, I guess. I'm over it anyway." I flipped my hair behind my back. "I'm going to make my move on Harrington today. After school at the station." I couldn't hide my smile. It was going to be perfect. He'd fall even more wildly in love with me and we'd get a one-way ticket to a beach tomorrow.

Ashley's mouth fell open, showing me half-chewed bell peppers and tomato. "Are you kidding me?"

I giggled. "It's true. Today's the day."

She gulped down her bite of lunch. Her eyes became deep thunderclouds suddenly blocking a high summer sun. "Paige, you're insane. Literally crazy. You have to stop."

I set my jaw. This wasn't the reaction I wanted, although I wasn't sure why I hadn't expected it. She didn't understand. I already knew she didn't get it, yet I still blabbed. I couldn't believe myself. "Don't call me that."

"What else do you want me to call you? It's true! He's *married*, Paige. With adult kids. A career. A life. He doesn't need you screwing that all up."

"I'm not. I would never. I'm making him better," I said defiantly.

"Oh my god, Paige, you are delusional. Do you even realize that all you talk about is men?" Her words bit into me. I'd never seen her so aggressive toward me. She'd always agreed with what I said, and I always agreed with her. A wedge had been driven between us and I couldn't stand it. She stared directly into my eyes. "Men. That's it. Nothing else. You used to have dreams and ambitions. Don't you remember that? We used to sit up talking for hours about our future. You wanted to be an animal doctor even though you'd never owned a pet before. I asked you why and you said, 'I want to be helpful and save lives.' Do you not remember that?"

I remembered that night perfectly. We sat on her roof staring at all the stars above us, the infinite space, so much of which will never be explored. We talked about how small we were, and that's when I decided I wanted to be a veterinarian. I wanted to make a difference in our teeny tiny world, and that's how I'd do it. "You know what?" I had said that night, "I wanna be a vet." Ashley had laughed, mostly out of surprise. "What happened to space? We were just talking about being on a rock floating around a giant ball of fire. I think you have ADD. Do you even like animals?" she asked. "Well, they never hurt me the way people did," I responded. She nodded, knowing exactly what I meant.

I looked at Ashley, my best friend, and shoved my thoughts about Will to the back of my mind, never to be mentioned to her again after this conversation. "I do remember that. And you wanted to be a dancer."

"Still do," she said, and I realized I hadn't asked her if she wanted to dance forever. I didn't know anything about her anymore.

"Paige," she continued, "what do you want to do when you grow up? Have you thought about that?"

I shrugged.

She balked. "Seriously? We're quickly approaching senior year. You're going to have to plan for college. Scholarships and what to major in."

My heart caught in my throat. I hadn't planned for a future other than one with Will. I legitimately had never thought about going to school, especially now, what with my mother in a drug-induced haze wandering who knows where and Glen's credit cards being almost maxed out. School wasn't a priority. Probably not an option. I had no idea what I wanted to do with my life as far as a career went and I told Ashley as much.

"Well, this summer, let's get you a job. And we'll work really hard together to get you scholarships so you can go. In this economy, you really cannot afford not to go to college. Especially as a woman, when a man will come up and take the job out from under you even though he's less qualified. Simply because of the floppy meat between his legs."

"Tell me how you really feel," I mumbled, desperately wanting to change the subject. Usually I loved talking about myself, but only what I'm good at.

She smiled. "I could go on, don't worry. But I won't. Because we're talking about you and your dreams."

"I don't have any."

"Then that's our goal. This year, we'll find out what you love and we'll play to your strengths. You can forget all about the middle-aged man with a wife and kids." Her tone was bitter.

I forced a smile and agreed just to agree. I didn't want to lose my best friend, but if she didn't support me in this, maybe she wasn't a friend at all.

Chapter 27

Usually when I flirted, it was subtle. I'd never had to do much work to get men to fall under my spell, but Will was especially difficult. So that day, after talking to the doctor about whatever nonsense he wanted to continue talking about, I flirted with Will, and I flirted hard.

I flipped my hair, I touched his hand, I made sure he caught me looking at his mouth. I laughed openly and made sex eyes at him. I wore my silkiest stockings under my skirt, and I kept rubbing my hands over them. "These are seriously the softest. I can't get over it!" My heart fluttered when he looked at my hands. As the minutes passed, I got bolder, sliding my fingers from my knees to my inner thighs.

He responded very well.

He fidgeted, torn between professionalism and lust. He bit his lip, looking me up and down. I could see in his eyes he wanted me.

Finally, I'd broken down his walls. I celebrated internally. For once, I didn't want anything more from him than himself. I wasn't flirting to get free booze or tickets or anything else. Just him.

"You want to get something to eat?" he asked.

"I guess I am kind of hungry." I couldn't believe I was actually nervous. Excited, but nervous as well.

He took me with him to a drive-thru during his break. Most of the time, I came and went pretty quickly, never sticking around for long, so we'd never had a lunch date together. Not that this was really a date – fast food at three in the afternoon – but it still felt special.

He bought me a bean burrito and parked in the back of the lot.

I stared at it, wishing it had at least a few veggies in it, thinking back to lunch with Ashley. I absentmindedly poked the planet on my chin.

"Tell me if this is too forward," he said between bites, "but I sense something. You know, between us."

I swallowed an excited squeal and forced myself not to dance. "Like what?"

"Like," and then, he leaned toward me over the center console.

I hurriedly dropped the second half of my burrito in my napkin on my lap and did a quick sweep of my tongue over my teeth to get out any tortilla bits.

He put his left hand just above my knee and cupped my face in his right. I thanked the kissing gods that his eyes were already closed or else he'd see the panic as I realized my first kiss with this man would taste like old beans and preservatives.

But when his lips touched mine, I hardly even noticed.

In sixth grade, Craig O'Flannigan kissed me. His mouth collided with mine. I'd thought I'd broken a tooth. He ran away to his friends; clearly a dare.

In ninth grade, Miles Shay kissed me. It was wet and clumsy. I wiped my mouth on the sleeve of my sweatshirt afterward and walked away without a word.

The last year and a half, I've made out mindlessly with boys and a couple girls at parties Ashley dragged me to. I'd take shots before the door had closed behind me, erasing thoughts of home and all inhibitions.

The last six years of my life, Glen would kiss me. Only sometimes, depending on what he'd been drinking and how much. His mouth was always sour. I never kissed back, but he was too drunk to notice I guess.

This kiss with William Harrington was nothing like any of those other times. This was sweet, caring, kind. He parted my lips with his tongue, only slightly, never overstepping or getting sloppy. He pulled away an inch, looked me in my eyes, and kissed me one last time.

He leaned back in his seat and looked at the creases in his

khakis. "Was that okay?"

I nodded, dazed. I chewed on my bottom lip, tasting him there. Not the taste of grease, but of this god in front of me. I wasn't sure what to do next. Usually boys expected you to go down on them after making out; they want to get the kissing out of the way so they don't get jizz in their mouths afterward. On the nights Glen wanted to kiss, he always wanted a blowjob after.

I reached for his zipper.

"Whoa," he chuckled uncomfortably, squirming away from me. "You don't, you don't need to do that."

I sat back in my seat, confusion etched in my face.

"Is that what he made you do?" Will looked straight into my soul. "Because you don't need to. That's not how it has to work. I'm really sorry," he whispered.

Tears welled up in my eyes. I rolled the rest of my lunch back up in its wrapper and put it back in the bag. "Can we go back? I'd like to go home now," I said.

We drove in silence and dropped me off at my dilapidated shack. I was too embarrassed and confused to look back at him as I ambled up my driveway. Did he not want me? I did what I was supposed to do and he rejected me. I didn't understand what this man wanted. First he kisses me, then he tells me no?

"Wait," he called from the passenger-side window. "Will I see you tomorrow maybe? Or the next day?"

I tried my best not to let bitterness ooze out of me when I turned to answer him. "Are you sure you really want me there?" My best wasn't good enough.

He knitted his brows together, completely clueless. "Of course I do."

I took a deep breath and plastered on a smile, shoving the pain from his apparent rejection down as far as I could. "Yeah, I'll be there."

He smiled back and drove away.

Chapter 28

"Did you see her today? She had her boobs pushed so far up into Harrington's face, I was afraid her nips would poke his eyes out. Jesus."

Woods laughed at her description. He had seen it and he thought the same thing, albeit much less eloquently. "Take a breath, Di."

She was pacing, her mouth a tight line. Harrington was her best friend, and she worried about him. Seeing him leave through the door with an underage girl he was clearly attracted to scared her. "I'm just so pissed!"

"At her or at him?" Woods had seen DiPascua lose her cool once before, in a situation very similar to the one they were in now.

She stumbled over her words. "At -- at him. At her! Both of them. I don't know." She plopped down in Woods' chair.

He sat across from her. He'd never sat where his clients sat before. Although Di was naturally intimidating, she looked even more terrifying from this angle. "I need to get higher chairs and a smaller desk. Maybe this is why other psychologists have couches. Maybe I should get a couch." He looked around the room, running his hands over the arms of the chair. He looked up at the detective. She stared hard at him, head cocked, eyebrow raised. "Sorry," he said, a grin stamped on his face. "Why are you mad at him?"

"He's such a fucking idiot, that's why."

"And her?"

"She's throwing herself all over him. Totally asking for it."

The doctor leaned forward, the grin melted from his face. Seriously, he asked, "Why are you blaming her? Every other case just like this one, you hate the man and protect the girl. She's a victim no matter what she did. With Will, however, you are upset with her yet he's only an idiot."

DiPascua sighed, rubbing the pads of her fingers back and forth across her forehead. "I mean, we can't see the whole story. We haven't even talked to him about it yet."

"That's what we can do today, if you think that's best."

She looked at him. "Of course I do. We need to nip this in the bud!" She slammed her fist against the desk, masking her anxiety with anger. She couldn't admit to herself, let alone the doctor, that she worried Harrington was just like the men they brought in: a pervert who deserved to be locked away for good.

There certainly was something about Paige, though she couldn't quite figure it out. She was manipulative, but she had her cracks. She wasn't exactly sociopathic, but she did show tendencies. Then again, she was a child in the eyes of the law, and maybe just hormonal. It was understandable and even normal for young girls to want to be with older men, but the other way around was just creepy.

Ten minutes later, Harrington walked through the door, without Paige. Di wanted to slap the smirk right of his face. "Get in here!" she roared at him.

Harrington's heart stopped. Making his partner mad was on the top of the list of things not to do, yet here he was.

"What did you just do, huh?" she yelled as Harrington closed the door behind him. Woods sheepishly stood in the corner, ready to mediate if it got too heated, although he wasn't sure he could hold DiPascua off if he tried.

"We got something to eat. I was hungry, I brought her with me. It was nothing." Harrington's voice was too high, too on edge.

"Detectives do not bring vics out for lunch." She punctuated each word with her fist against the desk. "They don't even do fake internships. Do you realize how long this has been going on? Weeks, Harrington. Weeks. You're spiraling. You're losing control and you're losing your mind."

Harrington lifted his fingertips to his lips subconsciously. "It's nothing."

DiPascua took a step back, deflated a bit. "Oh my god. What did you do?"

"Nothing! She--" he saw the look on her face and decided the truth was the best route to take. Di had an amazing way of finding out. All women did. "She kissed me. We went out and got burritos around the corner. I was asking her about how she was doing and you know, her future and things like that. What she wanted to do with her life. Then she leaned over and kissed me."

Di scoffed and shook her head. "And you just came back after that? Is that what I'm supposed to believe?"

He looked at Woods who looked back at him with a look that said *I can't save you. You got yourself into this mess.* "No, that's not it. She reached for my zipper." Both the doctor and DiPascua groaned. Harrington put his hands up, pleading. "It wasn't like that. That's all she's been taught. She thinks that's what you're supposed to do. You kiss then you give a bj. That's all she's been taught."

DiPascua sneered at him, fighting back hot tears of anger. "That's all she's been taught so you figured, hey, why not? Things get a little boring at home and a girl less than half your age unzips your pants and you figure it's a sign from the gods? You disgust me," she sneered.

"Just listen to me!" Officers and witnesses outside the office stared in. He'd forgotten that just because the door was closed didn't mean it was soundproof. He took a breath, lowering his voice. "I pushed her hand away. I told her she didn't need to do that, that it wasn't healthy. I said she took things too far with the kiss in the first place. She was confused. It's all she's known in her life. I'm a father figure and she didn't know how to act around me. She seemed to understand. I took her home after that. I didn't think it would be good for her to be around men right now. She needs to think through things, maybe call her friend and work through it."

"She needs a doctor," Woods spoke up, startling the detectives.

"She does, she certainly does. She's not okay. She needs help, but nothing happened." He didn't know how he could say nothing happened when clearly it did. She kissed him, and he was elated.

"You kissed her back, didn't you?" his partner whispered.

He swallowed hard. Looking at his feet, he said, "Yes, I did."

"You see perverts every single day. You have a daughter. How could you possibly act this way?" DiPascua shook her head, running her fingers through her hair. She pointed to the door. "You'd better leave before I rip your throat out."

Harrington sat at his desk, staring blankly at the photos of mountains and forests and beaches rotate through on his computer screen.

Di was wrong. There was no way he was like those perverts. Those men and women prey on little kids. They take children's innocence. They rape and hurt people to get off. Harrington didn't do that. What he and Paige had was consensual, nurturing. He wanted to help the poor girl move on from her uncle: a man who was *actually* like the perverts who walked through the station. He preyed on and raped a little girl. He truly did a number on her, too. He made her think sex was all she was worth. Harrington was the one who saw how much more she really was. She was intelligent, funny, adventurous. She had such a future ahead of her, even if she didn't know exactly what it was. That man broke her, but Harrington was put in her life to piece her back together.

He truly hoped that man would never wake up again. Every day he was asleep reduced the odds that he would open his eyes again. People woke up years later, of course, but the system wouldn't wait that long.

Paige would have to testify. She would go the self-defense route, which was perfectly true. She would have to go through all of the things that monster did to her, but maybe it would be therapeutic. Keeping her story all buttoned up was doing nothing but harming her.

Then, if he ever did wake up, he'd get locked up and she would finally be free.

Doctor Woods was suddenly standing beside Harrington's desk, a smirk tugging at the corners of his thin mouth.

Harrington jumped in his seat. Goosebumps prickled at the top of his head and waterfalled down his body. "Jesus!" he yelled.

"Oh I'm sorry, did I startle you?" Woods laughed loudly. It grated on Harrington's spine. "I've been standing here trying to talk to you for five minutes. Some world you were in there."

As Woods talked, he had that glint in his eye he got when he saw a challenge. This one seemed to be especially intriguing. Harrington imagined Woods physically picking apart his and Paige's brains, fat fingers in their grey matter, giggling to himself.

Woods wanted to talk to Paige again, then he wanted to observe her and Harrington together. Not behind glass. Somewhere that felt truly private. She was the type of person who started opening up in the interrogation room, but then remembered someone could be standing behind the mirror listening, so she'd clam up.

"Where do you propose we do this? We can't go to her house and mine's certainly off limits." Bile rose in his throat as the thought of Eva crossed his mind. She didn't deserve what he put her through, but he just couldn't seem to stop himself. Paige was one hell of an addiction.

"Take her to a coffee shop. Maybe one a little farther away, with outdoor seating. She won't expect to see anyone she knows. I just want to see how she interacts with you."

And how I interact with her, Harrington thought bitterly.

Woods sipped his coffee. His eyes watered as the hot liquid singed his lips and tongue. A whimper escaped from his throat.

DiPascua shot him a look from the passenger side of the car. He was thankful he wore the headphones to listen to Harrington's mic across the street. Otherwise, he'd be a sitting duck for Di's remarks. Nonetheless, heat prickled against his cheeks and under his arms.

Harrington sat at an outside table at the coffee shop, right in the view of DiPascua and Woods. He looked around every few seconds, unable to keep still. He had ordered a small frozen coffee for Paige. He'd downed his own black coffee and was working on shredding the cup to pieces when she came up.

"Oh my god, hi!" she squealed, her voice crackling slightly through the wireless connection.

As they embraced, Woods strained to hear what Harrington said through the muffled mic.

Suddenly DiPascua ripped the headphones from Woods' head. "I want to hear what this bitch has to say too," she demanded. Woods was not one to argue with the devil, so he held the headphones between the two of them.

Paige was all doe eyes and legs. Even Woods had to admit she was attractive. He had a hard time believing she was only sixteen. Sure she looked young, but he could see where Harrington would be swept away. Not that he'd ever admit that to Di.

He shifted himself closer to hear the voices coming through the headphones. Heat from DiPascua's neck pulsed against his own flesh. His heart beat a little faster as he pulled ever so slightly away from her. Di truly hated this girl.

Woods wasn't quite sold. No matter how seductive Paige was, no matter how mature she seemed, she wasn't an adult. And, frankly, she was a little unstable.

She couldn't be blamed for that, of course. A dead dad was enough to throw a kid off kilter, but add in a druggie mother and a rapist guardian, and there was simply no hope she'd be issue-free.

Di's fists clenched as she watched Paige put her hand on Harrington's thigh.

Harrington tensed. "Someone might see," his voice crackled through the headphones. Paige giggled. "Well," her voice was distant, muffled, "wouldn't it be nice to be able to be out in public and not have to worry if people saw us?"

Di punched the dashboard when Paige suggested Harrington leave his wife.

Murmurs of whether or not Harrington and Di slept together floated around the office. Despite his professional and personal vow to himself not to be involved in office gossip, Woods wondered the same thing. In the past, male/female partners who were as close as these two always got caught in compromising positions.

Sitting next to the female half of the duo, spying on the sweating male half, Woods still wasn't sure where her anger stemmed from. Was she jealous of the girl getting undivided and possibly inappropriate attention from a man she loved? Or was she truly upset that he was going to destroy his family to fuck a teenager?

And Woods was certain he was going to destroy his family.

Harrington had been miked before. He'd been put in precarious situations, sometimes illegal, before. He'd been in situations where his life depended on not breaking character. Every single time he was calm, playing the role like it was a second skin. Not a bead of sweat danced across his forehead. Other detectives joked that he should have gone into the undercover world. "Not with a family," he'd say.

Today, at the coffee shop, anyone watching would tell him to take up a different profession entirely. Maybe a warehouse job, or something where he didn't have to interact with people. He glanced at the car at least thirty times a minute. Had Paige been more perceptive, she would have figured out something was wrong. Fortunately for Harrington, she was the type to take things at face value. No one had played someone else around her. Everyone in her life was exactly who they claimed to be: dead, a vacant drug addict, a sexual predator.

Now she faced Harrington as he was to her: a supportive, loving man who would take care of her.

A shadow crossed Paige's face. Di stayed perfectly silent. Woods wasn't sure she was still breathing. "Don't call me crazy," Paige said through gritted teeth.

Harrington sputtered, lifting his hands in the air in surrender then putting them back down. "I wasn't calling you crazy, babe. Just the idea of leaving my family is crazy. I can't do that to them. If you were married as long as I've been, you'd understand."

The shadow lifted, replaced by a smirk. "Maybe you'll come around." She shrugged, unable to get the smile off her face.

Woods knew Paige had heard it. He looked at DiPascua, his stomach knotted. She was impassive, color drained from her face. She'd heard it too. They all had. Harrington hadn't realized he'd said it. A complete slip of the tongue. A slip a man like Harrington would never have made had he been in his right mind.

Babe.

"I have to go to the captain," Di said, monotone.

Woods hung his head, nodding in agreement. He flipped on the mic to Harrington's earpiece and told him to wrap it up.

Chapter 29

Will told me he had a big case to work on and he'd be pulling long nights. He said I could come to the station if I still needed to, but I should get out more, explore the world, socialize.

I knew he was trying to brush me off. "I don't care if anyone knows about us," I said.

He fidgeted, looking around. "I'm not..." he sighed. "It's not that simple. Just, you know, try to wean yourself away. You can't come to the station every day."

My hands shook. "But why not?"

He explained, gently, that people were suspecting something inappropriate between the two of us. Well, what did he expect? There *was* something inappropriate going on. I thought he loved the rush the way I did.

"Okay, that's fine," I said, and stormed away. I heard him call after me and sigh, but I ignored him.

I wandered around outside, killing time and cooling off. I couldn't believe he would act that way. I thought he was so mature, but here he was, blowing me off like some teenage boy who doesn't know how to talk to a woman. He really wanted to hide me away? He should be wanting to show me off. I was what boys and men alike dreamed of. Now I was a reality and suddenly he wanted to push me away.

I stomped to the park by our houses and laid in the grass, growing crunchy in the fall air. A breeze lifted up my shirt and rose goosebumps on my tummy. I wished it was Will's hands rather than a phantom. I closed my eyes, imagining him lying next to me. My anger dissolved.

He was just being influenced by other people. DiPascua could be extremely intimidating, so I understood. I would just need to be sneakier.

I stood up, brushed the grass and leaves off my clothes. I had decided I would go back to the station. I would let him know that I was on his level. We would be less obvious until he left his wife.

The station was quiet, which was rare. I was almost never there after six in the evening, but it was already at least eight. Most of the detectives had left, and there were nearly no crying mothers or dangerous men.

Will's desk was empty, so I meandered to the little kitchen. A sallow-faced detective whom I had never met before stirred his coffee. He didn't smile or acknowledge me in any way. "Sorry," I said to him, as if I'd wronged him by accidentally invading his space. Embarrassment - a relatively new feeling - flooded my body and I hung my head as I turned around to find Will somewhere else. I didn't know what that was all about, but I'd be considerably happier if it never happened again.

I went to the on-call rooms. They were cold, uninviting rooms with bunks in them. I had never seen anyone sleeping in there until today. I don't know who it was; they were turned on their side, facing the wall. Their frame was little, and I saw a lake of dark hair across the pillow. Definitely not Will.

I closed the door as quietly as I could. My heart still leapt at the loud *click!* I scurried away, hoping I didn't wake the sleep-deprived person inside.

I snuck around the corner to the bathrooms. The sound of a weak stream of water filled my ears. Someone was showering. I hoped it was Will.

I imagined walking into the bathroom, peeking around the corner, and watching Will, who hadn't noticed me yet. I'd gain confidence and step forward. He'd jump, at first, startled by the sight of someone standing there seeing him in his nakedness. But then, he'd relax, smile at me. He'd beckon me in. I'd strip and shower alongside him, our previous argument absolved.

I took a breath and stepped inside.

The space was different than I expected. It wasn't open with little pony walls like at the local swimming pool. The showers were in the back, with individual stalls turned away from the entrance. To see whoever was showering, I'd have to expose myself entirely, almost walking into the shower stall completely.

Draped over a duffel back in the far corner was a blue and white checkered shirt; Will's shirt. I couldn't stop the smile from spreading across my face.

I crept to the shower, the acid in my stomach suddenly rushing. The steam was oppressive. I wasn't sure if I could follow through with surprising him in the shower. I pictured the water running down his toned body, and I got a second wind. I swallowed the rising bile and squared my shoulders. I took a solid step forward, then another. I grabbed his shirt and held it to my face, breathing deeply, filling my lungs with the scent of him.

The water stopped.

I saw his arm reaching for the towel hanging on the rack outside the shower. My legs shook and carried me on their own accord. I practically flew out of the bathroom, his shirt still in my hands.

I was so concerned about getting out of there without Will seeing me that I ran head-on into a slender, muscular body. I gasped, bouncing off the person, falling flat on my ass. I looked up. DiPascua, unfazed, stared down at me.

"What exactly are you doing here?" she spat.

"I was just leaving," I sputtered, staring at her shoes. I was glued to the ground, out of fear or embarrassment, I couldn't tell.

"What's the rush?" She narrowed her eyes. I floundered around for words. I stopped dead when I saw her narrow in on the shirt still clutched in my fist. "Who's is that? Is that Detective Harrington's?"

The bile came back. It burned the base of my throat, but I couldn't swallow it down. I couldn't breathe, couldn't blink. The most intimidating woman in the world had caught me.

She yelled at me again, but I couldn't focus on her words. Slowly, the wheels turned in my stunned brain. Before she could hit me or arrest me (I'm sure she would have if she could figure out what for), I rolled to my left and bolted down the hall in the opposite direction she was standing. She yelled after me, telling me to stop and come back, but I ignored her. As my muscles pumped,

I wondered if that ever worked. If a fleeing criminal ever thought, "They told me I should stop, maybe I will."

I felt the eyes of the few people still in the building burning into me. None of them chased me. Peoples' need to not get involved saved me that day.

I ran for another block before I felt safe enough to walk. My lungs heaved. Quitting sports really did a number on me. I made a note to start working out again. Maybe Will and I could work out together, get all sweaty together, shower together afterward. I wrapped his shirt around my shoulders, something I could get used to.

Chapter 30

Di didn't hassle with chasing after Paige. It was pointless. The girl always came back.

She waited outside the showers for Harrington, capping her anger so she could make a logical argument about why this girl was trouble. A subconscious thought flitted through her mind, reminding her that Harrington was just as much to blame. She pushed the thought away. She couldn't bear to blame him when hating a girl with no future was so much easier.

Harrington stepped out in his jeans and a fresh button-up, looking bemused. He looked at the crease between his partner's eyebrows and shifted his attitude to the defensive.

"We need to talk," she said.

He gestured for her to lead the way.

She took him to their shared desk. Although she wanted a quieter, more private place to talk, this would have to do. All the people with actual offices had gone home for the night and interrogation rooms weren't as private as they felt.She pointed at the chair. He obliged and sat down stiffly.

"I have to go to the captain," she said bluntly.

Harrington stared at her. He had talked to Paige, telling her to leave him alone. She had. He was establishing space, a professional relationship. He had no idea what his partner was so upset about.

"I saw how you reacted toward her at the coffee shop," she

continued. "You responded like she was your high school crush."

Harrington put his hand up, signaling that he wanted to interject, but Di continued. She wasn't the type to be interrupted.

"She's conniving and manipulative. She knows you have a thing for her so she's using that to her advantage. You will totally fall for her. Christ, you already have. You need to get over it. This is only going to hurt you, on multiple levels."

As she mulled over her next words, Harrington seized his chance to defend himself. "This is what we're trained to do. We're trained to respond the way they want us to so they feel like we're connecting with them, like we're on their side. I'm just relating to her. I don't have a problem. Granted, she is a little clingy, but it's nothing--"

"A *little* clingy?" A bark of laughter escaped her mouth. "Man, you have no idea. She fucking *stalks* you. Don't scoff at me. I've seen her. If you're not here, she will leave. If you are here, she stays until you leave. She won't take a ride with anyone else. She won't even talk to anyone else unless she gets your approval. Today? Today she followed you into the shower! She wandered around, trying to find you. She walked into the on-call room, up to me while I laid there. She was checking if I was you! When she left, I followed her out. She went straight to the bathroom. You know what she did? She stole your fucking shirt! How creepy is that?"

"So that's where that went," he mumbled.

"Are you kidding me? You're not at all fazed by the fact that she's creeping around following you? She'll probably slit your throat in your sleep or something."

It was Harrington's turn to laugh. "She's not violent. She's just troubled. She feels abandoned and I'm a male presence that she needs but never had. It will all be fine. Just calm down."

DiPascua leaned in, putting her face in his. "Don't tell me to calm down. This is a big deal. If you were any other man who walked in here, you'd have had him arrested. You'd have wanted to beat the shit out of him. But you're too far gone to see it. I'm going to the captain." She grabbed her purse and stomped out.

Harrington stared after her. He tried to see it from her perspective. How he would have viewed it had he been the detective on a case where a middle aged man kissed teenagers. He would have punched himself. He would have gotten himself locked up on anything. Even a simple parking violation.

He sighed. He couldn't believe what he was doing. Everyone around him was right. He was a sick man.

But when he thought of Paige, that feeling went away. He wanted to be with her. He wanted to hold her, to do things with her, to travel, to take her out to dinner. He didn't see just a one night stand with her. He saw a future with her and it terrified him. Was he really sympathizing with the enemy? With the perverts who preyed on kids?

No, he couldn't be. He didn't feel this way about them all. Just her. He didn't watch kiddie porn or arrange to meet nine-year-old prostitutes. He wasn't attracted to children. He was attracted to this amazing woman.

He tried to focus on the case at hand. He shuffled his papers around, staring at the black shapes on them but registering nothing.

He looked at his phone. Disappointment filled his gut when he didn't see a missed call or a text from Paige. He was in trouble. Who he thought he was - the good guy - was in question. Di was right. He fucked up.

The next day, after a fitful sleep at the station, Harrington shuffled into Captain Douglas' office.

Harrington stayed standing. He had never been very chatty with the captain. They rarely exchanged more than a few words over the last ten years. Harrington thought he had power and control issues. He always threw his weight around, thinking about what would look good to the press rather than what would be best and most logical.

"Please, sit," Captain Douglas said, taking his own seat behind his oak-paneled desk.

"No, thanks, I'm okay." Harrington clasped his hands behind his back and bounced once on his toes. He smiled, taunting the man in front of him.

Douglas faltered. "Alright. Look, I'm not going to sugar coat it," he said, regaining his footing. "You're screwing up. It's been brought to my attention that you're getting inappropriate with a young victim and you need to watch yourself. You will be taken off the case if this continues. You should know better about professionalism. We can't have a scandal on our hands again."

"This is far from a scandal, trust me. Your reputation won't be tarnished."

"It's not me I'm worried about." At that, Harrington rolled his eyes. Douglas ignored it. "I'm worried about you and I'm worried about that girl. She's had enough to deal with over the last few years. She needs normalcy. You are not a part of that normalcy. Let her finish school. Let her have boyfriends her own age. This case won't progress for you unless the uncle wakes up anyway, so leave it. There is no reason for the girl to be talking to you until then. What she needs is a good lawyer. Female, preferably."

Harrington nodded, still smirking. "That all?"

The captain nodded and shooed him out. Harrington turned on his heel, and left the station without looking at anyone, especially not at his partner.

Chapter 31

Wrapped in a towel, I lined my eyes with absolute precision. Today was the day. I could feel it straight through to my core. I'd shared a deep and twisted secret with him. We'd established a level of trust. We'd reached the exact moment in a relationship when we were so intertwined that we could only go to the next step, never regressing.

I curled my lashes, applied mascara. No foundation or shadow. I didn't want to be greasy-looking later. Chapstick and a light gloss, so he didn't get lipstick all over himself.

I let my hair dry naturally. I wanted him to feel my natural beachy waves rather than hairspray and loads of sticky product. I sprayed my citrus perfume on my wrists and in my hair.

I knew which set of lingerie I'd wear. Black lace panties and a black lace bra. Simple, yet sexy. A pair of strappy wedges, a black skater skirt, and a teal crop top, black sweater, scarf, and I was ready.

I dialed his number before I left my bedroom. It rang three times before he picked up. "Harrington." My stomach jolted at the sound of his voice.

"Hey. It's Paige."

His tone changed immediately to one of familiarity, warmth. I smiled. "Hi, Paige. How's it going?"

"Fine." White space filled my mind. I hadn't thought of how to proceed.

"Good," he said. Silence. "What's going on?"

"Um, can we maybe go for coffee or something? I just need to talk to someone."

"Yeah, of course." He sounded distant, like he was reluctant to meet me.

"We can meet later if you need to. I don't want to interrupt work or anything."

"No, no, it's fine. I'm off today anyway."

"Well, I mean, if you're doing something with your wife…"

He laughed. "Paige, it's okay. We can meet for coffee. Should I pick you up?"

He met me outside my house fifteen minutes later. I reapplied deodorant and tried not to work myself up. I pushed my shoulders back, lifted my chin, and exuded all the confidence I had.

"You look really nice," he said as we pulled out of the driveway.

"Thank you. It's just natural," I joked, dramatically flipping my hair.

"It definitely is," he said, looking at me out of the corner of his eye.

My stomach shivered again. I looked out the window, hoping he wouldn't see the smile creeping across my lips.

We sat outside in the shade, sipping our lattes. A fall breeze brought goosebumps to my exposed legs. We made small talk for a little while, laughing at each other's bad jokes and nodding about the weather. Finally he asked me what I needed to talk about. I had my lies already planned out. "I don't really know how to put it into words. I guess I'm just confused about what happened."

"How do you mean?"

"I know I did the only thing I could. He wasn't ever going to stop. But at the same time, he's my uncle, you know?"

"It's completely natural to feel that way. He's someone you trusted and lived with forever. We see victims all the time who know their attackers and they harbor resentment for them while still caring for them at the same time." I fiddled with my coffee cup, hoping I looked shy and vulnerable. "You did what you had to do," he continued. "He was hurting you. You did the right thing."

"Thank you. It's definitely reassuring." I looked in his hazel eyes, noting the flecks of grey throughout his irises. I grazed my teeth along my bottom lip, suggesting to him heavily.

Surprisingly, he got the hint. I was so used to guys – including William – being dense.

"Do you want to go somewhere else maybe?"

I couldn't suppress a giggle. "I'd love to."

In the car, I slid my left leg, almost imperceptibly, toward him. He noticed and put his hand on my thigh, sliding higher.

I was surprised when we pulled into the back of a parking lot. "Um, shouldn't we go, I don't know, somewhere else? Just in case?" I could just imagine a cop driving by. It was the middle of the day. There were plenty of shoppers milling about. My heart thudded.

"There isn't really anywhere else. I mean, I can take you back home if you don't want to do this." He pulled his hand away.

"No, I definitely want to." I leaned my seat back, unsure of how to proceed. I never expected our first time to be this awkward.

This would have been a good time for him to drive a much larger car. We could have space. Instead, we were crammed into this little sedan, the emergency brake stabbing me in the leg.

But this is what I wanted, so I sucked it up. I grabbed his shirt and pulled him toward me. He slipped over the center console, banging his head against the top of the car. His face reddened. I giggled to make him relax, but I seethed inside.

A person walked by. We froze, Will crouched over me, a tiger about to pounce. The person glanced toward the car but ignored us. Will relaxed and lowered himself on top of me. His heart pounded against mine. Maybe I was wrong. The possibility of getting caught was exciting. I hiked up my skirt and pushed my panties to the side.

He fumbled with his zipper. His hands shook. I pulled his face toward mine. I kissed him hard, parting his lips with my tongue. I slid my hands to his pants, undoing them myself.

I'd never known myself to take charge the way I was, yet it felt completely natural. I wasn't scared or timid. I was someone new, someone I liked.

I cried out when he entered me. It hurt, almost like my body thought I was being attacked. It was a pain I welcomed, though, as if it was my first time. My first real time.

He finished quickly, his mouth slack, breathing heavily. He grunted, animalistic. I couldn't help but smile. I felt powerful knowing that he was so attracted to me that he could hardly last.

He laid on top of me, panting, sweat from his neck itching my skin.

He fumbled back over to the driver's side, pulling up his pants as he went. An odd mixture of disappointment and excitement filled me. It wasn't at all what I had planned. It wasn't perfect. I hardly felt anything at all, which left me completely unsatisfied and frustrated. He hadn't seen my lingerie. He hadn't held me afterward.

Yet I had him. I got what I wanted. Kind of. It should have been in a bed, and I should have been taken care of, but when I wished upon a star at night, I didn't specify exactly what I wanted. Next time I talked to a genie, I'd make sure to fill in any loopholes.

We drove away in silence. He kept inhaling, like he was about to say something, but could never quite seem to find the words. I didn't know what to say either, so I just stared out the window, screaming internally.

Suddenly, he reached into his pocket and handed me sixty dollars. "I don't know how much it costs, but you should probably use this. For, you know."

I didn't. "Are you paying me for what we just did?" I wanted to throw up, to run, to get as far away from this man as I possibly could.

"What?! No! Never! I just meant for, you know, because we didn't use a condom. Emergency contraceptive."

My nerves settled back into place. He went from sleaze to caring in one fumbling statement. I put the money in my bra to use for groceries. Obviously he didn't know Glen had put me on the pill.

A part of me expected him to take me back home, using me like everyone else, but we pulled up to a restaurant instead. "Are – are you hungry? I can take you back home if you want."

I smiled. "I could eat." Disappointment evaporated.

The restaurant was noisy and cramped, but the smell of hot food – real food and not the crap I'd been surviving off of since the situation with my uncle – sent my stomach into a frenzy, crying out to be filled.

We sat in a corner booth and scanned the menu without a word. I felt his eyes on me. I raised my eyebrows at him. He shrugged and went back to reading the menu. I think it was that moment when I realized he actually had feelings for me, maybe even loved me.

I wasn't sure how to handle that. I wanted to run. I thought if a man loved me, I'd feel whole. Instead, I was confused. It meant he was invested and had no plan of leaving. Suddenly, my dreams and fantasies were real, and happening all at once. I might really be able to run away with my knight to a sandy beach far, far away, something I never truly expected.

"What can I get you two?" a sweet voice said, interrupting my thoughts.

Our server was a girl maybe a couple years older than me. She wore her hair in a limp pony at the base of her head. I could see this job made her dead inside, but she tried to be sweet and not show it.

I ordered a mushroom burger with sweet potato fries and a starter salad. I bet Will doubted if I could eat it all, but I felt like my stomach was a bottomless pit. Despite not being sure if I could handle my new future, I wasn't a ball of stress. The knot in my gut had worked itself out and it had left plenty of space to be filled.

Will ordered a jalapeno burger and a milkshake to share. The realization that Will and I weren't father and daughter crept across our server's face. She couldn't suppress a smirk. I rolled my eyes at her back. "She gets no tip," I said to Will.

He laughed and said she was nice and he always tips. "I remember working my ass off for the measly change people left on their tables."

"She judged us. She knows and she judged us." He shook his head, smile still plastered on his face. "What? You have a thing for her too?"

He stared at me, eyebrow raised. "Don't be that person. Jealously is not attractive. But who cares if she judged us? People are going to judge. If not for our age, then for something else. That's the way people are: judgy. Don't let it bother you."

I nodded, unconvinced. The people at his work were the ones I was most worried about. DiPascua had really spooked me.

"Speaking of judgment," Will said, leaning over the table toward me, "I've had a bit of a hiccup at work."

The knot in my stomach wove itself up again. So she had talked to him about the shirt. I thought maybe a bond between females would have prevented that, or maybe she would just forget about it, but obviously when dreams come true, they only stretch so far.

The server set my salad down in front of me. "Here you go, hun," she said, clearly thinking me foolish. I picked up my fork, but couldn't eat.

"It's not a big deal, really, but, um, the captain has his eye on me. Getting involved with a victim of a case is not exactly something to be celebrated. He wants me to stop talking to you until there's a break in the case. Either if your uncle wakes up, dies, or after 30 more days of his coma."

I absent-mindedly stabbed at lettuce and cucumber. He was just like everyone else. But he couldn't grow a back bone and admit to using me. Instead, he blamed his boss. I brought a bite to my mouth. Might as well take what I could get out of him.

His face opened up into shock. "Oh! No, Paige, I'm not going to do that. I didn't bring you here to screw you and dump you. Hell no. I'm telling you that I plan on doing the opposite."

I laughed out of relief through my partially-chewed lettuce. The knot fluttered away. "You really had me worried there."

He put my free hand in his. "No, we just need to be more careful. I wouldn't do that to you. I – I really have feelings for you."

We locked eyes. I felt his hand grow sweaty in mine. The server brought our milkshake and our burgers, breaking our hand-holding. He wiped his on his pants.

Between bites, he explained that he didn't want to get kicked off the case. Otherwise, he couldn't monitor it whenever something did happen. He couldn't make sure that his partner didn't make me out to be a killer. "She doesn't really like you, if I'm being honest. It's probably my fault since she for some reason wants to protect me, a grown man." He chuckled. "She even said that you stole my shirt the other night. Like you're stalking me and taking my stuff. Isn't that ridiculous?"

Shit. "Yeah, no, totally. Crazy."

He looked at me suspiciously, a smile gradually moving across his mouth.

"What?" I asked, my voice too loud.

He shook his head. "Nothing. You're just cute."

I think I died then. I couldn't wipe the stupid grin off my face for the rest of the day, even after he dropped me back off at home, leaving me to my empty house.

Chapter 32

I texted him during my lunch. *Can I come over after school?*

Every three seconds I checked my phone. Ashley rolled her eyes every time. "What's up with you?"

I smiled wide. I couldn't tell her yet what I had done, what Will and I had done, but telling her a little bit couldn't hurt.

"God," she responded when I told her, "you guys are not 'official'. Don't even start. He's *married.* And by the way he's not texting you back, I'd say he doesn't think you guys are official either."

I kept my comments to myself. We were pretty official, I'd say.

Finally, my phone buzzed. *Not a good day. Maybe tomorrow. -W*

Why did old people always sign off like that? With the first letter of their name? And on a text? Like, obviously I know who I'm talking to. I didn't reply to him. I wanted to make him miss me. "Hey, you wanna hang out after school today?" I asked Ashley.

She stared wide-eyed at me. "Seriously? We haven't hung out in -- wait," her eyes narrowed to slits, "he just told you he can't see you today. So glad I'm your second choice. Awesome."

I mean, it was true, but I couldn't tell her that. "Shut up, no." It even sounded forced to me, but I blundered on, insisting that I wanted to spend time with her instead of Will. That Will wasn't even in the picture.

She eyed me suspiciously, but agreed to spend time with me,

just like old times.

I met her at her locker after the longest two hours of my life, sitting through two classes I didn't even remotely care about, now that I had no one to impress. She shook her keys at me and said, "Shall we?"

"Oh my god, you got it? And a car?" I squealed.

She looked offended. "Okay, *first* of all, why are you so surprised that I got my license? And no, I'm just driving my dad's old car. He said I have to 'earn' it, but I know he'll totally give it to me."

We flounced down the hall, barely taking notice of the eyes following us. Envy, lust, and hatred. A perfect trio. I pretended not to see Mr. Owens, but I could see him staring at me out of the corner of my eye.

At first, all I wanted to do was check my phone. I knew he hadn't texted me, and I couldn't help myself from wanting to text him, but I resisted. Then, good old Ashley took my mind off boys and set me straight.

"Wanna go on an adventure?" she asked, trouble written all over her face.

I smirked. "You know it."

She laughed and pointed out a sports car ahead of us. "Let's follow them."

The car zipped in and out of traffic. Ashley's SUV struggled to keep up, but she wasn't thwarted. My heart stopped every time she almost ran a car off the road, their horns trailing behind us. I laughed anyway.

I came so close to dying at the hands of my friend's bad driving, but it was exhilarating. My skin tingled with electricity. It was probably my body's response to its own mortality, but at the time, it felt like life, rushing through every atom of my being.

"Where d'ye think 'e's goin', mate?" Ashley asked, randomly picking up a bad Australian accent.

"Oi, probably to 'is mistress's 'ouse," I replied in my slightly worse Australian accent.

"Can't let 'im get away, eh?" She slammed on the gas. The car lurched forward dramatically and she gasped. Holding onto her accent, she said, "Ol' gal ain't what she used to be."

I laughed so hard I choked. It wasn't even funny, not really, but

I couldn't help myself. I was having *fun.* I'd missed her so much. With everything that had happened, she was always my savior.

We followed the guy onto the freeway. He weaved around cars, sped by semis, illegally drove in the carpool lane. Ashley and I couldn't stop laughing. She wiped her forehead. "Breaking a sweat there, are we?" I mocked.

"When you're following a perp," her accent dipped in and out, "you gotta keep your cool, but it's a tough life out here, man. You'll learn when you've been in the grind as long as I 'ave."

"Do you think this guy did it?" I asked, puffing out my chest and deepening my voice, carrying on the act.

"Crikey of course I do! Look at 'im! Guilty as hell, that one is."

The car sped across all four lanes, getting off at breakneck speed.

Ashley threw on her blinker and crossed the freeway too, not looking behind her. Horns screamed from every direction. She waved into the rearview, apologizing profusely to the people who couldn't hear her.

Another laughing fit seized me. "D'you reckon he sawr us?"

"Oi, we got a runnah!" Her face was flushed, tears of laughter glistened in the corners of her perfectly-lined eyes. She made siren noises. I had to crack a window. I couldn't breathe and the windows were fogging up.

He pulled into the parking lot of a grocery store. We parked a row behind him. We stared in silence as he got out, carrying his reusable bags with him. He never even looked at us.

"Huh," Ashley said. "That was certainly anti-climactic."

"Must be a sale on potatoes."

She stared at me stone-faced. "Must be another potato blight."

I broke into another fit. I had to cross my legs. "You're gonna make me pee!"

We followed two other people, one to their home, another to the mall. "Disappointing night, detective," Ashley said to me.

"Ah, maybe we'll 'ave better luck next time."

We picked up fast food on the way back home. She paid for me, even though I offered. "My mom gave me money for food," she said. The way she brushed it off, though, I kind of felt like she was paying for me just because she knew I only had Glen's cards and zero food in the house. I hadn't told her about the money Will had given me, and I didn't plan to. "You can get it next time."

We ate in the car and made up stories about the people passing by. "That guy right there," she said, nodding at a slightly-overweight balding white man, "totally spends his Friday evenings at the strip clubs."

"What? No, he's got a wife and two point five children at home. He's wholesome. He's had a long day at work, and he's picking up dinner for the fam."

"I don't doubt all of that, but he's also bored and depressed at home. His wife probably hates him, calls him a slob, even though she's probably not much better. So he goes and has hot titties shoved in his face once a week, to forget all his sorrows. Then he leaves, feeling worse about himself than he did before."

"That's kind of sad."

"Not if you see how creepy he looks. Just wait until he comes back out. He's totally got a creeper face."

He came out moments later with a family platter. Ashley was right, he did have that look about him. His wire glasses were a bit too small, he had a thin mustache, and his lips were overly red and lustrous. They glistened. "Nope, you're totes right. Total creep."

"Well shit," she said. "Now my mom's going to know I didn't buy us a salad from a respectable place like I promised."

A glob of mayo-ketchup mix slowly oozed down her shirt, leaving a streak of grease like a slug.

Ten minutes later, she pulled up in front of my house. It was already six, the autumn sun melting behind the mountains. I didn't want the night to end. "Know of any parties tonight?"

She shrugged. "Probably. You actually want to go out? I'm surprised. I thought you'd retired to old lady land already, what with your grandpa husband and all."

I grinned. "I'm full of surprises. I'll get ready? Text me when you find out."

"Get it girl," she yelled out her window as she drove away.

I wandered around the house, my body buzzing with energy. I hadn't felt that good probably in years. I plugged my phone in and blasted old Britney Spears dancing around in my underwear. When I was out of breath and I had listened to every song three times, Ashley texted me. *Pick you up at 10*

I had two hours. I put on my sexy playlist and hit repeat. I doused my hair in dry shampoo and washed my face, just to put about six pounds of makeup on it. I was doing it up big tonight.

Everyone stared as we walked into the party. For a second, I wondered if it was because we were too done up, but I shook off my insecurities. We were hot, in our skin-tight dresses and winged eyeliner.

"Let's get this party started!" Ashley yelled, and everyone listened.

I followed her into the kitchen. We each downed two Jell-O shots right away and grabbed a cup full of jungle juice. I looked around, waiting impatiently for the alcohol to kick in. I didn't know a single person there. I wondered who Ashley knew, but by the way she moved about the house, I guessed she didn't know anyone either. High school parties: where everyone is invited.

Suddenly, the room shifted. My legs and arms tingled. I got the giggles. The music I thought was shitty when I first walked in was all of a sudden so appealing. I started dancing alone, watching Ashley make rounds.

"Hey," a voice said in my ear.

I jumped and laughed when I saw a cute boy standing there undressing me with his eyes. "Hey," I replied, not interrupting my swaying hips.

"Can I get you a drink?"

I looked him up and down. He would do. "Another Jell-O shot. The pink one! I don't want that purple shit." I chugged my drink and set the empty cup on an end table. My dancing slowed while I digested. Too much liquid too fast on an empty stomach. I could practically hear the alcohol-doused fruit pieces swimming in my gut.

He pushed the little paper cup into my hand. "You know, no one else is dancing."

I ran my finger along the edges of the Jell-O to release it. He stared. "I don't care. I like to dance." I tossed the alcohol back and dropped the empty cup to the floor. I turned and pressed my ass into his crotch, using him as my prop. I imagined myself being in a sexy music video, surrounded by beautiful people at the beach.

What felt like seconds later, he whispered in my ear, "Want to go somewhere?"

I knew what he meant, but I wasn't ready yet. I grabbed his hand and followed my nose to one of the bedrooms. My eyes stung as I crossed the threshold. I could hardly see my own hand in front of me through the smoke. Someone shook my boy's hand and congratulated him on getting me. Congrats on your trophy, boy.

I took a joint from someone's hand and filled my lungs. My body floated. My boy took a hit from my stolen joint and told me that he meant somewhere private. He slid his hands down to my hips and pulled me toward him. "Fine," I said, leading him upstairs. I refused to let him ruin the way my body felt.

I fell onto the bed, pulling my skirt up. I didn't have time for foreplay, not that this boy would know what to do anyway.

He smiled like a kid on Christmas morning. I stared at the ceiling, letting my happiness and calm wash over me. I heard him unzip his pants. He fumbled with himself, missing a few times, before he finally entered me.

Seconds later, he grunted and fell on top of me. Set off the fireworks and release the balloons: this was a momentous time of this boy's life. I giggled at my own bitterness.

He looked up at me. "You think something is fucking funny, bitch?"

I sat up, rolling him off me. "Shh, it's okay." I walked away, his profanities and hurt ego trailing behind me as I made my way to the bathroom to wipe my legs off and freshen up. He stared at me incredulously, pants still around his ankles. I sauntered back to the smoke-filled room.

There was a giant bottle of cheap vodka on the table, surrounded by rolling papers. I was going to forget all my problems.

Chapter 33

I woke up in my own bed with a headache from the very depths of hell. I tried to sit up and thought for a split second I was dying. I'd been in a horrible accident and didn't realize it. I remembered pieces of the night before – vaguely – and hoisted myself to the bathroom.

I splashed water on my puffy face, and hurled into the sink.

I brushed my teeth, popped two aspirin, and crashed back onto my bed. I closed my eyes until the room stopped spinning. I checked my phone. Dick pics from two different guys, ones I was pretty sure I didn't screw the night before.

And two texts from Will.

No dick pics, sadly, but texts nonetheless. *Hey.* I rolled my eyes at that one. Couldn't think of anything better, huh?

I miss you.

That was it. That was all I needed. He was in love with me. He would leave his stupid wife and he would run away with me. We would get that beachfront house and make love every day. Glen and my mom would never bother me again. We would start fresh.

My hangover evaporated.

I miss you too. Can we get together? I texted back.

I stared at my phone. I checked our text history, then stared some more at the screen. It would alert me if anyone texted me, but in my mind, that wasn't good enough. I couldn't do anything else. If I looked at my phone, he would talk to me sooner.

Minutes that felt like days went by. I watched my battery life sink lower and lower. I got up to plug it in and find whatever there was to eat in the fridge.

Staring intently at my phone, I stepped in the spot on the carpet. I heard the crunch, felt it under my foot. Dried blood. No one had cleaned it. No one was going to clean it. Someone would need to replace the carpet and all the padding underneath. There would be a stain on the subfloor too.

My stomach churned again. I heaved, but nothing came out. I was thankful because I probably wouldn't ever clean that up either.

Tears pricked the back of my eyes. That horrible moment replayed in my head, my own mind betraying me. The fear and anger that had bubbled up inside me, escaping, making me stronger than I knew I could be. The connection of the bat against my rapist's head.

That's what he was. My rapist. I kept calling him my uncle, but he wasn't my family. Family wouldn't do that to their own, not a real one anyway.

The nausea subsided. My tears dried. Once again, I took power back. He was nothing to me.

My phone dinged, the sound echoing in my head, my hangover not as invisible as I had thought. It was Will, telling me he would pick me up at noon. His wife would be gone for the day.

I looked at the clock. 11:15. I grabbed some crackers and an old cereal bar, shoving them into my mouth, hardly chewing. I walked down the hallway with dignity. I didn't hop over the spot. Instead, I forced myself to stare at it.

It wasn't difficult, not this time. He got what he deserved. He should have gotten more. I hoped he would wake up, so he could see this new me, forcing him to live with the knowledge that he couldn't break me.

It would be nice if he died too, though. That's a terrible thing to say, but I didn't want to face him everyday again. If he died, I knew he would go straight to hell. I didn't want to deal with proving it was self-defense, but a few months of trial would be worth it in the end.

There was always foster care to contend with as well, but I only had two more years until I would be legally on my own. Compared to the years of living with that monster, twenty-four months of bouncing around families would be cake.

I showered quickly, washing the smell of drugs and alcohol and boys off of me. I brushed my teeth again, remembering how the first time we kissed, he could taste the burrito on my lips. I didn't want that to be his first thought too.

I blow dried my hair while I dressed. I looked at my clock again. 11:55. My hair was still damp, but I gave up, brushing mascara on my lashes. I smiled in the mirror at myself. Not perfect, probably not even good, but my phone beeped with a text from him – *I'm here* – so there was no time to improve. I grabbed shoes and ran down my driveway to meet him.

He held the door open for me. His house looked different during the day. Everything was so airy and bright. I loved it and wanted it to be my own.

"Do you want anything to drink?" he asked.

I ran my fingers along the top of the hall table, resisting the urge to slam the pictures of his family face-down. I didn't turn to him. "No, thank you," I said. I wished he'd hurry up and ravish me already, make me feel beautiful, wanted, loved.

I jumped when he came up behind me, putting his big hands around the base of my ribcage, at the tender spot just under my breasts. I felt him breathe in the smell of my shampoo, nestling his face into my hair. I thanked every god I could think of that I didn't have time to style my hair.

He pulled me back into him. I raised my arms behind my head, ran my fingers through his hair. Arching my back, I pushed my ass into his pelvis, grinning when I felt him stiffen against me.

I threw my scarf onto the floor. He pulled my top over my head. It was tight, and we chuckled when we struggled to get it past my shoulder blades, but it didn't deter us. He nudged me upstairs, running his hands along the backs of my thighs all the way to his bedroom.

We shed our clothes like they were burning us. The moment we hit the perfectly-made bed, I took control. I flipped to my stomach. I looked over my shoulder at him and whispered, "Bite my neck." I don't know what had come over me. I hadn't really seen it anywhere. I certainly hadn't experienced it. I just knew in my gut I needed him to.

He seemed all too willing to oblige. He bit lightly all along the top of my shoulder, right up to my ear. The base of my spine tingled each time his teeth grazed my skin. When he entered me, I couldn't help but cry out in euphoria.

I'd never thought sex would be enjoyable after what my attacker did. Ever. I thought it would be more of a duty than anything else, just like it was the night before at the party. Yet here I was, my entire body singing in rapture.

William held me to him afterward, our ribcages rising and falling heavily together. "I hope I didn't hurt you. I was biting pretty hard."

"What? No, it didn't feel like you were at all."

"I've never done that before."

"Neither have I."

He kissed me behind my ear. Tender, caring. That feeling hit me again. The feeling of the turning point in a movie where nothing will ever be the same. I wasn't sure if it was better or worse this time. Would there still be that delicious flirting? The sweet balance between safety and danger? We'd already plunged headfirst into peril.

I'd ruined his life. Right there, in that moment. It couldn't be brushed off as a mistake, a one-time thing. We went too far and it was all over. His career. His marriage. Even fatherhood. They'd never respect him if they found out. I was a kid and he cheated on his wife with me in their marriage bed. Not to mention he could go to jail for sleeping with me. Not that I had parents to give consent or press charges anyway.

Although, I could press charges, if I really needed to. I could use it as leverage. I wasn't sure for what yet, but it was nice to be in control of some part of my life.

Looking at the man sleeping next to me, the man I wanted so desperately, I couldn't imagine myself actually calling the police on him. I'd worked so hard to get where I was. The chase was over. He was mine. I couldn't throw that away.

Then again, if Eva ever found out and wanted me gone, she could say something. Then my only resort would be to say he raped me.

Chapter 34

I woke up to him staring at me. "What?"

"Paige, were you in my house the other night when I was gone?"

My stomach slammed against my uvula. "What? Why would you say that?" I tried to laugh it off, but I only made myself sound more guilty.

"Someone was in our house. They didn't take anything but the bed was messed up. I smelled oranges on the sheets and I couldn't place it, but it's definitely your perfume." He paused, waiting for me to answer. When I didn't, he pressed the issue. "It is, isn't it?"

I stared at him, frantically searching every fold of my brain to find a reason why my perfume would be on his sheets. I blinked, once, twice, told myself to breathe. "I don't know. I mean –"

Saved by the sound of keys in the lock. Never thought I would choose Eva over Will.

"Shit," Will whispered.

He threw his clothes on and tossed mine to me. I'd already figured out my escape when I came over without anyone knowing. Otherwise known as the night he apparently already knew about.

As soon as I squished myself into my tight-fitting clothes again, I hopped right out his window onto the roof and fumbled down the tree in his yard, wedges in hand. The cold grass stung the bottoms of my bare feet. I looked up to see him sticking his head out, brows raised. He laughed and shook his head when I waved back up at him. Then he was gone, back to his wife.

I called Ashley. I knew she wouldn't be as excited as I was, but I had no one else. She answered on the first ring. "Hello?"

"Hey, Ash. So, guess what just happened?"

"Should I be worried?"

I forced a laugh. "What? No, you should be excited!"

"Too late, I'm already worried."

"Stop ruining this for me! Anyway, so, I'm walking back home from Will's house right now."

"Shit, seriously? I'm definitely worried."

"No, it was great. We had sex. Like, actual, consensual sex. And it was amazing! He made me feel so desirable and sexy and pretty and he put me first. It was such a difference from every other experience I've ever had."

Silence.

"Um, hello? Ashley?"

"Paige, you can't be serious, can you?" She sounded strained and irritated, like I took her favorite pair of heels and sold them at a secondhand store.

"Why do you sound like that?"

"Paige, you're ruining a family!"

"It's not like he had nothing to do with it," I grumbled.

"What else is he going to do when a hot girl is waving her ass in his face?"

I was glad I hadn't told her about my first time with him if this was how she was going to react. She would really have a fit about having sex in a car in a busy parking lot. "He should have a little self-control maybe. If he was happily married and didn't want me, he wouldn't have done it. It's not like he's a child and can't make his own decisions."

"Okay, yes, you're right. He is a grown man. *You* are the child."

"Wow, thanks." I was half a second away from hanging up on her.

"No, but really." Her tone switched from accusatory to saddened. "Paige, don't you get it? He's a perv. You are sixteen years old. You are a child. By law. And, honestly, by the way you act too. It's one thing for you to obsess over him, but the other way around? It's weird. And what if you're not his first? What if he's into...weirder stuff. Like kiddie porn? You're completely right. He played a part in this; a major one."

I made a mental note to check his extracurricular activities more diligently. "Why does age matter anyway? It's just a number."

"No, it really isn't. Look at you and your uncle."

"That was fucking different."

"How?"

"He took things from me. Will never took anything. He only gave."

"Is Detective Harrington not taking anything from you? Think about it."

"He loves me."

Ashley sighed. "Remember what Glen told you?"

My stomach dropped. "I have to go." I shook. It took everything within me not to chuck my phone as far as I could. How dare she compare Will to that monster? I couldn't believe her.

I stomped home, tears burning my eyes. I wiped snot on my sleeve and stopped short at the driveway. My mother's car, parked just a little crooked. I looked up at the sky, completely defeated.

"Where have you been, missy?" my mom asked from the door. "I've been here all day worried sick about you." She sounded sweet, caring. Something was off.

"I was at a friend's house. School project."

"Honey, I could have helped you with your homework. I was here. I used to love helping you with your homework." She opened her arms for me and pulled me toward her. I didn't hug her back.

"What are you doing?"

"Hugging my daughter."

"That's not something you do."

"I know, honey, and I'm very sorry about that. Here, let's go inside. I'll make you some dinner."

I followed her, zombie-like. I was hollow. I didn't know how much more I could handle. Of my mother, of Ashley, of school, of any of it. All I wanted was to run away with Will, to live happily ever after on that beach somewhere.

She set hamburger patties to fry in a pan. Childhood memories washed over me. My dad used to grill the best burgers and hot dogs every summer. My parents' friends would come over with their kids. Everyone laughed and stayed late, not wanting to leave. That was back when we were happy.

"I went grocery shopping. You had nothing here. Glen took care of us better than that."

"Well, neither you nor Glen was here so I don't know what you want me to say." I thought about Glen's credit card bills in the mailbox. They'd be maxed out soon enough, but I didn't need a stocked fridge on survival mode.

"I'm just saying, you had it pretty good here. You're going to have to learn to take care of yourself a little sooner than expected."

I swallowed a scream and rolled my eyes so hard I saw lights.

She set a plate in front of me. One lone brown hockey puck. No cheese, no veggies, no bun. At least she put a mustard happy face on it. I smeared it with my fork.

"Now," she said, taking the seat across from me, "is there anything you want to say?"

I took a bite. Overcooked and bland. I might not have had much food in the house but I knew for a fact I at least had some pepper in the cupboard. "Is there anything you want me to say?"

"Well, I suppose I'd like to talk about what happened here, with your uncle."

"You already know. He was raping me, you did nothing to stop it, so I had to take matters into my own hands. Then you called me a slut, launched an investigation against me, and then ran off in a drug-induced haze. Now you're here and I don't know why."

Sighing, she set down her fork, food still untouched. Her eyes were clear, but she was so skinny, her skin grey, hair stringy. I almost felt sorry for her. "I wanted to come and see if maybe you wanted to tell the truth now. He might not make it and I don't want some crazed girl's lies to follow him to the grave."

I stood up. "You're a fucking idiot," I hissed.

I grabbed my backpack and a few clothes from my room, hopping over the black spot in the hallway, and stormed out to Will's house.

The sun was already setting. A cold fall breeze bought goosebumps up on my arms and legs. It was amazing how quickly the weather could change in this town.

My stomach rumbled as I looked at the house on Benjamin Franklin Drive. The lights were on inside. She was serving dinner. A bite or two of tough meat was hardly enough to tide me over for the night.

I should just knock on the door, I told myself. They would let me in. Will would convince Eva it was okay, that I was a good girl who had a rough life.

I could just make out their expressions. They were smiling. He looked happy. He leaned over and kissed her.

My heart fell. He was kissing her with the same mouth that was all over my body, just hours before. He really thought nothing of it. If he could just flip a switch like that, if he could turn around after making love to me, my scent still on him, and act like nothing was wrong, how could I trust him? How could I trust he would leave her like he said he would?

I crept along the house, moving to the side so I could get a better view of them. I relaxed. Obviously he was going to act like nothing was wrong. Otherwise it would raise suspicion. She would question him, try to get me arrested, ruin what we had. He had to be sly about it all until the right moment. Once the case was over, he would leave her.

I nearly pressed my nose against the glass. Her back was toward me, but I could see him well. I loved looking at him. He had so much power, so much passion about protecting people – protecting me – from creeps. He looked younger now than he did when I first met him. I smiled. I brought that out in him.

He looked at his wife, then his face fell, eyes widening. He could see me. I waved. He shook his head. The new-found youth dropped away, replaced with a grimace and panic.

It dawned at me that if he could see me, so could she, if she turned around. I ducked under the window and waited.

And waited. The sun was fully set now, stars twinkling at me, mocking me. I put on every piece of clothing I had, but I was still cold.

Finally, I heard the window open. "Paige? Are you still there?"

I bolted up. "Yes! Hi!" I couldn't reel in the smile on my face.

He looked over his shoulder. He nodded toward the back door. I ran to meet him. "What the hell are you doing here? What if she had seen you?"

From there, I could hear the shower running. We were safe for at least fifteen minutes. I pushed my way inside. "Could I have some leftovers? I didn't eat."

"What? No, you have to leave!" he was whispering, but there

was no point. You can't hear anything when you're in the shower.

I pushed past him and rummaged through his fridge anyway. I ate with my fingers, digging into the roast with potatoes and carrots. I didn't want to dirty a dish, just in case she noticed. I was acting like a pig, but I couldn't help myself. I was ravenous.

And turned on.

I rinsed my hands and sat on the counter, spreading my legs. I smiled.

I saw him consider it. He really did. But then he shook his head and told me to leave again. "I'll see you tomorrow."

I pouted, but I did what he asked. I didn't want to annoy him, not while things were going this well.

He didn't lock the door behind me. Was it an invitation to come back? Or maybe he just forgot, but I took it as an invite. I waited an hour. The lights went off in the bedroom. I walked right into that house.

I wasn't tired yet, too much adrenaline, so I did more snooping.

I found his work laptop by the front door in his briefcase. They made the things so small now, you would mistake them for a pile of papers. I opened it. The light from the screen made my eyes hurt. The log in screen stared back at me.

I tried every password I could think of, just like on the forgotten laptop in the home office. None of them worked. I tried my name, a combination of Eva and their kids. I tried things related to police and detective work. I tried qwerty and password. Finally, I tried Benjamin Franklin.

His desktop was filled with files. Current investigations, old ones, cold cases. I opened them, but immediately regretted it. Photos of people, mostly women, beaten bloody. Autopsy photos. Photos taken at the scene. I closed them immediately. I felt bad for Will. I didn't know how he could look at those things day in and day out and be as collected as he was. I certainly couldn't do it.

I opened the internet and looked at his search history. Most of it was work-related and what I assumed were names of suspects. There were searches for dinner places, for vacation spots. I clicked on some of those, imagining him taking me there, running away from it all.

There was porn. I clicked on those too, just to see what he was into. Barely legal, and some seriously hardcore stuff, though none of it scared me. He wasn't into anything violent, so that was a good sign.

Then, there, hidden between a recipe for alfredo and a news article about a recent shooting, was *Paige Harper.* He had looked through all my social media. There were clicks on my photos. I wish I could see how long he spent on each of my pictures, which ones really did it for him.

I heard rustling upstairs. I closed the laptop, in case they came downstairs and saw the light shining. I had seen what I needed to, so I didn't need to look any further.

The toilet flushed, more rustling, and then gentle snoring. I replaced the laptop in his case and crept back toward the back door. I could feel the cold seeping through the cracks and couldn't bring myself to sleep outside. There was no way I could go back to my mom's house. I couldn't go to Ashley's. I grabbed a pillow from the front couch and laid down on the floor by the door. That way I could make a quick escape if I overslept.

Far from it. My eyes shot open at every noise I heard, real or imagined. At five in the morning, I heard Eva get up. I snuck outside, forgetting to put the pillow back.

I made it through school somehow. My eyes wouldn't stay open, and every muscle and joint ached from sleeping on the floor. I had showered in the school gym, when it was just the janitor on campus. He was about a hundred years old and had seen it all, so he ignored me when I passed him in the hall. Ashley barely talked to me, and I couldn't focus on anything related to parabolas or sonnets. Finally, when the final bell rang, I ran, heading directly to the station.

Detective DiPascua pulled up a chair when I buried my head in my arms on Will's desk. "Paige, what is it? What happened?"

"Nothing, I'm fine," I said, my words muffled.

"Harrington isn't back from the field yet. He should be here soon, but he's got a pretty big case right now. Do you want to come back a little later maybe?"

She rubbed my back. Her voice wrapped itself around me, soothing me, making me think of when my dad would sleep next to me when I thought there were monsters in my closet.

If only I'd have known the real monster was right across the hall.

"I'm sorry." A little voice in my head wondered why she was here if her partner was 'in the field'. I raised my head and looked at her. She had her guard up. The moment of safety I had felt only a moment before was gone. She was faking it. She didn't really care about me. This was all for the witnesses.

I could play that game too. I put on my sweetest voice. "I just have nowhere else to go right now. I'll stay out of the way, I promise. Just please don't make me go."

"Okay, you're okay, shh," she cooed. She led me to the doctor's office. She propped me up on the couch and brought me a little paper cup of water. "Doc's with someone right now, but he'll be back soon. Just holler if you need anything."

I waited until her footsteps faded out of earshot before I sat up. I checked every corner for a surveillance camera. When I didn't find any, I tiptoed over to the filing cabinet. I was sure they'd started a file on me. That's what people in places like that do. That's why you can never date a shrink. They'll be constantly keeping tabs and analyzing you.

I pulled on the top drawer. Locked. I tried the middle. Also locked. I tried every drawer of the cabinet as well as the drawers on in his desk. Every single one was locked. Snooping was so much harder than they made it seem in the movies.

His office was immaculate. Not a single thing was out of place. No pieces of scratch paper with a note scribbled across it. Certainly no spare keys laying around. There was no dust nor any cobwebs. It was completely impersonal and entirely secure.

I pulled a bobby pin from my hair, stared at it. People picked locks with these things all the time, but I just couldn't see a key no matter how hard I tried.

"You alright over there?"

I jumped. Sweat prickled all over my body. "Yeah, sorry." I smiled when I saw Will's frame in the doorway.

"Zoning a little, huh?"

"I guess so."

He sat on the couch next to me, our legs touching. He checked over his shoulder for any gawkers. When he saw that everyone was immersed in their own business, he took my face in his hands and ran his lips over mine, lightly at first, then eagerly. He pulled an inch away and stared straight at me, eyes smiling. "Hi," he said.

"Hey."

He scooted back to a safe distance. "What's going on?"

"My mom's back."

"Ah," he said, nodding. "Why?"

"I don't really know. She wanted me to confess to I don't know what. To attacking him in cold blood I guess. Which I didn't," I was quick to add.

"No one thinks you did."

"Has she called here?"

"No, not yet. She won't get too far if she does. She's unreliable. If it came to going to court, a judge would never hear her. A lawyer wouldn't call her to the stand. That's if she shows up in the first place, which she's shown she can't be trusted in that way."

"So I'm safe?"

"You're safe. As far as the court is concerned. I don't know about at home. You might want to stay at a friend's until she gets herself sorted out."

A lead blanket thudded across my chest. "Couldn't I maybe stay with you?"

His laugh ripped through me. "No, I don't think so."

"Why not?" I squeaked.

"Eva would never allow it." He stood, leaning toward the door like he was ready to leave, but not without me. "Last night was bad enough. I can't have you sneaking around, let alone *staying* at my house." He laughed again, in his own world, imagining the look on Eva's face, I'm sure. He sighed. "I have to get back to work. You're welcome to come out there or you can stay in here."

Of course, I followed him.

I passed Detective DiPascua on the way to his desk. She stood directly outside the threshold. I hung my head, not looking at her. I wondered how long she'd been standing there, how much she heard. I could feel her staring at me. I'm sure she wished the doctor would have shown up before Will, so he could get inside my head. I celebrated a small triumph knowing I won that round.

I sat at his desk, doodling and hand-writing essays I would probably throw out later. I wish I'd thought to bring something entertaining when I ran out of the house. At least I had Will to look at.

As he worked, I stared at him, trying to figure out how I felt now that I had him. I mean, I finally had the man I'd chased for so long, the man I lusted after and longed for. A magic genie had granted my wish. But now I was in this limbo. We snuck around, only allowed to be romantic behind closed doors. I wanted him to leave Eva, to run away with me. Then again, did I really want to be with him? He was a cheater, a weak man who couldn't resist young girls. Now that I had him, I wasn't sure I wanted him.

"Do I have a file?" I asked suddenly.

"Just with what relates to the case."

"Anything ... personal?"

"Like a psych eval? No, you were never analyzed officially so there are no records. Why?"

"Just wondering." *Never analyzed officially.* Like I was some document to be picked over rather than a human being.

"Don't worry. As of right now, this whole thing doesn't affect your record as far as applying to colleges and looking for work. You're a minor anyway, so it won't stick around."

After the words were out of his mouth, we locked eyes. *You're a minor.* If a news story were to be written about me, they'd refer to me as *girl* rather than *woman.* No matter how much either of us denied it, there it was, out in the universe.

I dragged my eyes away from his to a blank space on his desk. "Okay, thanks," was all I could manage to say.

I spent the day wandering around the building. I took a walk around the block, stopped at a sandwich shop on the corner for early dinner alone, wandered back into the building. I found a break room with a TV and watched bad sitcoms until Detective DiPascua came in to talk to me. She didn't sit down.

"Is there something going on with Harrington that I should know about?" she asked. She was no bullshit, and it was both frightening and impressive.

"What do you mean?" I tried to sound innocent, but it came out too aggressive. I wish I knew how to handle myself around her.

"I think you know what I mean. I see the way you two are together, especially the way you are around him. And you know I saw you steal his shirt."

Hot acid flooded my gut. I squared my shoulders, tipped my chin up, and raised an eyebrow, emulating sexy, strong, respectable women I'd seen in movies despite feeling like I was going to puke all over myself. "He's been good to me. I needed someone like him in my life and he stuck around. There's nothing wrong with that."

"The way you look at him, there's a little more to it."

I shrugged.

She put her face in mine, narrowing her eyes. "Kids aren't given enough credit," she hissed, "because I know you know full well what you're doing. Harrington is a good man. Don't ruin his life."

As I watched her leave, sucking all the power out of the room, I realized that I did want Will, now more than ever.

I waited until the episode of a self-help talk show turned into the news before I sauntered over to Will's desk. "So," I said, replacing the innocent me with the seductive, sex kitten me. "When do you think we'll be able to get out of here?" I bit my bottom lip.

He stared at me, that damn monkey with the cymbals clapping away again in his brain. Finally, it registered. "Oh, actually, I'm just about done here for today. We don't really have any new leads yet. Want to meet me out front in ten?"

I swung my hips as I left, reveling in the familiar feeling of being desired.

When he came out fifteen minutes later, he stood next to me without looking at me. He told me to wait even longer, until he pulled his car around the corner, then I should walk to meet him. I pretended like we were in a movie. The dapper man taking the vixen to his lush home after a night of dancing seductively.

He took me to a motel. "Are you fucking kidding me?" I raged.

"What do you want? Some plush suite in a five star hotel? Eva sees my credit card transactions and I only have like forty bucks on me."

"I just didn't know I was some cheap whore. I thought maybe we could go back to your place, like before."

"Eva's home. I told her I'd be late, but she said she'd just order take out and catch up on some reading."

"Couldn't you have gotten her to leave?"

"Yeah, right," he scoffed. "'Oh, yeah, honey, I'm going to be late, but maybe could you leave the house? I don't want you there because I need somewhere to have sex with someone else.' Yep, sounds perfect."

I sighed. "Whatever. It'll have to do."

The room was bigger than I expected, with a king-sized bed. It was clean: no stains and no stale dead body smell. Basically, the opposite of what movies had led me to expect from a motel. My mood immediately improved.

I flopped on the bed and kicked off my shoes. "This is okay, actually. I guess I don't feel like a hooker."

He answered me by crawling on top of me, kissing my neck, shoulders, collar bones. He lifted my shirt over my head and unhooked my bra all in one swift movement. I gasped when he ran his lips and tongue from my neck to my navel. He pulled my leggings off. Spreading my legs, he kissed along my legs, spending extra time on the sweet spots right at the top of my inner thighs.

Then, impatience washed over him. He yanked my panties off. He fumbled with his zipper, not bothering to drop his pants before shoving my legs into the air and pushing himself inside me.

I panicked.

I tried to push him off of me, but he was too heavy. My heart crashed through my chest. I couldn't breathe, couldn't speak. My entire body prickled with sweat. I needed to run as fast as I could away from this motel, but I was trapped.

I covered my face with my hands and sobbed, the only thing I could do.

Will stopped mid-thrust. "What's wrong?" he asked. "Am I hurting you?"

I shook my head.

He tried to pull my hands away, but I refused. He pulled away from me and sat next to me until I composed myself.

"What happened?" he asked after I'd recovered relatively well: just shuddering breaths and leftover tears.

"I don't know," was all I could manage.

Will wrapped me in his arms, rocked me gently. "I shouldn't have been that forceful. It was my fault."

I pulled away to look at him. I wiped snot on the back of my hand. I had no idea what he was talking about.

He told me I have a trigger because of Glen. Everyone who's been abused has it. It's different for everyone. Apparently for me, it was going too fast and being pushed, being helpless; a feeling of entrapment.

"We can just lay here for a bit if you want," he said.

"No, I want to try again."

He asked me if I was sure. Even when I nodded, he seemed unsure. He looked around, not sure how to proceed.

I went to the bathroom to fix my tear-stained face. The panic and adrenaline had fallen away, leaving embarrassment in their wake. I stared at myself under the harsh fluorescent lights. My still-dripping nose was red and swollen. Flecks and smears of mascara coated my cheeks. I rinsed my face with cold water. I patted my skin dry. I already looked better, but not like a sex kitten. Not a confident movie vixen.

I took a deep breath as I watched the redness recede. *This is what you wanted*, I told my reflection. *Grow a backbone.* I fluffed my hair and turned back to Will, my signature make-men-melt attitude back.

"We could try something else," he said. "Maybe you on top?"

I pushed him onto the mattress without answering him. He couldn't suppress a smile. Thankfully, my little episode didn't stop him.

Will guided my hips. I'd never been on top before; it was both nerve-wracking and empowering.

"Don't worry, you're not going to hurt me," Will said.

I moved my hips faster. I grabbed his hands and pinned them above his head. I don't know if it was the sex or being entirely in control that felt so good.

We were panting, moaning. I closed my eyes. My hands moved to his throat. My fingers tightened.

He clawed at my back. I cried out. The world stopped turning.

I opened my eyes. Will's eyes bulged. A vein in his forehead pulsed. I let go of his neck and smiled.

He coughed. Not his annoying, this-is-awkward cough, but a real cough. "What the fuck?" he croaked.

I slid off of him and laid next to him. "I thought you'd like it."

Will rubbed his neck, finger marks blooming. "I'm all for a little kink, but, Jesus, Paige! That was insane!"

"Awe, I'm sorry." I started kissing his neck, but he pushed me away.

"I should probably go. I need to get back home." He started

gathering his clothes. "I can book the room for the night if you'd feel safer or I can take you back home now."

I stuck out my bottom lip. "Already?" I whined. "Fine. I'll just go home with you then. Although I have enjoyed our little romantic getaway."

He froze. His eyes bore into me. "Paige, I'm not taking you home with me. I'll take you to *your* house, but that's it."

I looked at the man standing in front of me, a man I knew but barely recognized. His muscles rippled beneath his skin as he pulled on his boxer briefs; a few silver hairs mixed with the black ones on his chest. When I looked at his face, though, something was off. His lips were a tight, straight line. His eyes, normally bright and happy, were troubled. It was as if he were actually *mad* at me.

Then it hit me. He didn't want to be with me. He was going home to Eva, to be with that witch instead of me.

I ran to the bathroom and vomited.

"You okay?" Will shouted from the main room.

I flushed, rinsed my mouth, and threw my clothes back on before he finished tying his shoes. "Yeah, I'm fine. Ready?"

A wall had been built between us, strong and unyielding. I stared out the car window in bitter silence as he took me home. To my home, not to his.

He was leaving me. This was it. I thought he needed me, but he was just tossing me aside like a used tissue. He was the same as my uncle.

As we turned the corner onto my street, I looked at him. "Why can't I stay with you?" I asked.

Will sighed, heavy and dripping with frustration. "Because I have a wife."

"That didn't stop you before. It didn't stop you an hour ago."

"Yeah, but if I brought you home tonight, she would know, whereas before, she didn't know. That's the whole point: not to get caught."

"Why don't you just leave her then? Why sneak around?" My voice trembled.

He threw the car in park once we'd reached my house. My mother's car was still in the driveway. "Because I don't think I can. This is a fling, nothing more. I shouldn't have done it in the first place."

Nothing more. The words echoed in my mind, mocking me. "Don't say that," I said, barely a whisper.

"Paige," his voice caught. He rubbed his hand over his face, refusing to look at me. "Look, we can't do this anymore."

Tears blurred my sight. "Don't say that!" I yelled.

Finally, he looked at me. "It's not healthy. I mean, what did you think? That we were going to get married and live happily ever after like some fairy tale?"

Anger moved through me like wildfire when he scoffed. "If you were never going to leave her, then why kiss me? Why fuck me? Lead me on like that?"

Finally, he looked at me. "I thought you were mature enough to understand that that's how an affair works."

The world dropped around me. I grabbed onto the dashboard to steady myself. My chest heaved. "No, this was not just some affair without feelings and emotions. You – you *care* about me. This is so much more than just sex and you know it."

A coldness passed over his face. "I think you misunderstood. I think I need to take myself off this case. And you can't come to the station anymore."

Everything stopped spinning. I looked at him with complete clarity. "No, I did not misunderstand." I sat up in my seat, glaring at him. "You started feeling guilty, and now you're trying to blame me for everything that's happened. You're trying to act like I've gotten to attached, but that's not really what's going on. *You* are attached to *me*," I spat.

"Paige, please get out of the car," he asked calmly.

"You just used me. Your marriage got a little stale, so you thought you'd look somewhere else. Then I came along. Little did you know you'd actually fall for me."

"Paige, get out."

"I'm going to tell. I'll – I'll say you raped me."

Fear flashed over Will's face, but only for a moment. "I have more evidence that you abused me rather than the other way around," he said, pointing to his neck. "All you have is that we had sex, nothing more."

"But I'm an attractive white female. My father is dead, my mother might as well be. I have no role models. I've been abused for years. You're an old man, a predator. Unhappy marriage, unhappy at work. You chose me because I'm a weak, innocent victim. The jury will side with me."

He slouched, melting into a puddle of defeat. He'd seen it time and again. He knew I was right. He rubbed his face with his hands, sighing.

I flipped my hair over my shoulders, straightening my posture. I patted his knee. "I understand, William, I really do. You're in a tough spot, but soon, Eva will get it and she'll allow you to move on. Even if she doesn't, who cares? What matters is that you and I will be together."

He stared at my hand. "I used to think you were different. That you were so level-headed and mature. That despite everything you were put through, everything that was done to you, that you'd made it out to the other side as a wise woman. Someone who was strong and aware. I was wrong. You're not aware of anything."

"Shh, you weren't wrong. You're such an intelligent man. Don't be so hard on yourself."

Will slapped my hand away. "Do you see what I mean?" He was yelling. It scared me. I'd never heard him raise his voice before, especially not to me. "I just told you you're fucking crazy and you turn it around like I'm just being hard on myself! Are you kidding me? Is this some sort of joke? You can't seriously be this delusional. Yes, I had sex with you. Yes, I had it in my head that we would have an affair and we could run away together. But the more I thought about it, the more I realized how stupid that is. And tonight did not help that situation. I have a family. I have a career. I should never have touched you. I will always regret that. But you can't really sit there thinking that we'll fall in love, can you? Especially after today?"

"I thought we had a good afternoon."

He laughed, condescending. "You tried to strangle me! I told you I didn't want anything to do with you anymore. How is that a good afternoon?"

I leaned toward him and put my hand back on his leg. "You're seeing it all wrong. We had a breakthrough. It was emotional, yes, but you helped me to see who I am. I cried and came back to you. I'm over what happened now. You cured me. You're the best thing that ever happened to me. Don't you see that?"

He rubbed his face again. "Honestly, yes, I do see that. But you are nowhere near the best thing that ever happened to me. And you're not cured. Trust me."

I moved my left hand slowly higher up his thigh. He flinched. I stopped sliding my hand upward, but I didn't take it away from his leg. "I can see you're distraught. I know it was emotional for you too. We'll talk later, okay? Give you some time to process everything and to think of a way to break the news to Eva." I leaned in for a kiss. He turned his head away. I sighed. "That's something you'll have to work on. See you later."

I trounced up my driveway as he peeled away. I couldn't believe what he had said. I knew it was the guilt talking, but still, for him to not recognize that was insane to me. He'd come around though. I just knew it.

My mother was still home – surprisingly – so I wandered into the garage, through the door to sneak into my bedroom and grab extra clothes and my gym bag. I heard her snoring on Glen's bed. He never wanted her, only me, and it ate her up inside, even now.

Chapter 35

Harrington pulled into his driveway after dropping off Paige. Paige, such a beautiful, intelligent, insane girl. He couldn't believe he'd fallen for her, that he thought she would have come out of her trauma unscathed.

No, that wasn't true. He could believe it, as much as he didn't want to admit it, even to himself. He was a perfect example of history repeating itself.

Two years ago, there was a victim. Chloe. Her mother was Japanese, her father black. Mixed, just like his own children.

But more beautiful, though guilt prickled at his brain every time he thought it.

Chloe was a perfect combination of the two, with bright almond eyes, big curls, and silky, flawless skin. Despite her godly faultlessness, she didn't feel she fit in anywhere. She floated around, never feeling a oneness with her peers. Everyone admired her, but when they'd tease that she wasn't "black enough" or that she wasn't "smart enough" to be Asian, she put up walls. She cut herself off and got into trouble. That's when she ended up at the station.

"These people accept me. It doesn't matter what race I am." Hot, angry tears streamed from her eyes. Harrington had to force himself not to wipe them away with the pad of his thumb.

"As long as you can get them their drugs," he told her.

"It wasn't like that."

DiPascua warned him right away. She told him to focus on getting justice, just like every other case that walked through the door.

He blocked her out, claiming that's exactly what he was doing.

The nights he turned away from his wife, lost in his own world, thinking about being wrapped in Chloe's arms, proved otherwise.

He allowed himself to feel. Love? Infatuation? Lust? Whatever it was, he allowed it. He didn't deny himself any longer. Eva grew suspicious when all he would talk about was the girl who had everything but gave it all up to feel like she belonged somewhere, but he didn't care. He ignored her.

Harrington pursued Chloe, but she rejected him, calling him a perverted old man. She threatened to turn him in, to get him fired. "I'm going to tell your wife who you really are," she spat.

And tell she did.

He walked into his home to see Chloe at his kitchen table. He smiled boyishly. His smile dropped when he saw Eva sitting across from her, fire burning in her eyes. "Chloe, you can go now. Have a lovely evening."

Eva started throwing punches the moment the front door closed. "How could you?" she screamed.

Harrington forced down bile. "I never touched her!" He swatted away her blows.

"That's not what she says, and the way you've been acting, I believe her." Her accent floated to the surface when she was angry. Normally he thought it was cute; this time it terrified him.

Chloe had told his wife that he forced himself on her. That he'd been inappropriate with her time and again. Finally, after so many rejections, he snapped. He held her down. She cried out. He muffled her screams with his palm.

Eva believed her. After so many years together, she really thought he'd be capable of something so atrocious.

Now, as he sat in his car in the driveway, he was about to face his wife again, the same allegations looming over his head. He'd have to be honest with her about the affair.

His life, already ripped and torn by his own hand, was about to fall completely apart.

Chapter 36

It was getting dark early. Fall afternoons had a way of doing that.
The sunlight filtered through fiery leaves. A chilly wind blew my
hair around my shoulders. I didn't feel it. I was too involved.
Ashley wanted to find out what I loved, what I had passion for.
Well, here it was.

I stood in front of Will's house, my bag over my shoulder. I
heard muffled yelling in Spanish, pleading in English. I smirked.
He was begging her for a divorce, I just knew it. Eva was such a
fighter, I respected that, but she'd lose this one.

I slinked to their back yard. I peeked in the kitchen window.
Her arms flailed, veins in her neck and forehead bulged. He
slumped at the table, tears brimming, threatening to spill over. His
chin quivered.

My heart thumped. He was so sweet to cry for me. Such an
emotional time.

I slipped the key from its place atop the door frame. Carefully,
quietly, I unlocked the door and slipped inside.

"Eva, please, I don't – I can't understand you. I'm sorry.
Please!" Harrington moaned as his soon-to-be ex-wife pummeled
him with a barrage of Spanish.

They never looked at me as I tiptoed upstairs to their bedroom.

I dug through their closet until I found a purple suitcase. I
opened it and threw Eva's clothes into it. A nice dress for a dinner,

three work dresses, heels. I moved to her dresser and threw in socks and underwear. I tossed sweats and a pair of slippers on top. I started zipping the suitcase closed when I remembered what was in her bottom drawer. I picked up the dildo with a sock and dropped it in the suitcase. "Because you'll probably be lonely out there," I said, trying not to laugh.

Silence fell downstairs. It was happening. He was leaving her. I zipped up the suitcase and snuck to the top of the stairs. From my perch, I could just see the side of Will's arm and the shadow cast by a pacing Eva.

"Please," Will begged, "just listen. I messed up. Huge." I heard Eva scoff. "I know there's no excuse and I've ruined what we have, but I never raped her. I would never. She's lying."

"But you fucked her," Eva spat.

"Yes, I did." A beat of silence. Another. "Only once, and it didn't go well. I know that doesn't make a difference because it still happened, but it wasn't a full-blown affair."

"Then what do you call it, you asshole?"

"A mistake."

I slid down another step. I couldn't believe what I was hearing. First of all, how could he say we only had sex once? I get lying to her to make himself seem more angelic, but if he's having honesty time, why lie about how many times? Not only that, but what we had was not a mistake. Nowhere near it. He loved me. My uncle always taught me that when men want to show you they love you, they have sex with you.

I could see Will fully now. His eyes were red and swollen. Lines pulled down his face; he looked so much older than he was. This woman was stressing him out. I needed to get him out of there, to save him.

He went on. "I was blinded by a beautiful girl –"

"A child bride," that witch interrupted.

Ignoring her, he said, "and I'm such an idiot for doing it. She was broken and I thought I could fix her. I didn't realize how messed up she was."

"And now she's threatening you with rape if you don't leave me." He nodded. "Sounds familiar."

"Chloe was different. I never touched her."

"But you wanted to."

He paused, so long I didn't think he was ever going to answer. "Yes, I did."

I slid down another step, shaking. Who was Chloe? I didn't know a Chloe. Was this one of the other girls Doctor Woods was talking about? I swayed, suddenly light headed.

"You want me to believe you about this other girl?" Eva made a gagging noise. "I invited her into our home! This is my fault."

"It would have happened anyway." His eyes snapped to her, immediately regretting what he'd just said.

"Well," she laughed humorously, "good to know."

"I'm sorry. It's true though. All of what I'm telling you is true. That day, when we came back from our anniversary, you know how you said someone was in our bed? I think – I think it was her. I denied it then and made excuses but I don't think there's any other explanation. I wanted her to be something she clearly was not."

"What am I supposed to do about it?"

"Help me. Just help me somehow. I'll give you everything I have."

I had slid down to the middle of the staircase by now, wrapped up entirely in what they were saying. The anger seemed to have melted off of Eva. Will could do that, melt you, no matter how much of an ice queen you may be.

But this, this was not going the way I had planned. Unless this was some weird, twisted way of telling her to leave, it seemed like maybe he was trying to patch things up with her.

Will sniffed the air, knitted his eyebrows together. "Do you smell that?"

"Smell what? Oh, don't worry, we're not talking about anything extremely important right now."

He held up her hand to hush her. I smiled. "Oranges," he said.

He stood. My lungs stopped working. "She's here," he whispered.

"What the fuck? Who's here? Will? Answer me!" she screamed.

I scampered back upstairs. I could hear his hurried footsteps behind me, then her bare feet slapping against the linoleum behind him. I was shaking. I couldn't get my legs to move fast enough.

I slipped into the closet and hid behind the door, willing my heart to quiet its thumping in my brain. Speckles of light flickered in front of my eyes, refusing to be blinked away.

"Paige!" he yelled. "Get out here, you crazy bitch!"

Will ran in, followed by Eva. I peeked through the crack in the door at them, the room spinning. This wasn't at all how it was supposed to happen.

Will stopped dead in the middle of the bedroom. I followed his gaze to the suitcase I left next to the bed. Eva squeaked as she slammed into Will's back, not expecting him to stop so suddenly. "Is that my suitcase?" she asked.

Will yelled for me again. I wanted to come out, but he seemed so mad. I didn't want to be in trouble. I thought he'd appreciate what I'd done for him.

I couldn't breathe. I panted like a cornered animal, the spots in front of my eyes growing stronger.

Then, blackness.

Chapter 37

A sliding sound followed by a loud *thud* sent Harrington running to the master closet. Behind the door lay a beautiful blonde who once sent fire through his being. Now, chills raised goosebumps across his entire body.

He dragged her limp body to the middle of the room. His wife couldn't decide whether to be fearful or angry.

"How did she get in?" she asked.

"I don't know," he replied, too baffled to do anything more than stand and stare.

"You let her in here. You thought I wasn't going to be home. You had her pack my things and you two were going to live happily ever after in this home I built for you!" Eva screamed. She hit Harrington in his gut. He grabbed her wrists, hard enough to bruise.

"Don't you dare accuse me of this! She must have broken in while we were arguing." He dropped her wrists, afraid of himself. He'd never been a violent man, especially toward women. Even toward guilty scum, he was reasonable.

He ran through every step he took since he drove home. He dropped her off, he drove straight home. He watched her go inside through the garage. She must have run here, trailing behind his car. He remembered closing the door, but did he lock it? He and Eva argued near the front, there was no possible way Paige walked in through the front without either of them noticing. How did she get in here?

The back. He and Eva left a key back there for the kids, in case something ever happened. They'd all but forgotten about it. Paige was stealthy. She could have passed right by them.

Eva pushed him, bringing him back to the present. "You can't just ignore me. You brought her back here after you fucked, didn't you?" Her words burned like acid. "Don't think I can't smell her on you! That I can't see what you two do while I'm away!" She wrapped her small, hot hands around his throat, covering the finger marks left by Paige an hour before.

He let her keep her hands there, feeling the burn of his raw skin beneath her fingers. "I'm sorry," he whispered.

"If I remember correctly," she said, folding her arms across her chest, "just a few minutes ago you said you had sex, but it was over. That it happened a while ago but never again."

"It is over. I just didn't want to hurt you more by telling you how recent it was." His excuse sounded weak and pathetic even as he spoke the words.

"How nice of you. Such a sweetheart. Well, you can have her. She's right here, ready for you. She's already got my bags packed."

"Eva! This is what I'm talking about!" He grabbed her wrists again, shaking her. Her eyes widened, but she didn't move away. "She's insane! She broke into our home while we were here. She tried to strangle me. She went through your things and packed for you, ready to send you off so she could be with me. And that's just today! I can't fight her alone. I need you here with me."

She spat in his face. "You can't fight her alone? Are you kidding me? She's half your size! She's a little girl. You wanted the crazy bitch." She yanked her wrists free. Folding her arms, she turned away from him, but didn't leave. She was testing him.

He put his clammy hands on her shoulders. "I'm going to call Di." He kissed her hair. He'd passed, but she still pulled away from his touch.

Chapter 38

I watched her standing there, her back toward me. She mumbled to herself in Spanish, motioning with her hands, like how people do when they're on the phone even though no one's there to see them.

She ran her hands through her hair. How long did this bitch seriously think I'd be passed out? I'd regained consciousness the second I started falling, before I even hit the ground, but apparently she thought people fainted and then fell into a deep sleep that only true love's kiss can break.

I really would have liked if Will had kissed me. When he wrapped his strong hands around my arms to drag me out of the closet, my body shuddered. He was saving me.

Yet he dropped me on the floor and said all those things about me. That wasn't saving me. If anything, that was incriminating me, throwing me in front of the Ice Queen to be executed.

I didn't know what he wanted from me, leaving me here, supposedly unconscious, in the same room as the woman he wanted to divorce. I didn't know how much longer I could let him play innocent. It made me antsy enough hearing him say those things to her, like he wanted to stay with her and wanted me to disappear. All I could figure was that he wanted to be the hero. He wanted to leave his hands clean of the mess of the divorce. That's why he told her about us. So maybe then she'd leave him.

I didn't mind seeming like the crazy one in her eyes, as long as it made him more comfortable with himself. He could tell her I was crazy, he was innocent, yet she'd still leave him. Really, it was ingenious. People always think women are crazy, no matter what they do.

As soon as I heard his voice downstairs, I stood up. Eva spun around, gasped. She started to scream for Will. I lunged at her, slamming her against the wall, pinning her there with my forearm against her throat.

"Will and I are going to be together," I whispered. "Stop getting in the way."

She clawed at my arm; I hardly felt it, even as drops of my blood popped up to the surface of my skin. I pushed harder.

A strange gurgling noise escaped from her as she gasped in vain for air.

When I hit Glen, it was a snap decision. I knew I'd defend myself, but I didn't know how. While it was satisfying to see him laying there bleeding, after all he'd done to me, this was different. I looked at Eva as she struggled against me, so weak, yet trying so hard. I thought she was a powerful woman when I first met her, but now she was like a baby bird, fragile and so easily crushed. Her streaming eyes bulged. She turned a strange hue of purple, one vein in her forehead threatening to burst.

I didn't hear Will screaming my name. I didn't know he was in the room until he hit me hard from the side. I went down, and there he was, on top of me.

I smiled at him. "Hi, Babe. It's okay, we can be together now. She understands."

His eyes widened. "Are you kidding me?" he said, his voice unusually high. I found it extremely unattractive.

"Cuff that bitch, Will!" Eva screamed through tears and an irritated windpipe.

"What the hell were you thinking?" he whispered to me.

He still pinned me down, knee on my chest. Eyebrows knitted, eyes wide, lips pulled back. He actually looked confused. I waited for him to wink at me or give some signal that he was leading Eva on, that he was on my side and he would work it all out so we could be together.

But he gave me nothing.

"Don't you want to be together?" I asked, voice quivering.

"No, Paige, I don't. Not anymore." He looked over his

shoulder, checking on his wife. He leaned closer, placing his lips close to mine. "I did, at one time, I really did. But not anymore."

Tears welled in my eyes, threatening to spill over. "You don't mean that."

"Come on, Will, what are you waiting for?" Eva croaked. She was getting nervous, pacing in and out of my line of vision behind my prize.

"I do mean it. Paige, you are insane."

"Don't call me that." The hot tears spilled over. Frustration, anger, confusion, all of it overwhelmed me.

"I thought I could help you. I thought you were a little broken doll that could be fixed, but I was wrong. You're so much worse than I thought. You need help."

The tears poured from my eyes now. My mouth curved downward and I couldn't swallow my spit. I couldn't believe I was ugly-crying in front of this man. He'd never love me if he saw me like that. Men liked pretty girls, happy girls. That's what Glen always said.

Yet I couldn't help it. Nothing was working out. I had all these dreams and aspirations and none of them were coming true. I was so embarrassed.

"I'm sorry, Paige. This isn't how I wanted this to turn out," Will whispered.

He held me there until his partner arrived to make the arrest. Eva screamed at him the entire time, but he wouldn't budge. In that moment, I think he really cared about me.

Chapter 39

"They sentenced me to this therapy crap and to stay in foster care because my mother shouldn't be a mother. They found her guilty of neglect and found so much crap in her system, she probably had a hell of a time detoxing in jail." I shrugged. "And I believe the rest you already know."

My words hung heavily in front of me.

"I know there's a lot you're not telling me," the doctor finally said.

I rolled my eyes. "God, I've been talking to you for forever. I've poured my soul out and you're going to say I'm leaving stuff out?" I crossed my arms and sat back in the chair, refusing to look at either the director or the psychiatrist.

"What you are saying and what other people say don't match. Even if I didn't have their testimony, I can tell you're hiding. You play with your ear every time you lie, and you pick at your nails every time you lie by omission."

"How am I supposed to feel safe if you're calling me a liar?"

I was losing it and he remained completely calm. "I don't mean it maliciously. That's the way you are. You're afraid to be yourself, so you make up a different persona. It's your way of escaping your reality."

I could feel the blood pulsing through my veins in my arms and thighs. My lip bled from biting it. After all this, this man in front of me didn't know the first thing about me. I couldn't believe he was calling me a liar. Although, I guess I shouldn't be surprised. No one ever gave me enough credit. Not even Will.

"I think we should talk about something else," I said.

The ancient psychiatrist took a deep breath. "Where do you think your need for control comes from?"

I didn't have control issues. Things just went my way. "I like to get what I want, and it's easy for me."

"Clearly it's not. The whole reason you're here is because you lost control and you acted out, multiple times. You spiraled, and could still be spiraling."

I didn't like his tone. It was accusatory. He didn't know me, or what I had been through. He had no idea what it was like to be me.

"Okay," he continued when I didn't reply to him, my body shaking with bubbling anger. "We can stop here. Next time I want you to tell me about the trial."

I looked up at him. "You already know all about that."

"Not from your perspective. I know it was strenuous, but I need you to open up to me about it. Your thoughts during it, how you felt seeing the men you have history with on the stand."

I thought about Will, the way he looked in his freshly pressed suit. I missed him.

The feeling washed over me suddenly and fiercely. I got up and walked slowly back to my room, trying to hold myself together.

I curled up on my bed facing the wall. Thankfully my roommate was out. I hugged my knees and sobbed into my pillow.

I couldn't believe I missed him. I didn't think I would ever feel that way again, not since my dad died. Missing my dad physically hurt. Even after all these years, it still tore me apart. It was as if I couldn't cry hard enough. I needed to scream, but even that wouldn't reduce the overwhelming sense that my insides needed out.

Mostly I ignored it over the last couple of years, not allowing myself to feel it. If the feeling crept up, I would distract myself. I would call Ashley, or go find a party somewhere.

Now, alone in a sterile dorm room after losing everything, that feeling came back. I wanted to turn myself inside out. It wasn't anything I could tell a therapist or anyone else. They wouldn't understand.

I missed Will. I missed my dad. I missed feeling safe, even for a moment.

Chapter 40

I sat in a holding cell, waiting for Ashley's parents to come get me. I wasn't sure they'd come. My mother certainly wouldn't. I had no one else. Literally no one.

The officers had fingerprinted me. They were gentle, not like in the movies where they rough up hardened criminals. DiPascua stayed by my side, telling me she would try her hardest to get a hold of my mother for me but she couldn't promise anything. She assured me she was trying her best to make it all go away. "I want a counsel and release, but Eva is pressing charges and won't let it go."

I didn't know why she was being so nice to me. She wanted to bring me and Will down right from the beginning. "What about Will? What does he want?"

She looked at her feet. It was the first time I'd ever seen her defeated. "Jesus. You don't stop, do you?" she mumbled. She looked at me, square in the eye. "He thinks you need help. He doesn't want you to go to Juvenile Hall, but he thinks you need counseling."

"Can't you guys do something? To make sure I don't go to juvie?" I didn't think a girl like me could handle a jail cell no matter how young the inmates were.

"I can try my best, but I'm not your guardian. I can't call too many shots in this case. Luckily you're a white girl and you're pretty."

"Thank you."

"Not a compliment, sweet thing," she snapped. "The fact is that being white and a girl put the odds in your favor. If you were trashy or ugly, that would hurt you. You're not. You're in school, no priors, and you keep yourself up. You're not doing or dealing drugs. You didn't have a reputation for sleeping around until word got back to your school, but even that is just typical rumor that won't hold up. Things look good in that respect. You had the cards stacked against you as far as your mother and father, and with your uncle raping you, that helps too." She shrugged. "Course, it would have been better if you had actually reported the rape, any of the times you claim it happened. Especially the one that led you to beat said uncle over the head with a bat, but maybe no one in the room will think about that. Anyway, that's all playing to the sympathy card. It also gives you a reason to have become an obsessive stalker and to attack a woman."

My heart dropped. Is that really what she thought of me? I was lying about the rape? I was an obsessive stalker?

"It was a one-time thing that the courts will view as something that can be cured with therapy," she continued. "So that's what we're going for. The hiccup is that your mother is MIA. She's flighty. She wanted to press charges against you for your uncle. That will be brought up. There's no doubt of it. It will show that you're unstable by default. And boy have you proven that." DiPascua rested her hands on her hips, her stance wide. Her confidence was back. She was all business and the more she talked, the less she cared for me, that much was obvious.

After she left, shoes pounding into the tiled floor, I called Ashley. "Why is this call coming from the police station and not from your phone?" she asked, judgment dripping off of every word.

"Hey to you too. Look, I'm in trouble and they can't find my mom. Could your parents come help me? They could be, like, my unofficial caregivers or whatever."

"And why should they? Obviously you wouldn't be there if you didn't do something really stupid. Considering how stupid you've been lately, I believe it."

I took a deep breath. "Because you guys are literally all I have."

I'd waited so long in the holding cell, I almost thought I was dreaming when Ashley's parents came to get me. Ashley wasn't there.

I stood beside them as they filled out paperwork. "When it rains, it pours, right?" the officer said to me.

I smiled, shook my head in confusion.

"Well, first your uncle, now this, and your mom's going to be charged with neglect once we track her down."

Mr. Hale dropped the pen and stared at the officer. "What does that mean for Paige?" he asked, his voice bloated with worry.

"She'll probably go into the system unless someone becomes her guardian," the officer said, each word wrapping around the real meaning: if you don't adopt her, she'll end up as another troubled kid in the system.

The car ride to Ashley's was filled with a heavy silence. Mr. Hale stared straight ahead. I doubted if he truly saw the road. Mrs. Hale stared out the passenger window, punctuating the silence with deep sighs. I imagined Will sitting next to me, getting me through it all.

Ashley ignored me until dinner. I could tell she was working through everything in her head: exactly what to say and how to say it, imagining all the rebuttals I had, planning her responses. Finally, after a few measly bites of mashed potatoes, she turned to me, fork in hand.

"What exactly happened?" Her eyes were narrowed to slits under heavy brows. It was her serious face, one she got when she was mad at her boyfriend or studying hard for tests. One I knew not to mess with.

"I don't know. It was weird. Will and I were going to run away together, you know? So I went with the plan we made together. I went over to his house, but he and Eva were fighting. So I went upstairs to pack her bags."

"You packed the woman's bags? Are you kidding?" Ashley interrupted.

"Yes, it was a part of the plan. See, it would show that he was serious. He was leaving her. Well, making her leave him. Then that way he and I would have the house until we figured out where to go. She has family she could stay with, but he doesn't really have anyone except his partner, but that looks kind of weird to the job. And we definitely couldn't live at my house, not with the blood stain and with my mom being there sometimes." The words spewed out of my mouth. I sounded manic. "So anyway, I waited for them to finish fighting but they kept going on and on. He's like, 'Eva I love her sorry' and she's like, 'But I thought you loved me' and she called him all these names and it was just awful. She is so awful to him. She doesn't deserve him. I do though. I really do. We care about each other, you know?"

Ashley and her parents stared at me. No one touched their food.

"And then finally they came upstairs," I continued. "Eva saw her bags were packed and freaked on Will and on me. He couldn't do anything because then she'd cry domestic abuse, so I stepped in. I got her off of him and held her against the wall so she couldn't hurt him anymore. She was hysterical. Absolutely nuts. She scratched at me," I held up my arms for them to see, "and all sorts of stuff. She was like a wild animal. I was scared, I really was. That's when Will called his partner, but Eva came up with some story about how it was my fault and I attacked her and I should be arrested. And now here I am."

I took a breath, a sip of water.

"I don't believe you," Ashley said. She stood up, covered her plate with foil, and put it in the fridge. "I think I'm going to turn in early. See you guys tomorrow." With a flip of her hair in my direction, she walked down the hall to her bedroom, every step calculated.

I continued eating every morsel on my plate while her parents picked at theirs. "This is so delicious. Thanks so much," I told them.

Ashley's mom shook her head. She threw her napkin on the plate and flitted to the bedroom she shared with her husband, muttering, "I can't take this."

"Look, Paige," Mr. Hale said, "I'm afraid this is only temporary. We can't have this sort of behavior going on. You've been going down this road for a while now, and we tried to help, but I don't think there's much more that we can do. We'll support you however we can, but if your mom is charged with neglect and you have to live with a guardian, it won't be us. I truly am sorry. A year ago it would be different. Now, though, we just can't. I hope you understand."

I tilted my chin toward the ceiling. What I understood was yet another person I trusted was about to abandon me. "Foster care it is, I guess." I washed my plate and went to crash in the spare bedroom before he could say anything more. I could tell he felt bad, but feeling bad didn't make it go away. The simple fact was that I had no one.

I met with my lawyer, Willow Parker, the next day. I walked to my appointment at the court instead of depending on the Hales for a ride. I didn't want to burden them any more than I already had.

"Mrs. Harrington won't let up," Parker said. I winced at the sound of that woman's name. "I've tried to cut a deal with her, but she is one persistent woman."

Boy, was that true. "So what's going to happen to me?" I tried so hard to sound like a strong woman, like DiPascua. Instead, I just sounded like a scared little girl.

"Well, next is an adjudicatory hearing. Basically," she explained after seeing the look of confusion on my face, "you're going in front of a judge. Not a jury, but you'll still present your case. They have people testifying against you. It's not going to be pretty, I have to warn you. We'll be okay though. It'd be different if you'd murdered someone, but you're good." She was trying to make a joke to lighten the mood. It fell flat when our eyes met and she remembered that my uncle could still potentially die. She cleared her throat.

"What does Will say?" I asked.

"He agrees with his wife. He thinks you need to see someone. Honestly, that's pretty good. He doesn't want you getting locked up, and he has a pretty big influence here."

I couldn't help but smile. I just couldn't understand why he wouldn't get it all over with. Why he wouldn't come to my rescue.

Chapter 41

I sat at a giant table in front of a giant man wearing giant robes in a giant room. I suppose they did it on purpose, to make you feel smaller than you already did. To remind you that you're just a kid who had made barely a ripple in this ocean of a world.

I dressed in Ashley's pencil skirt and button-down blouse. I didn't have any sort of clothes that would be acceptable to wear to a hearing. At least it got her talking to me a little, telling me what I should and shouldn't wear. The way she looked at me when I left that morning pulled something in my gut. It was almost as if she still wanted the best for me.

The prosecutor called the first person to the stand. Dr. Woods. I rolled my eyes. I knew he'd been evaluating me all those times he wanted to talk to me. I was glad I hadn't said much to him.

The attorney asked him what type of person I seemed to be in the few times he'd seen me. "Oh, she's a very bright girl," Dr. Woods said. "Very intelligent. So much potential."

So far so good, until the prosecutor asked him about my mental state and if I posed a threat to anyone.

"She has obsessive tendencies," he said.

I rolled my eyes again. No I didn't. He clearly wasn't a very good doctor.

The prosecutor asked him to elaborate.

He claimed I wouldn't leave Will alone, which is the dumbest thing I ever heard. "She came to the station nearly every day when

Detective Harrington was working. He told her multiple times she needed to go home, or to get back into sports, but she wouldn't listen. Just kept saying she would feel better at the station." I wanted to scream at him. Will *asked* me to come to the station after school to be his intern. He wanted me there. I just wanted to shake that pudgy little man!

"I thought Detective Harrington told Miss Harper that she could intern at the station?" the prosecutor asked.

"Ah,yes, that was a bit of a mess. He did tell her that, so that she would come in on her own to talk to me. When that plan unraveled after two days, he told her she couldn't come back. He very blatantly told her she needed to stay home and she could only come down when summoned. She ignored him. She ignored all of us."

Dr. Woods said that when he talked to me, I only talked about Will, and that I had delusions about being with him. When asked to elaborate on my "delusions," he claimed he overheard me talking to Will about our house on the beach, that I called him my husband.

If anyone was delusional, it was the doctor. I flipped my hair and tuned him out. Pure idiocy.

My jaw literally dropped when they called the next witness. Mr. Owens glided up to the front of the room to be sworn in. He glanced at me before sitting down, back straight. What a handsome man.

"She was obsessed with me," he said.

"You're an attractive man, I'm sure you have plenty of girls swooning over you," the prosecutor said.

He tried to hide a smile. "Sure, every teacher has that problem, but in those situations, it's innocent. Young girls find stability in older men, and it's our responsibility to not encourage it. Support them and be a strong male figure, but never breach that trust."

"How was the situation with Paige different?"

"She'd make lewd comments constantly."

"Such as?"

Mr. Owens took a breath, not wanting to say whatever was coming next. He could be such a prude sometimes. "Well," he said, "she told me how 'hot' I am and she asked suggestively when she could come over to my house. Things like that. The comment made to me that made me file my third request to have her removed from my class was, 'When you gonna make me suck that big dick of yours?'"

A collective intake of breath, shifting of bodies in their chairs. I could feel everyone's eyes burning into me. Sweat prickled under my arms.

My lawyer shot me a sharp look. She scribbled on her notepad and passed it to me. *Anything you want to tell me?*

I passed the note back. *He's lying.*

How could he say that to everyone? That was our secret. Obviously he was hurt that I didn't want to be with him anymore, so he lashed out.

"She would follow me," Mr. Owens continued. "She'd wait for me after school, saying she didn't want to go home, which I completely understand. Whatever went on in that house was not healthy, which is why I allowed it to begin with. But then she wouldn't leave me alone. She'd wait for me outside the bathroom. She'd wait by my car. She'd have the older boys with licenses drive her around, following me to my house."

How did he know about that? I was very careful. I made sure to ask different boys so the cars would be different and he wouldn't know. And those boys would do anything for me. They'd kill if I asked them. If they were nice enough, I'd go down on them, but usually I wouldn't. It made them mad, but frankly, some of them were gross. I have standards.

My lawyer sighed. She raised her eyebrow at me. I shrugged in response.

"Guess we'll just run with it," she mumbled. She stood up to make her argument. To Mr. Owens she said, "Assuming what you say is true, and she did make that comment to you, notice how she said 'When are you going to *make me*,' not "When will you *let me*'. Clearly she has been influenced by the abuse she has suffered. Instead of removing her from your class, shouldn't you have tried to get her in to see the counselor? As a teacher, shouldn't you have been her protector, rather than someone to push her away?"

"She was too far gone. I'd tried everything I could with her. She was in the principal's office practically ever other day," he fumbled.

"You knew about her uncle. Gossip spreads through high

schools like wildfire. Instead of seeing her as the little girl she is, a girl who needed help, you played victim, like she was hurting you. But really, you were hurting her by not providing her with resources, isn't that right?"

He rubbed his face with a strong hand. "Yes, I should have been. I didn't see it. I obviously failed her."

Chapter 42

Harrington stared at Paige's lawyer. He'd been on the stand hundreds of times for work, but he was uncomfortable up there, sitting next to the judge. He should have felt more comfortable without a jury. Should have felt better that he wasn't the one being charged. Nonetheless, he fidgeted, wiped his forehead frequently. "She seduced me," he said.

"You're the adult here. You should have known better," Parker said. "You should have been like Mr. Owens, and set boundaries. Instead, you crossed right over them like they were nothing."

"It wasn't like that."

"Oh really? Then, tell me, Detective Harrington, what exactly was it like?"

For the first time since he entered the room, he looked at Paige. In that moment, his walls crumbled. "She was someone I could fix. She was so broken. She'd suffered a great hurt that no one should ever feel. I wanted to protect her, to show her that there are good men in the world."

"And you're one of those good men? A middle-aged man who preys on young, vulnerable girls?" Parker's voice rose. Although she was court-appointed, she really cared about her clients, about getting the bad guy.

"That's not how it was. I wasn't preying on her. I was helping her. I was showing her what it was really like to love and…and to be loved."

Paige hadn't felt like smiling since the day she'd been brought in, but now, drowning in this oversized courtroom, she felt her lips being tugged upward. *He admitted it in front of everyone*, she thought. *He loves me.*

Parker continued. "You loved her? It's funny but that's exactly what rapists say to their victims."

The prosecutor threw a fit. The judge told Parker to watch herself.

She spent the next few minutes painting Will as a rapist and a sick man. She had it all wrong. Paige wanted to cry out for her to stop, but she couldn't. She'd been told specifically not to speak out of turn.

Paige wanted to run to him, to hold him, to tell him it would be all right. She wanted to protect him from all this, just like he had wanted to protect her. She picked her nails and fought back tears of frustration.

Parker went on. "Did you have plans of the future with Ms. Harper? Things that would make an impressionable girl have false hope?"

Will sighed. "I did. That makes me look so awful, that I would go out on my wife and leave her, but that was the plan. I really considered it. I don't think I'd ever really do it, but when your marriage is falling apart, you look for ways out."

Paige gnawed on her nails, trying to cover her goofy grin.

"Then what happened?"

"Paige went crazy."

"How so?"

"She followed me around with her friend. She wouldn't stay away from the station. I told her time and again to go home, I had work to do. I told her to stay after school in a program, or to find a job, or to volunteer. She ignored me. She told me she was my unofficial intern and it was her duty to get me coffee."

"But I thought you liked her?" Parker cooed.

"I did. At first, I wanted to see her. I enjoyed her company. But then she started getting obsessive and not listening to me when I told her to leave. Then, she actually broke into my home and slept in our bed."

Paige's face burned. She'd hoped he'd believed her when she lied to him, or that he'd completely forgotten the whole ordeal.

"She was delusional," he went on. "I'd tell her something, and she'd hear something entirely different. She would make up stories that she convinced herself were true."

"Could you give an example?"

Will wasn't looking at Paige anymore. She fidgeted, trying to get him to look again, but he refused. He couldn't bring himself to. Those feelings of infatuation had burned out. All that was left were the ashes of a life that could never be again.

"She'd always talk about us living on a beach. That in two months we'd be rid of Eva and we'd be free to live in the Hamptons or something. She really thought I was buying us a house there. She'd always ask me if I'd heard back yet about the bid. I'd tell her that wasn't real. There was no house and we wouldn't be living there. There was no way I could afford it, even if I did want it. But still she lived in this fantasy world."

"If she's this 'crazy' as you say, then why have sex with her? Because, according to your story, you had sex with her *after* you knew all of these things about her."

Harrington stared right at Parker, not skipping a beat despite his heart dropping at her words. "Honestly, I don't know. I think it's like what happens to victims of domestic violence. They remember the good things and convince themselves the bad isn't so bad, that it'll stop eventually."

"Hm, so now you're the victim, is that right?"

That damn cough again. Paige felt a twinge in her stomach when she heard it. "When we had sex, she lost it. She was crying, so I let her cry without pressuring her to continue. That happens with abuse victims. If they feel threatened at all, they'll panic." He never broke eye contact with Parker. "I wasn't going to force her into anything she didn't want to do. I would never do that. But then, when I told her we should just lay there, that she should talk to me about it, she wouldn't take no for an answer. She pushed me down on the bed and held my hands above my head. She forced herself on me. Then she choked me." He lifted his chin slightly, showing the court a glimpse of the finger-shaped yellowing bruises above his collar. "I couldn't get her off of me. I was shocked and scared and torn. I didn't want to hurt her."

Parker halted. She hadn't known this information. Paige had never said anything of the sort. At first, she believed Harrington was a piece of lying scum, but with this new story, she wasn't so sure. A man like him would not lie about being raped, but she had a job to do. "So what you're saying is that you were raped? By a sixteen-year-old girl?"

"Yes, I am."

"She's sixteen! You're twice her size! Look at her! You expect the court to believe that?"

No matter what he said next, Harrington was going to sound weak and defensive. It didn't matter that he had nightmares of that night. Dreams of faceless forms holding him under water, him clawing to get free but never could. That he, who once had so much confidence, hated himself. He wanted to personally kill each and every one of the men who assaulted women. Yet this fragile doll in front of him was actually a monster.

Parker stepped toward the stand. "You booked a motel room with this girl under your name, paying in cash so there would be no paper trail. You had every intention to sleep with her, and you're going to sit up here under oath to claim *she* raped *you.*"

He stared at the lawyer in front of him, suddenly understanding what the girls he put on the stand went through. They had to relive the worst moment in their lives in front of people who most likely didn't have any sympathy for them because in rape culture, it's always the victim's fault.

Harrington hung his head. "It's true. I was pinned and in shock, like I said. She wanted me to take her to my house to stay with me, but I told her no, not after what she'd just done. She threatened me, to tell my wife and my superiors and to bring me down. She said she'd tell them I raped her, even though the opposite was true. So, I took her home--"

"You drove your rapist home?"

"Yes, I did. Just like in domestic situations. People are forced to see their attacker every day. I still felt confused and I didn't know what to do about the blackmail. I didn't want to abandon her at the motel. So I took her home. Then I decided I would go home to my wife to tell her everything. Just come clean, so Paige wouldn't have any leverage on me."

Parker paced slowly in front of the stand. "Why not run away to the Hamptons? Why stay and ruin your own life by confessing to your wife that you'd had an affair with a teenaged victim?"

"Because by that time I realized I couldn't leave my wife. I couldn't be with this young girl. I realized just how young she is. She's not ready to be with me. She needs therapy and to run around and be with guys her own age, to have a normal life, not to be with someone like me." His breath caught in his throat, realizing what he'd said.

"Not with someone like you." Parker tilted her head back, almost imperceptibly, then rested her case.

The prosecutor stepped in with his rebuttal. "Let's go back to the day when she raped you. She could have killed you. You knew she tried to kill her uncle. Why would you be torn?"

"Because, like I said, I had feelings for her. And I don't think she tried to kill--"

"So this wasn't some one time thing? You weren't taking advantage of her, you were in love with her, is that correct?"

He nodded, choking out the word *yes* and the lawyers made their closing arguments. A quick day in court.

Chapter 43

"Paige, do you think these sessions are helping you?" my doctor asked, looking into my eyes through his square frameless glasses.

I worried my blatant admission to lying overstepped my bounds in this room, especially since I freaked out about being called a liar during my last session. I crawled back within myself for a second, fearing he'd judged me. I swallowed and let myself be vulnerable again, forcing away the fear of being judged.

I didn't answer right away. Had they helped? All I'd been doing for one hour at a time was retell what happened over the last couple of months of my life.

I looked over at Stacy in the corner. I'd completely forgotten about her during every session. Her blank face showed nothing of her thoughts. She could have been thinking anything from "Yeah, you stupid whore, is this helping your self esteem?" to "I could really go for a cheeseburger right now". I missed when she teared up at my pain, when she sympathized.

Thinking back to when I'd first started the sessions, I cared so much about what this woman thought. Not that her opinion would change what had happened, but just that I didn't want to be seen as weak or stupid around her. She was in charge of so much, and I needed her to think nothing was wrong with me.

But the thing was, I was starting to see that my life so far has been way more fucked up than I let myself think. Instead of pushing the painful emotions down and turning to sex or anger or

231

both, I'd let myself recount what happened. I let myself feel raw emotions. During the sessions, I'd cried. Before sitting in front of this ancient man spewing my darkest thoughts and actions, I couldn't tell you the last time I'd cried from any emotion other than anger.

I felt like a different person from when I'd begun the therapy. I was lighter, yet so much more knowledgeable. I knew myself, what drove me to act the way I did. The way I do. It's helped me change my whole mindset.

Yet when I looked at the man in front of me, I realized I didn't know why it had helped. All he'd done was make me mad. The director had said nothing except, "Paige, dear, I know this is a little different, but I have to stay in here during your sessions. I'm sorry, but there simply is no way around it."

These people hadn't driven me to new discoveries about myself. They hadn't told me any secrets about myself. They hadn't unlocked some door to a new life. They'd just sat there and listened. I was doing all the work myself and it was stupid they just sat there while I found myself. There was no effort on their side whatsoever. I could literally do the same thing with anyone at all and they wouldn't even need fancy letters after their names to hear my problems, and I let the two of them know it.

"It just seems a little pointless, don't you think?" I said irritably. It was the first time since I'd started pouring my guts out that I'd been annoyed with anyone. It felt familiar and comfortable. "Coming here all the time. I could have talked to someone else. Maybe someone who actually cares about me."

"Yes, you certainly could talk to anyone else. Do you have anyone else around with whom you feel comfortable enough to share your deepest thoughts? Anyone who would listen attentively to every word you say?"

I fought. "Well, yeah, of course. You think I don't have friends?"

"Acquaintances, sure. People you know from school. Ones you say hi to at the movies. Boys who do your bidding for you. But friends? People you share everything with on a daily basis? People you couldn't imagine life without? People you feel so comfortable with and trust so much that you feel safer with them than you do with just yourself? No, I don't think you have anyone like that."

"I have Ashley."

"Do you? Or did you drive her away too?"

My chin quivered. Frustration. Embarrassment. Realization of the truth. He was completely right.

He went on, passing me a tissue without otherwise acknowledging my slow breakdown unfolding before him. "This is why you turn to older men. Your teacher. The detective. They were safe and strong. They were males to replace what you had lost when you lost your father. Yet you crave the attention that you never got from your mother. You twist your experiences with men because of your uncle. You think the only experience you can have with a male is sexual. You need to be sexually desirable to them in order to feel loved. Is all of this making sense?"

I nodded.

He pushed his glasses higher on his nose. "It's not all men, of course. Only the ones you see your father in. Strong, protective, caring. This is completely normal, I assure you. Parents nurture. We as humans need to be nurtured throughout our lives. Now, you never developed relationships with people your own age because you didn't have much of a childhood. You were forced to grow up so quickly that people your own age bore you. If you were to talk to quote 'anyone else,' you wouldn't feel you could open up. You'd be either trying to make yourself sexually attractive to the person or you wouldn't feel you'd been heard. Or you could also feel judged. You need to be held in high esteem, which I'm sure stems from your relationship with your mother. Does this assessment sound accurate?"

I rolled my eyes. It sounded like a perfect assessment, but I didn't want to accept it. "Okay, so fix me. That's why I'm here, isn't it?" I almost forced myself to yell. I held on to my anger like a loving friend, like my only friend, but it was slipping away, replaced by hurt. Anger was such better company.

"You have to fix yourself, Paige. I can only help you along. It's going to be painful and you're going to fight it, but eventually, if you keep working at it, you'll improve. You've already made vast improvements."

I pushed my shoulders back, bettering my posture. I took a deep breath, tipped my chin up. "I have, haven't I?"

"That being said, you have to be completely honest with

yourself."

I stared at him. Here we go again. I braced myself for him to call me a liar, just like last time.

He leaned forward. "Paige, I have the files. I know the police version, and I know your version. Somewhere in there is the truth, and you know what that truth is. You can bend the truth with me all you want, but you won't get better until you admit the truth to yourself."

"I have no idea what you're talking about."

"Paige," he said between gritted teeth. "You are not a stupid girl. Stop acting like it."

I hung my head. He sounded like my dad when he got mad.

The psychiatrist sighed, counted to three under his breath. "Paige, I see the potential in you, but I don't know if I can help you."

Panic stopped my heart. If he couldn't "help" me, then I would end up somewhere else, like in a psych ward or something. If this man gave up on me, I would lose. "No, I'm sorry. I'm just emotional. It's hard, you know? Let's keep going. Something I realized last night is that I can use my sexuality as power."

He looked at me like I lost my damn mind, but he humored me. "What do you mean?"

"Well, it's always seen as a bad thing to be sexy. Like you're going to get raped or whatever if you're a sexual woman. But that's not true. Sexuality isn't something to be feared and it has such a power over men. Sorry, but it's true."

"Yet it didn't give you power with your uncle. He took your power away because of your sex."

I picked at my nail polish. "It kind of did give me power then though," I mumbled.

"Pardon?"

"It did kind of give me power. He had to have it. He couldn't live without it. And now he's in a coma because of it."

"That's a very interesting perspective."

"I used to have the perspective you have. But the night I hit him was the night I took it back. I refuse to let him have any part of me."

"Paige, I just don't think you're getting it. You're twisting things to make them fit how you want, even if it doesn't make a bit of sense."

I folded my arms and looked at the clock. Five more minutes. "Can I go?"

I didn't wait for an answer and stormed out into the hall, but I hovered just outside the threshold, listening to them. "She doesn't see it, does she?" the director asked.

"See what?" the psychiatrist said.

"That she's lost it. I mean, does she really believe the crap that comes out of her mouth? Can she really be that delusional?"

"We're not here to judge. We're here to help. But in this case, I think the only thing that will help that girl is to be committed. She's way beyond what I can do."

I climbed up to my bunk in my dorm. My roommate was reading below me. A mousy little girl name Marie. You could tell from the moment you laid eyes on her that she'd been abused and neglected every which way. The first day here, I told her to stop being the victim and to take control of her own life or else she'd be stuck here forever.

"I'm working on it," she squeaked.

"Can't even tell."

Today she asked me how the therapy session went, as she did every time I had session. "Same as always," I said, as I did every time I had session. It had become our ritualistic greeting.

"You got a call when you were in there," she said, never taking her eyes off her book.

I sighed and walked to the main room. All calls were monitored. It was a breach of privacy and everyone complained frequently about it, but there was an undercurrent of appreciation for it. If they weren't monitored, the people in this place would have access to their drug dealers. The majority of them would be drugged out of their minds and sent off to rehab. As it is now, only a few manage to work around the system.

"Hey, I had a call today?" I asked the telephone lady. No one knew her name. She was in charge of our meals, our medication if we needed it, our visitation hours, yet she was nameless in our books.

"Yes, let me find it." She dug through her box of papers until she came across mine. "It was the hospital. Your uncle's awake."

"Okay." My fingers started tingling. "So now what?"

"Now you wait until you hear back from the authorities to see if he's pressing charges."

I thought of Will. He wasn't on this case anymore. I couldn't talk to him. He was always so calming to me. I wish I had him to tell me what to do.

"Will I have to see him?" I asked her.

She shrugged. "Depends, I guess." She leaned forward and looked into my eyes. It was hard not to look away. I felt myself crumbling. "I'll let you know when I know. I'm sure they'll be calling again soon."

I nodded and dragged my feet back to my room. My entire body coursed with electricity.

"Whoa, you okay?" my roommate asked, sitting up.

I shook my head. She ran toward me and my face smashed into the floor.

I woke up on the bottom bunk, Marie and the telephone lady staring at me. Marie held her hands up to her little O of a mouth while the lady shoved a glass of water into my face.

"There you are. Welcome back to earth, hon."

I sipped. A metallic and dusty taste washed over my tongue. Tap water. I pretended to gag and handed it back. "Thanks."

The lady mumbled something about me being an ungrateful bitch. She waddled out of the room, huffing.

My head felt light and empty, but I hadn't forgotten what I'd been told: my uncle was awake.

I waited impatiently for news, pacing my room. Marie peeked up at me from her book every few minutes. She twirled her hair in her fingers. She was as nervous as I was.

An hour passed before I was summoned downstairs. It took all I had not to run, both excited at the prospect of never having to see him again and terrified that I'd be forced to allow him to lay his eyes on me again.

I shook as I approached the director of foster care. I couldn't read her expression.

"He's asking for you."

I swallowed down bile. She must have seen the color drain from my face because she put her hand on my shoulder. "I'm sorry," she whispered. "We don't have to go. Not right now anyway."

"No, let's go. Might as well get it over with."

My stomach tied and untied itself in knots for the entire drive to the hospital. It was only maybe a fifteen minute drive, but it felt like it went on forever. My palms were wet and my body trembled uncontrollably.

Stacy kept her hand on my low back up to the automatic doors of the hospital, steadying me. Right before we crossed the threshold, I spun and threw up in the bushes.

The director asked me if I wanted her to accompany me to see Glen. More than anything, I wanted her to be there. I wanted a crowd to protect me. Someone to protect me. Instead, I told her no. I chose to face him alone.

He was propped up on a mountain of pillows, clearly waiting for me. His hands were folded in his lap. His forehead shined with a thin film of grease. "Hi, little girl," he sneered.

My stomach roiled. "My name's Paige."

"Of course it is, but you're my little girl."

I tasted blood. I'd chewed a hole in my bottom lip. I couldn't answer him. I just stared like an idiot, silently praying he'd slip back into a coma or better yet, have a heart attack. Then he'd be dead and it wouldn't be my fault.

"Well, anyway," he continued, looking at his overgrown fingernails, "I wanted to make sure you were going to behave when I get back home. I don't want any more trouble from you, do you understand?" His face contorted into a slimy smile.

I nodded slowly, trying to figure out an escape route for when he was released. I only had a couple days. They wanted to monitor him, to make sure his brain functioned well. Clearly he remembered me, what he did to me, and what I did to him. Even if he couldn't remember how to wipe his own ass, those three memories were all that mattered to me. In that moment, staring at his distorted grin, at the peach fuzz growing back over his wounded temple, at the sweat beading at the base of his throat, I wished I had killed him. I didn't care if I had gone to jail for it, if I'd been tried as an adult. Going back to that house with him was worse than any prison. Even my mother couldn't save me.

"Good girl," he said. "Now, you can go back and pack up your things. I've been told a lot has happened since I last saw you. A lot we need to discuss. But for now, I'm so tired from all this information. I'll see you soon."

He adjusted his pillows and turned to his side, facing away from me. I shook with anger at the way he just dismissed me. I looked at his monitors, at his IV bag. I thought about pumping his system full of morphine until he overdosed and died, but hospitals monitor that sort of thing. I looked around for a rope or a knife or scalpel or a gun just laying around, but there was nothing.

Even if I went to police, saying he'd raped me, that I couldn't go back to him, they wouldn't hear me. They wouldn't believe me. Even if he raped me again and they did a rape kit, confirming the rape, they would find some way of letting him keep custody of me. It was just rough sex. I planted the semen. They would take one look at my history and say I was crazy enough to do something like that.

I was repeatedly told I was manipulative and unstable. Just like my psychiatrist said, I would be committed. That was the next step if I messed up.

Psych would be better than jail, though.

I would kill him. I had to. There was no other way. I couldn't live another year and a half that way. Not after I'd been free. I could plea insanity.

A calm crept over me. It would be over soon.

Chapter 44

"Ms. Harper, you have a visitor," the telephone lady said, not stepping into the room.

My uncle was early and I wasn't packed yet, but I trudged downstairs anyway, my feet lead. I swallowed all the things I wanted to say to him, the snide comments, the anger and hurt I was feeling. I just needed to be patient. I would bite my tongue and be a good little girl until the time was right.

I peeked around the stairwell. Standing in the main room, arms crossed, was not my uncle, but a man I hoped with all my being I'd see again.

Will's eyes met mine. He smiled. "Hi, Paige."